THE PINK CAGE

DERBHILE DROMEY

To Kay
Hope you enjoy
this
Best wishes
Derbhile

PUBLISHED IN 2011 BY BOOK REPUBLIC, A DIVISION OF MAVERICK HOUSE PUBLISHERS.

Office 19, Dunboyne Business Park, Dunboyne, Co. Meath, Ireland.

http://www.bookrepublic.ie
info@bookrepublic.ie

ISBN: 978-1-907221-24-8

A CIP catalogue record for this book is available from the British Library and the Irish Copyright libraries.

℘ THE PINK CAGE ℘

Derbhile Dromey

BOOK REPUBLIC

A BOUTIQUE PUBLISHING PRESS

❧ Dedication ❧

To my late father, Muiris Dromey, who reckoned I'd be able to relocate to the South of France with the proceeds of my first novel. I'm on my way.

❧ Contents ❧

☙ Prism ❧

BEATS BLASTED THROUGH the door to Jazz's apartment. As I let myself in, they took shape. The Chemical Brothers, *Come With Us*. Jazz always listened to The Chemical Brothers when he needed to release tension. No doubt he was still pumped after kickboxing class.

The clatter of my rucksack on the polished floorboards alerted Jazz to my presence. He appeared at the door of the living area, close enough for me to discern the wet sheen of his close-cropped dark hair. Steam from his shower still wafted from his skin. It was a black T-shirt night tonight; the T-shirt clung to his body, emphasising the sculpted muscles. Because it was Prism night, the T-shirt bore the legend M-Jazz, his DJ name, in green letters. The name was a nod to his guilty love affair with old-skool rave. I realised I hadn't seen him since his break up with Jenny almost two weeks earlier, a yawning gap of time.

"Astrid, don't dump your shit in the hall," he said, with an exaggerated sigh.

I picked up the rucksack, yanking the top strap. It skittered across the floor, into his studio. In the living area, I laid my overcoat on the black leather armchair near the dining area, the one I inhabited.

"Time for chips," I said, rubbing my hands.

"I'm getting Chinese."

Friday was takeaway night, Jazz's only departure from his strict diet of grilled fish, chicken and vegetables.

"Can't we at least engage in a little friendly debate about our choice of takeaway? Chings' chips taste of pig swill."

"You get what you like."

I made for the galley kitchen, where I kept my stash of vodka. It was empty.

"What happened to my vodka?" I asked. "You decide to indulge for once?"

"No. You drank it. You replace it."

He was clearly still in tragedy mode; the mourning was a little more protracted than usual.

"Right. I'll get my supplies. I trust you'll have mellowed by the time I return."

Twenty minutes later, I returned armed with two bags of chips and a naggin of Smirnoff. Though I was more of a Stoli girl, I was forced to make do with the meagre selection at the local Spar. I held the bags aloft.

"Got you some too. Since you always want to pick at mine."

He held up his hand. With their sluggish zoom, my eyes registered the phone pressed against his ear.

"She's back now, Mum," he was saying, "I'll put you on to her."

He handed the phone to me. I plopped onto the armchair and answered Ora's well-worn repertoire of questions. She always felt the need to play the role of mother. Yes, I had everything. Yes, it was great that Jazz was able to bring me to the airport after the club. No, I could survive on a couple of hours' kip. No, I wasn't nervous. I had to go now, my dinner was getting cold.

Ora's anxious tones gave way to Matthew's sonic boom. Matthew failed to realise that he didn't need to raise his voice when he was on loudspeaker. He was suspicious of telephones, viewed them as bombs likely to detonate at any moment. As I spoke, Jazz took the bags of chips and shook both of them onto a plate.

"Well, I'm sure that the gods will protect you and that you'll show those people a thing or two," Matthew said.

"Of course." A grin leaked into my voice. "I'll slay them."

"All right then. Try not to maim yourself."

ORA BROACHED THE idea of the skiing trip during one of my monthly visits home. It was a Saturday morning. I was lounging on the window seat, my throne. The document I was proofing rested on my bent knees, inches from my face. My red pen, tool of the proofreading trade, was in my right hand, my monocle in my left. An heirloom from Matthew's student days, the monocle was my long-time, trusted companion. It was heavy and substantial; I was quite fond of the Sherlockesque air it gave me. It turned the black squiggles on the page into words. A capacious earthenware mug, empty now, stood on the floor beside me. Despite the length of my body, I could nestle into a comfortable groove on the windowseat's faded yellow cushions, created from years of curling up with various tomes.

Ora stood at the table, her back facing me. The wood was scored with intersecting lines, jumbled routes to nowhere. She was inserting her latest batch of photographs into frames, readying them for collection by clients. The photographs were all of children, her specialty. From this perspective, they were daubs, a sea of formless faces interspersed with bright dashes of colour. The beams of February sunlight that spilled through the wide, east-facing windows shaded Ora black and grey.

"I've got a proposition for you, Asi."

I've tired of asking her to stop calling me that.

Her voice was even quieter than usual, muffled by the curtain of grey-streaked hair that curled around her face.

"Yes?"

I stretched my hands above my head, still feeling the effects of Thursday night's gig at Eclectica, followed by a quick romp in the nightclub staff-room with Carl, who was always happy to oblige. I never brought my ballers back to mine; I still thought of the house as part Matthew's.

"I heard about something you might be interested in. It's a skiing trip."

Ora's voice was almost a whisper now, her words directed at the photo frames. Shards of memory prickled. I pushed them down and carried on with my document. It was an awkward beast, showered with Rorschach blots: the proofreading equivalent of wading through concrete. And it was due on Monday. Why couldn't these academics learn to type?

"You know that lunch I was at, where they asked me to do the photographs? I was telling you about it last night. There was a very interesting lady sitting beside me. She was wearing the most magnificent cream blouse. I'd say it was real silk."

Ora's conversational style was crab-like; she scuttled from side to side until she reached her end point. My pen hovered over one of the ink splodges. The monocle was of little use, the paper brushed against my nose as I attempted to divine what lay beneath.

"She's involved in a lot of charity work; she's so generous with her time."

My dictionary was wedged into the space between my hip and the window. I thumbed through it. *Etiolated.* That was the word under the ink splodge. Blanched or whitened due to lack of exposure to sunlight. Quite an apposite word for me to be defining.

"Anyway, she was telling me about a skiing trip she raises money for."

She took a deep breath.

"It's called Sightskiers. They go to Austria every year."

Her words activated my internal firewall.

"It's just, it sounds wonderful."

Her voice was at its most emollient.

"You get your own guide and everything. And free boots and ski hire, free lift passes. She said there's a place left because someone dropped out. I told her I'd mention it when you came home."

"Forget it."

I stalked towards the percolator; another cup of coffee beckoned. The percolator dated from circa 1956, but made the best coffee known to man.

"Well, it's bound to be better than the last time."

The percolator clattered onto the worktop; the wood sizzled as it made contact. I picked it up. A welt now marred the worktop's smooth surface. I busied myself with a cloth in a futile attempt to remove it, cursing under my breath. Words bubbled up in my throat, became trapped.

"Fine then. Sign me up."

"Are you sure? I mean, I do think you'd enjoy it."

"Whatever."

I poured the coffee and slathered Brie on day-old bread with savage strokes. As I made my way back to the windowseat, Matthew came in from his study.

"What's all this? I heard some sort of clattering noise."

"Astrid's going skiing. I heard about this trip at the lunch, Sightskiers. Isn't that exciting?"

Matthew gave one of his explosive snorts.

"What on earth for?"

I shrugged, "Any excuse for a shade-shopping spree."

"Some sort of charitable venture, is it?"

"Well, it's for the blind. I mean, not exactly the blind," Ora said, twisting her hands together.

Matthew's gaze penetrated my skin, made me squirm.

"I didn't raise you to become a trained monkey for the satisfaction of do-gooders. Why should you wish to submit yourself to such a scheme?"

It was impossible to give him an answer.

JAZZ AND I sat at opposite ends of the mahogany-effect dining table, our plates resting on straw place mats. Jazz still ate like a fat-boy, inhaling the food, his cheeks bulging. I pushed the plate of chips at him but he ignored it. His eyes were fixed on the widescreen television on the other side of the room. One of his Japanese films was playing. They were all the same to me, a blur of daggers and strange angled shapes. Sometimes, for amusement, I crouched in front of the television and tried to read the subtitles. It was rather like reading a book accompanied by moving images, but the words always disappeared from the screen before I finished reading them. The only sound came from the aural spaghetti junction of shouting voices on the television. Silence was a modus operandi for Jazz and I, but there was a different tenor to this one. It was suspended in mid-air, stretching into infinity. I speared my last chip.

"Time for some beats," I announced. "Since I suspect I will be enduring a musical famine for the week."

I crossed the room and opened a pair of wooden

doors underneath the television to reveal a Bang & Olufsen sound system with a vinyl player on top. I selected *Jackpot* by Tocotronic (*KO Kompakt Remix*), crouched over the vinyl player and inserted the needle into the groove. Then I stood back and let its clean, clinical beats fill the room. The Teutonic vocal was appropriate for the occasion.

Jazz loaded the dishwasher and went to sit on the couch, which was upholstered in the same black leather as my armchair. His legs were stretched in front of him, crossed at the ankles. Jazz liked to listen to beats with the television on mute, so he could watch the moving images at the same time. It baffled me, this conflict between sight and sound. This time, he made no move to press the mute button.

"Turn that off. I'm watching this."

Jazz was particular about his pre-club rituals. They kept his mind clear for the set. I put the record back in its casing and slid it into its correct place on the shelving that lined one wall of the living area. The shelves stretched to the ceiling and contained all the records and DVDs Jazz owned. I poured myself a belt of vodka and set the glass on the coffee table, making sure to place it on a coaster. Jazz was already wound up tight enough; I didn't want him to provoke him further. I switched on the lamp beside the armchair and angled it so that the light pooled over me without shining directly into my face. The lamp was a sleek metal contraption. Jazz claimed to have bought it because it looked cool, but he never used it. I settled myself down with my monocle and my much-thumbed copy of *The Hound of The Baskervilles*, which I planned to bring on the trip for a little light reading. I didn't read for pleasure much these days; my eyes were always beat after proofreading.

"Might as well get the party started anyway. Since there'll be precious little partying when I slum it amongst the Cabbage Patch Kids."

"I wish you wouldn't call them that. Especially since you pretty much are one," said Jazz, not looking away from the screen.

I downed my shot.

"Oh my eyes work just fine, St Geoffrey. Perhaps you're confusing me with someone else."

14

Jazz turned towards me. Blue lights from the television screen illuminated his face.

"If your eyes work so well, why haven't you DJ'd in front of anyone except me since that Eclectica thing?"

His words found their mark, expelling the air from my body.

"What about White Nights?"

Good recovery. He couldn't dispute the cult following of my Internet radio show, with its dedicated band of Mittel-European listeners.

"You only got that show because you shagged Carl." Carl, aka DJ Lucius. Resident DJ at Eclectica.

"Yeah, well he's hot."

Jazz wasn't a fan of Carl's.

"He jerks you around. And he steals your sets."

"Stick to the point, Jazz."

"I just think this trip is a good idea."

"Why?"

"You might stop being cruel to people. Especially blind people."

"Fucksake, when did you become such a sanctimonious prick?"

I swung my legs around and stood up, setting my monocle and book down on the coffee table. Time was ticking on and I needed to get ready.

I DECIDED TO keep things simple that night, so I opted for a pair of denim hotpants and a red beaded top, accompanied by knee-high red boots. Then I applied industrial-strength hair gel, getting up close and personal with Jazz's mirror as I sculpted my hair into artful waves. Under the bathroom lights, my hair was the colour of day-old snow. I slipped on my Ray-Bans: a traditional choice, but I needed durable shades for the rough and tumble of the club. These ones had the added bonus of arms which were the exact same shade of red as my top.

At the club, we fell into a routine honed over the three years of Jazz's residency. We hooked Jazz's laptop, the nerve-centre of his operation, up to the club's decks. Unlike most clubs, there was no warm-up DJ, so Jazz was free to reign supreme over his DJ universe, tweaking the decks to his specifications. Though the decks resembled the vinyl behemoths of old, the records were designed to receive digital signals, which enabled Jazz to play music directly from his laptop while still indulging his sentimental fondness for vinyl. Jazz also lined up his emergency CDs, which contained a copy of his set in case of needle failure. Then we hooked up the amps and tested the sound levels, over and over again, until Jazz was satisfied.

As the first beats of Jazz's set began, I made for the bar. Simon the barman slipped a double vodka my way. Instead of his trademark mellow beginning, building the vibe up with deep, soulful numbers, Jazz gunned straight for hands-in-the-air hardcore. Though punters were starting to drift in, the club was almost empty. With nothing to absorb the sound, the beats hurled themselves against the walls.

The DJ box was high above the crowd, on a mezzanine floor which ran along the four walls of the club and which was seldom accessed by the punters. At Prism, God truly was a DJ. Lurid shapes danced on the walls, the prisms which formed the club's logo. The shades blocked out the worst of the glare, but all I could see was the flash of the lights, interspersed with darkness: black white black white black. Good thing I knew every inch of the club. At various intervals, I sidled up to the bar for refills, or paid visits to the DJ box to help Jazz adjust his sound levels. I also brought him pints of iced water; the DJ box was an alcohol-free zone. He was working the decks pretty hard, inserting extra beats, layering records over each other, spinning them back and forth. At times, the needles jumped under the strain, but only I was able to detect the sudden jerks, the little breaks in the otherwise smooth flow of beats. The bass line throbbed, like the beating of a heart, almost obliterating the melodies. Jazz wasn't inclined to indulge in turntable trickery as a rule. Still, the crowd were well up for it; the dancefloor was filled with heaving bodies. There was no-one like Jazz for reading the pulse of a crowd; he was a pied piper, leading them over the edge into oblivion.

He didn't even look up when I approached. No shouted words of thanks, no casual hand on my arm. I figured he was deep in the zone. Besides, the noise was loud enough to induce bleeding eardrums. I figured he could fend for himself and took up residence at my usual spot, leaning against a pole at the edge of the dance floor. Light haloed my body, casting a glow over my translucent skin. I didn't have to wait long. A shadow bobbed in front of me and a hot, damp hand grabbed mine. He pulled me out onto the floor and his hands moved to my waist. He blew hot beer breath into my ear. My hands roamed down his back. His T-shirt was soaked in sweat. It had the slick plastic veneer of a sports top. Jazz segued into a tune I didn't recall seeing on his set list. Such deviations were a frequent occurrence; he liked to make the crowd silent partners in his song-selection process. The harsh, industrial beats were accompanied by a searing vocal, a nameless cry of love. It filled every crevice of my body, lifted me higher until I was airborne. My shadow and I writhed to the beat, our hips grinding. My hands kneaded his jean-clad buttocks. His tongue moved from my ear to my mouth, turning my insides to liquid.

The beats came to a sudden halt and the club turned back into a drab room. A babel of voices filled the vacuum left by the beats. As the lights came up, my shadow morphed into a troll. He grabbed my hand again, but I pulled away.

"Can't. Got to go to the airport. Maybe next time."

Lucky escape. I went back to Jazz and we packed up. As we walked to the car, his laptop case thunked against my leg, sometimes with force, but he didn't appear to notice.

"So who was the sucker tonight?" he said, placing his laptop with care on the back seat.

"Some old geek. Reckon at least thirty-five."

"Suppose you didn't bother to find out his name."

From time to time, Jazz took it upon himself to comment on my random ballers. It was irksome. After all, it wasn't as if Jazz waited for the waxing of a new moon to move onto his next conquest.

"Whatever bug is up your ass, get rid of it."

"You think you're shit hot in those clothes of yours.

Well you're not. You have no idea how wrong you look. Freaky Friday, that's what the regulars call you. They all lay bets on who can get it on with the albino chick. And they don't buy that crap about your mother being Scandinavian either."

It was unusual to hear Jazz utter so many sentences in one sitting.

"Whatever, Jazz. You're just jealous."

Jazz drove fast. The air in the car filled with beats, the sort of meat-market crud he knew I hated. At least it drowned out the silence.

WE BOTH HOVERED at the door of Jazz's bedroom. I ran my fingertips along the contours of his face. Despite hours at the gym, a trace of fatboy pudge lingered on his cheeks. As my hand reached his hair, he shook it off.

"Come on, Jazz. I want to play."

He reached out and put his hands on my shoulders, manoeuvring me so that I was pinned against the wall. In that moment, he towered above me. His fingers dug into my flesh. This was something of a departure from our usual drill.

"Do you know why Jenny broke it off with me?"

"She realised Depêche Mode wasn't a fashion label."

"Because of you."

I figured he was due one his biennial rages, so I decided to ride it out.

"'Your head is full of Astrid, I can't compete.' That's what she said. Not that you care. You don't know what it's like to love someone."

His voice remained level, but it crackled with menace, incipient thunder. His face was very close to mine, close enough for me to see that it was set in granite lines. Rock formations sprang to mind: *igneous basalt sandstone limestone sedimentary quartz mica feldspar metamorphic*. His breath was hot; the scent of sweet and sour chicken lingered.

"If I wanted to get your attention, I'd have to do this."

He thrust his tongue into my mouth. No time to react, no time to think. I was only aware of the hardness of the wall behind my back and the treacherous leap of my body as it arched towards his. I pushed him away. Chips and vodka churned in my stomach. My shades became dislodged and perched on the edge of my nose. The rock formations in my head gave way to a verse of the *Aeneid*, the same verse over and over, Dido and Aeneas, Dido and Aeneas.

Rattled, I shouted "What do you think you're doing, you twisted fuck?"

"Isn't that how you like it? Scuzzy and skanky."

I moved to adjust my shades; my hands shook and they fell to the ground. Without them, I was naked. My eyelids fluttered, captive hummingbirds attempting to take flight. Jazz leaned over and picked up the shades. His hands were gentle as he put them back onto my nose. My eyes stilled and locked with his. I kept forgetting how big his eyes were. They were warm, chocolate brown orbs.

"You ruined it for me, Astrid. She's the sort of girl I should be with."

The menace had drained from his voice, his words were now directed at his shoes. I saw him in our kitchen that first day; geeky and lost.

"She was right, you see. About you. You keep getting in the way. I don't know why I'm even telling you this. You're not going to understand."

"What a wonderful plot for a Greek tragedy, Jazz. Perhaps you should gouge your eyes out with sticks. And while I would love nothing more than to indulge you in your little fantasy, I'm afraid I must try and get some kip before my journey to Cabbage Patch Land."

I stretched my hands above my head, affecting a yawn. Jazz turned away. The door of his bedroom shut with an emphatic click. I went to the studio and yanked clothes out of my rucksack: a plain white T-shirt, jeans and my favourite jumper, worn into a faded comfortable nothing shade as a result of frequent washing. My glasses were still on the coffee table. I gave them a quick clean and put them on. It was a relief to be rid of the red top; the label scratched my neck. I retrieved my overcoat and ran my hands over the fine grey wool. It was an heirloom from my mother. My iPod was in one of the pockets; I fished it out and sat on the black leather couch, drawing my legs into my chest and resting my head on my knees. The couch doubled as a pull-out bed, but I made no move to set it up. The taste of Jazz was still in my mouth. My eyes closed and soothing Bach took me to a dark, deep place; an ice fortress. A place first discovered in the pink cage.

THE GATES WERE not high, but I couldn't climb over them. They stood between two red brick walls and were made of grey convoluted metal bars. I traced the metal with my finger, following the patterns it made as far as I could. The bars were the same colour as the sky. At the top, the metal turned into words. I didn't know what they said: they were up too high for me to see. There were spaces between the bars, but they were too narrow to squeeze through. The gates clanged shut after the car drove through them. I listened to the scrunching sound the tyres made until I couldn't hear it any more. My hands wound around the metal. It was cold and hard and my fingers burned, but I held on until hands pried me loose. There were red marks on my palms, from the metal. I didn't make a sound. Vikings never cried out when they were wounded in battle.

THE TWO STEPS leading from Jazz's apartment get me every time. Under normal circumstances, I could prevent a major spillage, but with a rucksack weighing me down, I didn't stand a chance. As my legs began to give way, a hand gripped my arm. Jazz stood behind me. He was still wearing his Prism clothes.

"Christ, Astrid, you know I'm supposed to bring you."

"Didn't want to put you out, seeing as I keep getting in your way."

From the depths of my overcoat, my phone emitted a jangling mishmash of sounds. "My taxi awaits."

He shook his head.

"Don't you ever get tired of fighting?"

I didn't respond, just turned and clattered down the stairs, my back straight. From a distance, I heard the door slam.

✑ The Twelve Labours ✑ of Hercules

THE CABBAGE PATCH Kids were hard to miss. As I strode through the departure area, squinting at pillars, I almost tripped on a phalanx of canes.

"Oh there you are," said a penetrating, nasal voice. "Sorry, I suppose we are a bit in the way."

A figure separated itself from the madding crowd and bustled towards me.

"Cliona Smith," she said, pumping my hand. "We spoke on the phone."

I looked down at a squat body. Her bristling dark hair was cut in an almost military crop. Her thick glasses reflected the airport's lights and her jaw jutted outwards. Something about the set of her face was familiar.

"Not late, am I?" I said.

"Well, not exactly. Could everyone move to the right in case more people trip over us."

Another figure floated towards us, a greyish creature with hair the colour of dust. He hovered next to Cliona, resting a hand on her shoulder.

"This is Kim," Cliona said.

The figure stepped forward and gave me a dishcloth handshake, his fingers making the briefest contact with mine.

"Nice to meet you," he said.

He was nitrogen: colourless, odourless, tasteless. We moved towards the group, whose canes tapped in unison. Two men were conducting a fierce, clamourous conversation. Their wrinkled apple cheeks and white beards gave them the appearance of prophets, but I sensed they lacked the required wisdom. They were so similar in appearance that it was impossible to tell one from the other.

"God, it's early, isn't it?" said one.

"Yeah, too early for me eyes to be open," the other one said.

"Your eyes are no good to you open anyway."

Their laughter came in gusts. Kim tapped them on the shoulder and they turned around.

"Guys, Astrid's here," Kim said.

"Howya?" the two men said with one voice.

My hand was pumped again. Their identikit heads bobbed up and down; wide grins split their faces in two. Two names hovered in the air, Tom and Eamonn, but failed to attach themselves to either one.

"Haven't you lovely long fingers," said one, giving my hand an extra squeeze.

His crony guffawed. I snatched my hand away.

"And here are the other two," said Cliona.

"How's it goin'?" said a deep voice.

I turned towards the voice and came face-to-face with a latter-day Roman God; guitar case slung over his shoulder, built like an exclamation mark, a battered face topped with crisp black curls. He wore a glaring high-vis jacket and a bilious-green sports top, but I could get over that. The tightness of his jeans led me to wonder what lay beneath. A sharp, musky smell of sweat rose up from him, 99 percent testosterone: just the way I liked them, with that little element of edge.

This guy had an easy grace that Jazz, with his iron-pumping and his no-carbs diets, could only dream of. He was tall enough to dwarf Jazz and no doubt he met Jazz's scuzzy and skanky criteria.

"Well, now that everyone's here, we'll proceed to check-in," said Cliona.

Ave, Caesar. I resisted the urge to click my heels together.

"Astrid, will you take Mia?"

I caught a glimpse of a nymph-like creature, hidden behind the other bodies. Cliona thrust her towards me.

"Take her?" I repeated.

"Yes, yes, we have to get going."

A small hand attached itself to my arm. I turned around and saw dirty blonde hair falling into blank blue eyes, a long red skirt and an almost-transparent white blouse. I also saw that everyone else was gone. There were no markers, just grey walls and blinking signs that hovered beyond the reach of my erratic eyes. Two fingers of pain jabbed at my skull. I loped forward through the sea of blank faces, trying to spot the red jacket Cliona was wearing, pulling Mia in my wake. Her weight slowed me; her pink suitcase was almost as big as she was. For such a tiny creature, her grip was vice-like. Bodies brushed against me. I pushed past them. Had to keep going. Trolleys appeared out of nowhere, unexploded landmines lying in wait. I stepped around them, yanking Mia's arm.

"Sorry, could you slow down?"

The voice at my shoulder was like a wisp of smoke. Ora's voice was a foghorn in comparison.

"Can't. Have to keep up with the others."

As I spun her around a corner, the jacket appeared, a lighthouse beacon in a dark sea. The next moment, my face crunched into a solid wall of flesh.

"Nice to meet you again," said that deep voice.

"Oh. Sorry," I mumbled.

It was a mercy he couldn't see my flaming cheeks. Blushing created an interesting raspberry-ripple effect on my skin.

"You might as well introduce yerself properly so, seeing as you're trying to cause me grievous bodily harm."

A stream of laughter gurgled out of him.

"Astrid Johnson."

"I'm Johno. Nice to meet ya."

I reached for his hand and shook it. His fingers were long, with knobs of bone that pressed into my skin. Not girl's fingers these. Not like Jazz's. The pressure of his hand was firm, but not crushing. Cliona shattered the moment.

"Try to look where you're going, Astrid. You can't fling people around the place willy nilly."

Her voice was weighed down with umbrage.

"Guiding is a serious responsibility. It's important for blind people to feel secure. Isn't that right, Mia?"

Mia looked down at her suede boots.

"It doesn't matter," she said.

Pity I had to relinquish all sharp objects.

CHECK-IN WAS THE first flaming hoop to be jumped through. I flung my bag onto the conveyer belt, then Mia's, since her twig arms were incapable of bearing the weight. After that, the metal detector lay in wait. As I marched Mia towards it, something slapped into me. It was a piece of luminous tape.

"You have to sort of zig-zag through the barrier," said Kim.

We joined the shuffling line, let ourselves be shunted forward. The two guffawing cronies stood behind us, with Johno, Cliona and Kim forming a triumvirate at the head of the pack. Kim murmured something in Cliona's ear. She gave a short, barking laugh.

"Reckon I'll start mooing in a minute," I said to Mia.

"What?" she said, in a vacant voice.

"You know, cattle."

We were now at the top of the line. A man in a high-vis vest was bearing down on us.

"Never mind. Get out your passport."

I unearthed my own passport from the cavernous pockets of my overcoat. The high-vis man gave it a cursory glance before turning his attention to Mia. She didn't have her passport in her hand, as I expected; she was rummaging in a pouch which ran in a diagonal line across her body. I snatched the pouch and burrowed through it. My hand connected with it in an instant. I plucked it out and handed it to the high-vis man.

"D'you need any help, love?" he asked.

"No," I said, stalking past him.

The others were already through. I quickened my pace, to ensure they didn't elude me again. When I reached the metal detector, I yanked off all my metallic objects, while Mia stood beside me, unmoving.

"Aren't you going to put your stuff on the belt?" I said.

She said nothing.

"Haven't you ever flown before?"

"Not without my parents," she almost whispered.

Ye gods.

"Right." I moved over to her. "The tray's in front of you. Put your bag, coat and jewellery onto it."

She did so, with agonising slowness. Then I propelled her forward, through the detector. As I followed her through, the beeper sounded. A friendly frisk from one of the airport staff revealed coins in the pockets of my jeans, change from my taxi.

"Shit," I muttered, lowering my head in a vain attempt to cover my scorching cheeks.

By the time we were finished, the others were already making for the gate, their canes beating out a steady rhythm. I followed them, tugging Mia along with me. Every vein in my body was screaming for coffee, a double espresso for courage.

"Any chance of a pit stop?" I asked.

"Maybe when we find the gate," said Cliona.

We walked over to the display. Kim, the sighted stooge, offered to scan the blinking screens. At least he had his uses. I yanked Mia through a maze of corridors and escalators. When we reached the gate, thankfully there was a coffee stand.

"I could murder a cup of tea," said one of the guffawing cronies.

"I know, yeah, it's like a three-ring circus around here," said his friend.

"There's no time, we have to board," Cliona dictated.

An orderly line of people were snaking towards the gate. I looked at my watch. 9.35am. Flying had never been such a Herculean labour before. But then every other time, Jazz was there with his butterfly touch, steering me through the maze, making hurdles disappear. Still, I was able to manage without him. *My eyes work just fine, St Geoffrey.*

THERE WERE CORRIDORS everywhere. Long corridors that looped around, like the model train-set Matthew had shown me once. My feet made an echo as I walked along them. The echo came from the ceilings, which were as high as the cliff on the beach at home. The air in the corridors was dry and hot and smelled of cabbage and polish. It crept into my nose and made me sneeze.

The corridors were full of light, but it wasn't the light of a sunny day at home. It bounced everywhere and I couldn't escape from it. It was even on the floors. The light came from thin lamps that dangled from the ceiling. When it was quiet, they buzzed. Sometimes I passed bigger girls in the corridor, who held sticks in front of them. The sticks made tapping sounds. I heard them everywhere. Sometimes I walked to the sound of the sticks: tap-tap, tap-tap.

When I looked at the floors, I saw my face. Some of the floors were speckled grey; some were covered in red and cream squares. The walls were almost white, but not quite. If I dragged my feet on the floor, my shoes squeaked. Sometimes I tried to skid along it, or hop on the red squares, but they always stopped me. They said I might hurt myself; I didn't know why. So I counted the squares instead, red then cream. There were statues in the corners. It was hard to tell if they were men or women because they all had long hair and wore robes. The pink ladies said they were called Our Lord and Our Lady. I guessed it was because the statues belonged to the school. The corridors were divided by big, heavy doors. They all had panes of glass in them, as if they couldn't decide whether to be doors or windows. The handles were made of metal and there were pieces of metal at the bottoms. They were heavy; too heavy for me to push.

I knew why there were so many corridors; they needed them for all the rooms. The rooms were big, with white or green walls. There were no books or samples, just a lot of objects. There were so many rooms. More rooms than in our house in Wexford, or the other house in Dublin. More rooms than I had ever seen before.

I ATTEMPTED TO sink onto the seat. Across from me, Johno's long body was welded into a window seat, hemmed in by Tom and Eamonn. I had to content myself with sitting beside my new shadow. Kim and Cliona settled themselves in front of us.

Kim hovered over Cliona as she strapped herself in.

"All right?" he asked.

"At least we got everyone through without a hitch," Cliona replied. "You know what these airlines are like. And there appear to be some loose cannons in the bunch."

"God, it's a big plane, isn't it?" said one of the grinning cronies.

"Sure, they have to fit everyone in," replied the other.

They felt an obligation to comment on everything, rather like the chorus in a Greek play, but with less finesse and at a considerably higher volume. I took off my jumper and put on my seat belt. Beads of sweat rolled down my neck, making my T-shirt sticky. My eyes closed and I let my body go limp. I felt a tug at my sleeve, heard a mewling voice in my ear.

"Astrid, isn't it?"

"What?"

I kept my eyes closed.

"I'm sorry to bother you, it's just, I think I'm sitting on something."

I yanked her seat belt out from under her and clipped it on. Her mumbled thanks were drowned out by the sound of take-off. The steward began his safety drill. Cliona proclaimed, for all the plane to hear, that it was "inaccessible to the vision impaired."

"Sure it doesn't matter," Johno shouted over to her. "We're fucked if it goes down anyway."

"Guy's a total Gaylord," I muttered to myself.

"What?" said Mia.

She was gripping the armrests.

"The steward. A blatant homosexual."

Figured it might be useful to befriend the natives, even if I had no plans to become one myself.

"Oh, I get it. Gaylord. I never heard that one before."

Giggles exploded out of her, a succession of pink helium

balloons. I sensed that many things were unfamiliar to her. The plane lurched into the sky. Mia tightened her grip; her knuckles turned white.

"Trying to fly the plane?" I asked her.

"I always do that. To stop the plane falling over."

Such idiocy didn't merit a response.

I SUPPOSE I wasn't very nice to Jenny. There was nothing objectionable about her; she wasn't interesting enough for me to dislike. She was just one of Jazz's interchangeable nut-brown maidens. Mind you, she lasted longer than most, six months. Jazz even gave her a key.

It's just that I hate people watching me DJ. My style is somewhat unorthodox; there are some who misinterpret it as clumsiness. My show for that week was dedicated to classic 80s electro. I was listening for the bird's-wing beat that acted as my cue to fade in the next track, a delicate manoeuvre. My fingers located the groove in the vinyl and I hunched over the turntable, guiding the stylus towards it. As I inserted it into the groove, the skin on my back prickled, alerting me to a presence. The stylus juddered. I turned around. Jenny was standing in the doorway.

"Oh it's you Astrid," she said. "Sorry, I thought it was Geoff."

Her hands dug into her pockets.

"What are you doing here?"

"Geoff asked did I want to come round for something to eat before you guys go to the club. Do you know where he is?'

"Gone to get the takeaway."

I concentrated on reinserting the needle.

"Sorry to disturb you. I thought he'd be back by now."

The track made a quiet entrance. I increased the volume. Her footsteps moved towards the living area, then I heard the sound of the television. A moment later, Jazz's key turned in the lock. I heard voices, the rattle of bags. Decided it was safe to emerge.

"Here's your chips," Jazz said, handing me the bag.

"Hey, I never knew Astrid DJ'd," Jenny said.

"Yup. DJ Ice White, that's me," I said, shaking the chips onto my plate.

"How d'you get that name?" she asked, swallowing a mouthful of burger.

Her voice was eager, searching. She fell into the category of 'Jazz's girls who tried to befriend me.'

"Can't you guess?"

"Oh."

She blushed. Jazz gave one of his martyred sighs. In spite of all his kickboxing classes, he has never grasped the fundamental rule of battle; attack is the first line of defence. I ate my chips with relish, to the soundtrack of their kung fu film. Savage flames of triumph licked through me.

AT THE SOUND of seat belts being unclipped, I tilted my chair back as much as it would allow and reached for my iPod, preparing to lose myself in electric dreams. But before I surrendered, the trolley came around. My morning coffee fix was by now long overdue. But by the time I helped Mia wrestle with her sandwich and picked her purse off the floor, my coffee was tepid.

Cliona and Kim fussed over their food, utensils rattling. I looked over at Johno. Wires protruded from his ears. He was an iPod fan, just like me. I switched on my own and opted for Orbital, *Chime*. Its beats filled my nostrils with the smell of creosote and sweat. The smell of the DJ Shack. The sound on the iPod was slick, but I still heard the faint crackle of static. A wave of tiredness overcame me. I switched to the Prodigy, hoping their bomb-blast lyrics and beats could stave it off. They achieved the desired effect and lifted me into a psychotropic universe. Intermittent tugs at my sleeve punctuated my dreams, but this time I was able to push them aside.

JOHNO'S GUITAR CAME towards us, a gaudy Irish flag waving at the neck. As it reached us, I yanked it off and handed it to him.

"Jaysus, you're a strong girl," he said.

His voice was husky, a mixture of coddle and caramel.

I leaned towards him. This sort of conversation was easier in a nightclub, camouflaged by flashing lights and red beaded tops. He opened the case and ran his hands over the guitar's smooth brown surface, checking for nicks.

"Good thing it's only me banger," he said. "Didn't want me good one getting wrecked."

"This guitar of yours," I purred into his ear, "does it make you a rock god, in your estimation?"

"Nah. I'm more a 'trad lad.'"

Laughter gurgled from him again. Good thing I wasn't drawn to him for his sense of humour.

BLINDING SUN GREETED us as we left the terminal building, necessitating a changing of the guard from glasses to shades. I also donned a soft black hat with a brim wide enough to deflect rogue rays.

"That's us," Kim said.

A figure stood in front of a taxi-bus, holding a sign with a winking eye and the word Sightskiers printed on it.

"Oh, so it is," said Cliona. "At least they're on time this year."

The phalanx crossed the carpark, following the sign. The canes gleamed in the sunlight; the balls at the ends scraped the tarmac. As my shadow and I fell into step beside Cliona, I noticed that her cane was shorter than average.

"Where's the rest of your cane?" I asked her.

"Oh, it's a symbol cane," she said, with a flourish.

A symbol of what?

The bus loomed ahead. We stumbled towards it. Kim helped the Greek Chorus slide into the back seat. I threw myself onto a windowseat in the middle row, pulling Mia in my wake. Johno submitted to being helped into the seat beside her. The Greek Chorus commented on the seating structure of the bus as they settled themselves in.

"It's mad the way it's all long seats, isn't it?" they said. "Not little poxy ones like on the buses at home."

Their voices were audible above the roar of the engine, as the driver took off. I leaned against the window, my eyes closing. The Greek Chorus changed tack and began reliving the flight, treating it as a passage from *The Odyssey*. Johno gurgled his approval. His laughter merged with the engine. My phone began emitting random bleeping noises, indicating the arrival of a text. I jerked awake. Jazz?

"That's a noisy yoke," said one of the Greek Chorus.

The sun bounced off the phone's silver cover. I flipped it open and turned away from the window, but the sun still slanted across the tiny screen. Creating a shield over the screen with my hand and upper body diffused the sun's rays. It was my usual trick at times like this. I brought the phone to eye level.

Welcome to Austria. No other messages.

"They can do marvellous things with phones now," Cliona's voice gunned at me from the front row, where she sat beside the driver.

"Assistive technology has levelled the playing field for people with disabilities. I switched to a Talks phone recently, it makes all the difference."

"Don't they all do that? Talk?"

Guffaws from the cheap seats.

"I meant the screen reader software," said Cliona, with exaggerated patience. "You could get the Zooms version. It magnifies the screen."

"Why would I want to do that?"

"I'm only trying to help." Cliona sniffed.

She began to extol the accessibility of various types of mobile phone. My phone had space for hundreds of mp3 files. That was all I cared about. I tuned her out, went to the message menu and began to type:

Stk in Cbage Patch Hades.

Jazz always teased me about the brevity of my texts: "There's text speak and then there's Astrid text speak."

The text still took me an age to type. The tiny silver buttons on the keypad jostled for space, the letters were faint hieroglyphs on the screen. Still, typing the message gave me a brief feeling of release. I punched in Jazz's number and his face appeared. It reproached me.

"Forget it," I muttered, as I put the phone away.

For the rest of the trip, I gazed out the window. The roads grew steeper and houses gave way to forests of fir trees with snow coating the ground and branches.

THEY BROUGHT US out to a bus with words painted in blue on the side. The words were the same as the ones on the gates. When we got to the bus, they said we were going for a swimming lesson. My stomach fizzed. I already felt sand under my feet, heard the whoosh of the waves.

The van stopped at a grey-white blob of building, just like the school. There was no beach. Instead, the pink ladies brought us into a room that smelt of Mrs O'Brien's cleaning.

Hands pulled down my clothes and put on my swimming togs before I had time to think. I didn't know how they found my swimming togs. Maybe Mrs O'Brien told them. They looked different in here, less blue. I didn't wear a hat when I swam at home, but they said I had to wear one here. They gave me a hat which stuck to my head.

We walked through a small stream of water, into the swimming place. The ground was hard and full of tiles that zig zagged. Pools of water gathered on the tiles. I didn't have to hold on to the pink ladies, like some of the other girls. Instead, I took little steps to stop myself from slipping. The pink ladies asked if I was all right and I said yes. One of the pink ladies gave me rubber bands to wear on my arms. They were a bright orange colour and they pinched my skin.

The water wasn't the same as the water on the beach at home. It didn't stretch forever; it was a bright-blue rectangle, with bits of white in it. The white bits came from the bright lights on the ceiling. There were no waves; it stood still, waiting for us to splash it. I didn't care that it looked different. It was water. My feet pulled me towards it; it was soft and gentle. The armbands squeaked as I took them off. I stretched my legs and pushed myself out into the centre of the pool, where there was no ground. My legs and arms splashed up and down; I made water shoot into the air. Then I let the water close over my head and blew bubbles. The pink ladies and the other girls vanished. I floated in a silent, blue world.

A hand pulled my arm, so hard I thought my arm might come away from my body. My head pushed upwards; my body lifted out of the water. The lights seared my eyes as I reached the surface. I yelped and covered them with my hand. One of the pink ladies crouched in front of me.

"Child, we thought you were drowned," she said.

"I was just swimming. I want to go back in."

I tried to wriggle away, but my legs made scissors on the wet floor. The pink lady picked me up before I could fall and wrapped me in a towel which was soft, but too tight.

"We'll get you dry now, you'll be grand."

I was brought back into the dressing room. Her hands yanked and pulled at my clothes. I told her I could do it myself, but she didn't hear me. For the rest of the lesson, I sat on a bench at the side of the pool, beside the pink lady. There were little rainbows around all the lights. They weren't there before. Looking at them made my eyes sore.

DUSK WAS FALLING as we reached the hotel; the sky was the same no-colour as my jumper. The hotel's rough-hewn walls gleamed with a fresh coat of whitewash. The windows were hidden behind green shutters. Curved red tiles peeped out from under a covering of snow.

As I stepped out of the bus, cold rippled through me. It was fortunate that my overcoat provided excellent armour. I turned up the collar and pressed my chin into it. My cheeks tingled. I snatched up my rucksack from the back of the bus and started walking towards the hotel, anticipating the warmth within. But my progress was halted by the voice of my shadow.

"Astrid, can you help me find my bag?"

I glanced at the pile of bags still remaining in the bus. Her pink monstrosity eluded me. The bags tumbled around in satisfying disarray as I scrabbled through them. Cliona's click of disapproval as her foot made contact with an escaped casualty was even more satisfying.

"I'll help you with those," said Kim.

He located the pink monstrosity, lifted it out and placed Mia's hand on it. Her cane was in her other hand.

"Right," Cliona said. "Drop your bags in your rooms. We'll be meeting in the bar in 30 minutes."

This announcement was greeted with cheers from Johno and the Greek Chorus. Cliona bulldozed through their cheers.

"The guides will be there and we will hold our welcoming ceremony."

I shot forward, propelling myself through the big wooden door. A blast of warmth hit my face. The door opened onto a long, dark hallway with a spiral staircase at the end. Mia inched forward, see-sawing between cane and bag. The wheels of her bag began a crazy dance, as if they were punters at Prism.

"Give me your bag," I said.

"What?"

She was already panting. I snatched her bag and strode ahead. She tugged the straps of my rucksack. My leg made contact with the first step. Spiral staircases were not my friends, pretty though they were. I tried to heed Matthew's advice about following the curve of the wall with my shoulder, but with two bags, it was impossible to maintain balance. Expletives poured from my lips in a steady stream, as my shins thunked against each step. Our room was at the top of the stairs. I opened the door and let the bags fall, resting my weight against the doorframe. There was a preponderance of wood in the room: wooden furniture, wooden floors, a wooden ceiling which swooped downwards, creating a cave-like effect. Wooden shutters framed the narrow, triangular window. A small ledge underneath it offered meagre seating space. A vast white bed filled most of the room. I stepped forward and stretched out my hand. The bedspread felt rough; its texture reminded me of childhood blankets. As I explored further, I found the join where two beds dovetailed into one. A wardrobe leaned against the wall, a dark, hulking presence which stood guard over the two beds. Two matching lockers stood by the beds, each with their own chest of drawers.

"Which side should I pick?" Mia said.

"We'll be pretty cosy whatever side we choose."

I clattered across the polished floor with my rucksack, squeezing through the matchstick-thin space between the wardrobe and the inner bed. Mia stood by the door, gripping her pink monstrosity. I opened the door of the wardrobe to reveal a cavern, with rickety shelves tucked into the left-hand corner. A mirror was fitted into one of the doors; it was dotted with age spots. I yanked my clothes out of the rucksack and placed them on the top shelf, proud of the military precision of my packing. Aside from my ski paraphernalia, my rucksack contained a selection of my most alluring clubbing clobber: hotpants, miniskirts, skinny jeans, slinky tops, sawn-off boots. All designed for strutting. There were eight pairs of shades: one for each night, plus my skiing shades. And then the motherlode. My silver dress; my secret weapon. I already envisaged a use for it.

There was no time for delay. Johno's response to the call of the bar was bound to be swift. I arranged my clothes on the shelves, and from the slender pile I plucked out a clingy T-shirt sprayed with a blur of silver swirls and a pair of skinny jeans. Best not to reveal too much on the first day. Besides, it was cold. I compressed my disembowelled rucksack into a corner of the wardrobe and turned around. Mia was still standing at the door.

"Why haven't you started unpacking yet?"

"I don't know where to put my things."

"Why not start with the bed."

"I don't know where it is," she almost whispered.

I leaned against the wall, praying for the gods to give me strength. Then I walked over to her, yanked her suitcase out of her hand and hefted it onto the bed nearest the door, straining various ligaments in the process. Her packing style was less circumspect than my own. She inched towards me; her hand brushed against the back of my T-shirt. She found the clasps and tugged at them. The suitcase opened to reveal neat squares of clothes with a strong pink theme. She ran her hands over them.

"Imagine I'll be skiing tomorrow," she said. "I never thought I'd ski."

I shared her incredulity.

"Cliona came into our class, you see. That's how I found out about the trip. She's such an inspirational person."

She gave a reprise of Cliona's visit to her class. Then she segued into a monologue about the clothes she planned to wear each evening. My thirst was building. It was time to cut the monologue short.

"Right, we better start transferring these to the wardrobe."

I picked up one of the squares and turned to face her. But she didn't move.

"I don't want to put them in there," she said.

"Why not? Room for a small child in there."

"I want them to be where I know where they are."

I put the pile back into the suitcase, thinking of the limpets on the beach at home. Limpets were genetically programmed to cling to rocks. It was all they were able to do, but they did it with remarkable tenacity. Once they clamped themselves onto a rock, it was impossible to remove them. On the rare occasions when they did move, they left a scar, so that they could return to the same spot. I looked at my watch.

"Whatever. We have to get going. Commander's orders."

❧ Matthew Goes Away ❧

MATTHEW AND I lived in a house by the sea, in a place called Wexford. It perched on top of a cliff; the garden sloped towards the sea. It was long and low and bits of it stuck out. When gales came, the house moaned. The floorboards rattled and leaves fell off the creeper on the grey walls. The creeper was supposed to protect the house, but the wind was too strong.

The rooms were stuck together in clumps along a corridor which stretched from one end of the house to the other. There were the rooms we lived in, the rooms we slept in, and the rooms that echoed. We never went into the rooms that echoed. All of the rooms smelt of dusty books and seawater. Most of the floors were made with wooden floorboards, but the floors in the bedrooms were covered in brown carpet with splodges of orange on it. The bedrooms Matthew and I slept in were beside each other, so he could come to me in an instant if I woke in the night. Most of the time I didn't wake; the waves made a lullaby which sent me to sleep.

The house was full of treasures. There were folders filled with old brown photographs and gleaming statues from Africa. My favourite statues were the ones on the chess set in the corner of the living room. They were black and white. I liked to pretend that they were warriors fighting a battle. Matthew told me the names of each of the pieces and said that I could learn to play when I was a little older. There were colourful pictures on the walls. They felt soft, because they were made with wool instead of paint. Matthew said they were called tapestries. The skeletons of plants and animals were everywhere; they lived in little glass cases. There were so many books that there wasn't room for all of them on the shelves, so some of them were stacked into piles that leaned against the walls. The books were thick and heavy, with hard covers. The covers were cracked and stained greyish-brown. There were words on them; I liked following the pattern they made with my fingers. When I opened them, clouds of dust flew into the air and made me sneeze. Matthew told me to be careful when I turned the pages; they were as thin as the wings of birds. The words on the pages were so close together that they became blurred. Sometimes there were drawings in the books. The ones of the skeletons were my favourite. Most of them were animal skeletons, but some of them were people. Each book had a piece of ribbon that stuck out when the book was closed. Matthew explained that the ribbon was used to mark your place in the book.

EVERY MORNING, MATTHEW and I made our way along the cliff path that ran from the bottom of our garden down to the sea. It wound its way around the cliff like a piece of string. The path was very steep, but Matthew didn't hold my hand when we went down it. Instead, he showed me the places where it was safe to put my feet. He walked a few steps ahead and waited until I found them, always making sure I could see him. At first, I fumbled and groped my way along, while Matthew grunted and told me to hurry up. But it wasn't long before I learned where all the places were and I was able to fly down to the beach. The cliff was so high that when I reached the bottom, I couldn't see the top.

As soon as we landed on the beach, we ran straight into the sea. Every time we swam in the sea, it was a different colour. Sometimes it was grey and sometimes it was blue with green spots. Matthew said the green spots were the places where the sun was able to shine through. The sea was always cold, but when we started to swim, we forgot the cold. When we first started swimming, Matthew lowered me into the water, keeping his hands on my belly so I didn't sink and showed me how to move my legs and arms. After a while, they moved together and I didn't need him anymore.

Afterwards, Matthew wrapped me in a rough towel and rubbed me until my skin tingled. Then we walked the length of the beach, to the sound of the howling wind, until the feeling came back into our legs. The beach lasted forever. Matthew walked fast and I galloped alongside him, determined to keep up.

There were big rocks in a corner of the beach, near the cliff, and smaller stones and shells scattered along the top of it. Nearer the sea, the beach was covered in red and brown seaweed. The seaweed was my favourite part of the beach; it smelt of salt and metal. I liked its crisp surface and the little pods that burst when I pressed on them. Matthew didn't like it when I pressed the pods, so I tried not to do it too often. I didn't like the wet seaweed so much, but Matthew said that was the kind with the most nutrients. During our walks, Matthew collected his samples. He put on rubber gloves and searched the beach for fish bones and pieces of seaweed, which he put into a silver bucket. He looked for tiny creatures in the seaweed, in rockpools and under stones. When he found creatures that he thought were interesting, he took pictures of them with a brown camera in the shape of a box. Sometimes he just looked at them for a long time with his magnifying glass.

Matthew taught me to identify shells, rocks and fish by their feel and birds by their song. He placed the shells and stones in my hands and told me their names. I held them close to my face and examined them. He told me to be careful of the crabs which buried themselves in the stones, because of the pincers they used to stop their enemies from hurting them. He knew how to touch them without hurting himself. There were a lot of animals on the beach. Matthew said it was because the cliff gave them shelter. He knew where they all lived; he said they lived wherever they could find food. We waited by the rockpools where the fish lived. He said we had to stay still, so we didn't frighten them. Sometimes the sun made a reflection on the rockpool which hurt my eyes, but when I wore sunglasses, they stopped hurting. The fish moved too fast for me to see them, but Matthew let me look at other creatures through his magnifying glass. Most of them were grey blobs, but Matthew said they were fascinating.

On the days he had a lot of work to do, he gave me the task of collecting my own samples. When I found samples that pleased him, he said,

"You're turning into quite a scientist, aren't you?"

Sometimes he forgot to come back and look at my samples. When that happened, I wrote my name on the damp, greyish-brown sand with a pointed stick, over and over. I liked the way it looked.

We went to other places too. Matthew liked to go on what he called 'field trips.' Sometimes we went to other beaches where Matthew collected samples and other times we visited places full of old buildings and stories. Matthew knew all the stories. He described the places to me, showed me things I didn't know were there. But the beach was my favourite. It was my playground.

When we finished our walk, we returned to the house and ate porridge for our breakfast. Then Matthew went to work in his study. He wrote about his samples and he looked at shells and seaweeds through his microscope, because the creatures that lived in them were so small. Sometimes, he let me look into the microscope, but I couldn't see any of the little creatures.

While Matthew did his work, Mrs O'Brien looked after me. She came every day from her house in the village. I liked to twirl her hair around my fingers; it bounced when I let it go. Her hair was dark with bits of silver in it; it wasn't all silver like Matthew's. She wore an apron and always smelled of flour. When I touched her face, my fingers sank into the folds on her cheeks. Sometimes her sons Michael and Joseph came with her. They were older than me, but they played with me. We rolled down the garden until we came to the hedge at the end. They showed me how to play football; they told me to keep my eye on the ball, but I didn't know how to do it. Their favourite game was to make me guess how many fingers they were holding up. They tried to trick me by bending their fingers, but I was never fooled—until they stood further away and I wasn't able to see their fingers any more.

When Mrs O'Brien left, Matthew cooked meat and vegetables in a big pot. They were soft and slid down my throat. After we ate our lunch, Matthew gave me my lessons. The lessons were full of sandpaper letters, expeditions to Africa, and bones. We worked in Matthew's study, at a table that was so big, it filled almost the whole room. A cloth was spread over the table. It was full of holes, but there was so much paper on the table that you couldn't see them. When I asked Matthew why he had so much paper, he said he needed it for the stories he wrote about animals. Some of the animals lived in Africa and the others lived on beaches in Wexford. He wrote about them because he was a zoologist, which meant that he studied animals.

Matthew's typewriter and coffee cup stood at one end of the table. I worked at the other end, at one of the few clear spaces. I sat on a green chair that sank in the middle and used a stack of cushions to bring myself up to the level of the table. Matthew wrote letters at the top of a sheet of paper and told me to copy them. I liked the way they looked, with their thick black strokes, but I couldn't make my letters look the same. So Matthew made new letters out of sandpaper. He pasted them onto sheets of white paper, which he spread across the table. Then he placed his hand over mine and we traced the shapes the letters made. His hand was so big that it swallowed mine up. His fingers were hard and rough like the sandpaper, but they were also gentle. When he guided my hand over the letters, I was able to see them.

After that, it was easier to copy the letters, but it took a long time. I wrote until my head became heavy and fell on top of my hand. Even though I was careful, the letters still wobbled. I saw the shapes they made in my mind, but my hand couldn't do what I asked. Matthew never became impatient, he just told me to keep trying.

I read stories to Matthew from books with big black letters and pictures drawn with bright colours. The stories were boring, about animals that talked or women in towers who waited for men to climb up and rescue them. I preferred stories about battles. But Matthew said I had to read these stories so I could learn the words. Soon I knew all the words in the books.

When the reading and writing were finished, it was time for the abacus frame, which helped me learn about numbers. I clacked coloured balls from one side of the frame to the other, adding them, then taking them away. I liked the sound they made.

After that, we traced the map of Africa. The map was in an atlas with thick pages that stuck together. The map was drawn with thick black lines that wriggled across the page. Matthew showed me where the lines went.

"It's important to be able to make your own way in the world, Astrid," he said.

There were many places in the world, but Africa was the one we visited most often. Matthew put his hand over mine and we followed the trails that he once followed, through countries with strange names. Matthew knew how to say them all. As our hands moved along the lines, he told me stories about animals that rolled around in swamps and drank from watering holes. There were giant hippos and elephants, warthogs with ugly faces and flies that lived in the animals' skin.

A full-size human skeleton watched us while we worked. It had once belonged to my grandfather, who was a doctor. Matthew used it to show me all the parts of the body. I loved the smooth, cool feel of the bones under my hand, the way they fit together.

During my lessons, I repeated everything I learned until Matthew was satisfied. If I made mistakes, I had to do the work again. When he was pleased with my work, he said, 'That'll do.' Whenever he said it, balloons burst in my stomach, spreading waves of warmth through me. But he didn't say it very often.

"The world won't give you a second chance," he told me. "It works on the principles of survival of the fittest. I don't want to give people the opportunity to perceive you as weak."

I loved it when Matthew talked to me like a grown-up. I repeated his words over and over in my head, trying to figure out what they meant. His voice was deep and sounded as if bits of gravel were stuck to it.

After lessons, we ate bread and cheese, followed by small apples with wrinkles all over their skins, which tasted sweet and sour at the same time. Then he gave me a bath, soaping me and rubbing my skin until it turned pink. Afterwards, he carried me into my bedroom and tucked me into bed, where he told me tales of gods and warriors. My favourite stories were from the Viking book. The Viking book was different from the books downstairs; it wasn't as thick and the pages were wider. It had a hard, bright-blue cover, with a picture of a big ship on it. Red letters flowed across the top of the ship's sails. They said *Norse Myths and Legends*. Matthew told me that Norse was another word for Viking.

I always opened the book to the first page, even though there was nothing written on it, except for the strange, curly letters on the top corners. I held the book close to me and tried to read them, but they weren't like the sandpaper letters. When I asked Matthew what they said, he didn't know. I wondered why. He knew the answers to all the other questions I asked him.

On the next page, there was a map of all the places where the Vikings lived. I mouthed all the names as Matthew said them; our fingers voyaged along narrow fjords. I was fascinated by the gulping sounds Matthew made when he said the names.

On the left-hand side, the pages were filled with black, spiky letters. The first letter on each page was bigger than all the others. There were decorations all around them, so they were hard to read. But I could read some of the words. On the right-hand side, there were drawings covered with thin pieces of white cloth. There were more ships, big men fighting with swords and stones covered in curly writing, just like the writing on the first page. The pictures were full of colours: red for blood, blue and green for the sea and yellow for the warriors' hair, which was almost the same colour as mine. There were raised lines around the edges which made a frame for the picture. I liked to run my fingers over them.

Matthew described each picture for me, filling in the gaps my eyes missed. I leaned close to him and turned the pages while he read tales of battles and banquets. When my eyes grew heavy, Matthew closed the book and said, "Good night, little Viking."

He leaned over me and I reached out to touch the blurred outlines of his face, to check that it was there. The rough hairs on his cheeks tickled my fingers, making me giggle. He laughed too; his laugh rumbled and made his body shake.

One night, he didn't laugh. Instead, he held me tight and said,

"You can be whatever you want, little one. Don't let anyone tell you otherwise."

I DIDN'T KNOW where my mother was. Mrs O'Brien was Michael and Joseph's mother. They called her Mammy. I knew I must have a mother too, but she didn't live with us. One night, after he closed the Viking book, I asked Matthew if he knew where she lived. He always answered my questions.

"Far away," he said.

"Does she live in Valhalla with the Vikings?"

"It's possible. Now go to sleep."

He kissed me on the forehead. I reached out to touch his face, but my fingers touched the air.

SOMETIMES WE WENT to Dublin, because Matthew had to work. It took a long time to drive there. The roads were narrow, with bumps that made the car jump up and down. I liked that. While we drove, we listened to radio programmes that came from across the sea and told us stories about faraway places and people. I didn't understand all the stories, but Matthew explained them to me.

There was a library in Dublin, where Matthew went to get books. Sometimes he just collected them and brought them home; but other times, he wasn't allowed to take them out, so he read them at a big table. When he did that, I sat across from him, reading my own books. After we were finished with the library, we went to an office, where Matthew showed his samples to men who wore suits. He said he didn't like doing it, but he had to, because the men gave him money for his samples and the notes he wrote in his book. While Matthew talked to the men, I stayed in a corner and completed tasks which Matthew gave me. If I finished early, I came over to sit beside him. He said if I was good, we could go to the Zoo, the Museum of Natural History, or the Botanic Gardens, my favourite. So I didn't make a sound.

When we went to Dublin, we stayed in Matthew's other house, which was made of red bricks and stood at the bottom of a garden belonging to a bigger house. Matthew used to live in the bigger one when he was young. There was too much furniture in the house and all the furniture was green or brown. But the furniture was comfortable; the chairs sank with a soft sigh when you sat in them. There were a lot of books in the Dublin house too, but they were the colour of bird feathers: green, yellow, brown, red and blue. They felt softer too, like velvet.

FROM TIME TO time, a lady with a clipboard came to visit. She always wore brown clothes and used big words like 'needs assessment' and 'developmental goals.' I asked Matthew what they meant and he said they were nonsense words. The lady's visits made Matthew cross. He always shouted at her.

Sometimes letters came, saying that I had to go to the clinic. Matthew didn't like the clinic. He muttered under his breath when the letters came. When I went there, I played games. I piled bricks on top of each other, matched shapes, recited words. The games were fun, but it was strange to play them with people watching. After the games, I sat on Matthew's lap while a man in a white coat shone lights into my eyes. I didn't like that part. The lights made me yelp and wriggle in Matthew's arms. He said they had to use the lights to find out how my eyes worked. He told me to be as still as a Viking warrior and rubbed my arms until I stopped wriggling. Matthew asked the people questions all the time. He shouted at them too and told them they were treating me like a lab rat. When we came home from the clinic, Matthew always said, "They seemed surprised you weren't mentally defective."

I didn't know what he meant, but he always laughed when he said it, so I laughed too.

ONE MORNING, MATTHEW didn't get up. When I knocked on his door to tell him I was ready to go swimming, there was no sound. I ran downstairs and checked in the study. Sometimes he went in there during the night and forgot about the time. But he wasn't there. I ran back upstairs and knocked again. This time, there was a rustling sound. I pushed the door open. At first, I thought there was no-one in the room, but when I moved closer to the bed, I saw a bump under the white blanket. It was the same shape as the mountains in the atlas, the high ones that were covered in snow all year round. When I reached out to touch the bump, it moved. I crept around the side of the bed. Matthew's head poked out of the blanket. His eyes were closed.

"Matthew? Aren't we going swimming?"

He opened his eyes. It took him a long time.

"Not today, little one."

He put his hands on my shoulders. They were so hot they burned my skin, even though I was wearing my pyjamas.

"Astrid, I'm going away for a little while. I have a fever and I need to go to a hospital in Dublin, where they can give me special medicine."

His voice sounded different; there was extra gravel in it. And he spoke so fast that the words ran into each other.

"Could I come with you?"

"Not this time."

My head spun. Matthew never went to Dublin without me.

"Where will I go?"

"You're going to stay with Mrs O'Brien. I trust you'll behave well for her."

I wanted to touch his face, but his hands were still on my shoulders and I couldn't reach.

"You must go now. The ambulance is coming. It's just for a short while. You mustn't worry."

My head cleared. Matthew never told lies. He was coming back. Nothing else mattered.

❧ Guides & Warriors ❧

As I opened the door of the bar, I was greeted by a blast of male laughter. The bar was long and spacious, with an L-shaped counter in the corner. A brown lamp hung from the ceiling, its light casting a soft glow. The bar was a woodland glade; its walls were lined with dark, burnished wood and my feet sank into a soft green carpet. The windows were obscured by thick curtains of a darker green. Wildlife congregated around several of the scrubbed tables; the Cabbage Patch Kids were joined by large, lumpen men with battered, lived-in faces and voices that rose to a dull roar. Glasses of beer the colour of sputum sat in front of them. The air was thick with testosterone.

"Oh good, you're here," said Cliona. "Now we can begin."

There was a seat between her and Kim at a small table. I plonked Mia onto it and went to look for another seat. It was hard to spot a gap in the closed ranks. I went to a couch seat located as far as possible from Cliona's table. It was upholstered in the same green as the carpet. There was a space on the edge of the seat, right beside Johno. The Fates were indeed kind. When I sat down, the seat sagged under my weight. Foam trailed along Johno's upper lip. I fought the temptation to wipe it off with the tip of a finger, place the finger in his mouth.

"No need to rebuke you for being late then," I murmured.

"Sure I'm always quick when there's beer involved. One of the fellas brought me to me room and I just shoved me shite in the wardrobe and came straight down."

"You're not sharing?"

"No. All on me ownio. Lucky for the rest of yez, my farts are dire."

He chortled; the Greek Chorus joined in.

"Weren't you well able to find your own way down," said one.

"We've a grand room,"

"Bigger than last year."

"Yeah, but still small enough to hear you snoring."

The sound of Cliona banging the table with a spoon cut through their laughter.

"If I could just have your attention for a moment. I'd like to welcome all you Twilight Warriors to Mosenbach, for what I hope will be yet another resounding success for Sightskiers."

A sudden memory impaled me, of a pit-bull face below a headline which read 'Cliona's Crusade: blind athlete to climb four peaks in 24 hours for charity.'

"What's with the Twilight Warrior motif?" I hissed at Johno.

"It's what she calls us."

"Why?"

"Don't you know? We're such brave little fighters," he gurgled.

I removed the napkin from a nearby knife and fork, snatched them up and turned them into fencer's foils. Their clanking underpinned Cliona's earnest account of the trip's origins. I let my thigh rest against Johno's; it was rock-hard. Even harder than Jazz's. I imagined running my fingers up and down the length of it. Snatches of Cliona's monologue punctured my reverie, 'give something back... empowerment through skiing... helped me to accept my blindness.' Her talk climaxed with a litany of sponsors and fundraisers.

"Last of all, I want to thank my wonderful partner, Kim. Without him, I could never be the warrior I am today."

She raised their joined hands in a sort of victory salute.

"She deserves a medal," said Johno.

"What on earth for?"

"For bein such a brave little fighter."

We both sniggered. Cliona's voice rose to a crescendo, "Remember, it doesn't matter how often you fall, you can always get up again. At the end of the day, we're here to enjoy ourselves and to grow from each other's company." No-one was allowed to challenge her position as Queen of Cabbage Patch Land.

Everyone cheered. Didn't know why; she was no Marcus Aurelius. My limbs became restless; her words induced a longing to escape. As she sat down, Kim put his arms around her and they began to whisper and fondle each other.

"I've tears in me eyes," said Johno, "tears of boredom."

I returned the knife and fork to their napkin. There were kinks in the napkin which refused to straighten. As I attempted to smooth them, I became aware of a presence beside me. I didn't turn around; the task required my full attention. But then I felt a tap on my shoulder. A man was sitting on a chair beside me, a stocky creature whose face was almost obscured by a covering of reddish-brown hair. One of the friendly natives of the forest. His muscles threatened to burst out of his football shirt.

"Astrid, isn't it?"

"Yes."

"I'm Martin."

He held out his hand and I submitted to another bone-crushing handshake. His hand was a slab of meat; pink and glistening. It swallowed mine.

"You're stuck with me, I'm afraid."

"I don't know what you mean."

"Sorry, it's the accent. You can take the boy out of Blackpool... I'm your own personal guide."

Ah yes, the guides. A minor detail. Reckoned I could shake him off within two days.

"Astrid. Haven't heard that before. Where's it come from then?"

"It's kind of Viking."

"Your parents Swedish or what?"

"Something like that." He was a subscriber to my Viking myth.

"Saw you having fun with the stairs earlier. Would have helped you out, but you were nearly at the top. Anyway, my hands were full with the lads. Awful beasts, them spiral jobbies. Trip on them the whole time meself."

I stood up, knocking against his knee.

"Listen, I'd love to stay and chat, but I have to freshen up for the night's festivities."

"Be seeing you later then," he said.

The undergrowth parted to reveal a flash of teeth.

I LAY ON my bed, trying to orchestrate the next manoeuvre in my plan of attack. But I was unable to summon up the necessary energy. Instead, I stared at the ceiling, counting the dark splodges on the wooden beams above my bed. Three on the first one, four on the second. The handle of Mia's suitcase brushed against my waist. She spread a dress in front of her, running her fingers along the folds with delicate strokes, in case it might tear. The dried sweat under my arms formed sedimentary layers. Mia was talking; her words merged to form a gushing stream. I fought to keep my eyes open, but tiredness nailed them shut.

IT WAS DARK. I looked around, fuddled to find myself confronted with white walls, rather than the faded floral wallpaper of my bedroom in Dublin. I rubbed the thick layers of sleep out of my eyes and sat up. The room was empty. I switched on the lamp by my bed and looked at my watch. 9.00pm. 8.00pm Irish time.

Every Sunday, 8.00pm to 10.00pm, I morphed into DJ Ice White and broadcast my radio show, turning Jazz's studio into my own lair. I kept the lights off, letting myself be guided by red numbers, waves of sound, the feel of the cross-fader, the blinking laptop screen. Unlike Jazz, I was a laptop girl all the way. Easier that way, less fiddling. Less room for error. Even though the show was pre-loaded, I still liked to be present, to supervise the show's progress, to immerse myself in its soundscapes. And on the rare occasions when I received requests, I was able to respond in an instant. I sat in the big black swivel chair in front of the desk, my head bobbing up and down to the beats. My comfortable earmuff headphones enabled me to detect minute changes in rhythm.

The show featured an eclectic range of deep and minimalist house, intelligent techno, trip-hop and electronica. The bleeping, boreal beats of Finland, Sweden and Iceland were my specialty. Thanks to the nights spent with my Viking book, the strange Nordic names tripped off my tongue with ease. Sometimes I visited warmer climes, where the beats were mellower, more full-bodied. I interspersed these electronic warblings with obscure factoids about the music and its creators; my voice weaved in and out of the beats. Most of the tracks were quite rare, sourced through hours of careful cybertrawling. In honour of my snow-capped location, that week's edition of White Nights featured plenty of geyser-hot Icelandic electro.

Jazz never came in during the show, but on occasion, the sound of his films leaked through the wall. Sometimes I kipped on his couch after the show finished, but more often that not, he walked me to the DART. On the way to the station, we made desultory conversation about our sets, or swopped views of current entries to the dance and electronica charts.

WE WEREN'T DOING anything. Jenny just happened to stumble upon our little post-club ritual. I always stayed with Jazz when I didn't score at the club, or my regulars were unavailable. We were in the studio, relaxing to mellow beats. Jazz was laying his set down for the following week. He liked to do it on Sundays while the previous set still filled his mind. He also liked to correct glitches that were inaudible to everyone else but him. And me. He was planning one of his retro nights for the following week, a homage to acid house. Not my preference, but I figured he was allowed a rare moment of self-indulgence. Besides, the punters flocked to the retro nights, which meant more random ballers for me.

"Time to blow the dust off your Roland," I said.

Jazz lifted his vintage drum machine out of its hiding place under the sound-desk and hooked it up. He relished an excuse to play with it. We lined the beats up in logical sequence; so he could navigate them as if they were points on a map. Our movements were swift and silent; I anticipated Jazz's every move. We were both still in our kaks, though Jazz was due to go to an afternoon screening at the IFI with Jenny, who shared Jazz's taste for obscure Japanese films. I was wearing an extra long Prism T-shirt which skimmed the tops of my thighs. Jazz was in his boxers. My laptop was balanced on my knees. I pressed my face close to the screen and attempted to click on my selected track, but the mouse kept dancing out of reach.

"Come back, for fucksake," I muttered.

"Huh?" Jazz muttered, turning around.

I clicked on the screen a few times, and then looked up.

"Check your email," I said. "There's a gem waiting for you."

It was a warped yet fabulous reinterpretation of an acid-house standard that I knew was a favourite of Jazz's. Jazz cranked up the volume and adopted his default listening pose, pressing his knuckles into his cheeks.

"Where did you find that?"

The awe in his voice was gratifying.

"One of my cybertrawls. Am I good to you, or am I good to you?"

We high-fived, our classic ritual whenever either of us pulled off a major DJ coup. As the first verse played itself out, I faded up Jazz's next track.

"There's a couple of places you could loop this in. Like here, where it slows."

Jazz liked to punctuate one tune with tantalising hints of another. A standard DJ trick, but he pulled it off with finesse. And a little help from me.

"Oh yeah," said Jazz. "That'll go down well. Cool."

He removed a CD from its case.

"Better give this a whirl," he said, sighing. "Can't believe I got lumbered with it."

The cover had the garish, try-hard veneer of a demo.

"What is it?"

"It's Glenn's cousin's, so he'll be on to me."

Glenn managed the sound studio where Jazz worked: he knew Jazz was a soft touch for DJ wannabes.

"Some 15-year-old fuckwit with his first set of decks?"

"Something like that."

Jazz loaded it onto his computer. The speakers squealed.

"Must be feedback," I said.

"No, it isn't."

Jazz's mouth was set in a grim line. When it came to sound, purity was his mantra. The record descended into sonic chaos. Swirling guitar chords clashed with a thick layer of breaks, creating an oil-on-water effect which was exacerbated by the rodent-like quality of the vocals. Jazz's hands turned into fists. I stood behind him and placed my hands on his shoulders, massaging away the knots from the previous night.

"That's quite a mash-up," I said diplomatically.

"More like a train wreck."

"No, it's the aural equivalent of regurgitated meat."

The mellow beats of Jazz's laughter filled the studio. I enjoyed making him laugh; it was a rare privilege.

"Let me add something to the mix," I said.

I loaded up an extra-deep number which I planned to play later. The dark-caramel voice offset the hamster vocals.

"That's an improvement," Jazz said, grinning.

My hand brushed against his as I adjusted the cross-fader. The downy hairs on his arm stood to attention.

"Let's do the ultimate test," I said. "Play it backwards."

Trashing Jazz's demos was one of our favourite games. Jazz adjusted the settings and the hamsters began their chorus again.

"Tell me this; how is it possible that it sounds exactly the same now as it did on the first play? That breaks numerous scientific laws," I stated.

"Yeah, well, the punters love this kind of Scooter crap."

"In that case," I said, holding the CD aloft, "it must go in the bag for next week."

"No way," Jazz mock-growled.

He made a grab for the CD, but I danced away. As I attempted to insert it into his CD case, he pinned me against the wall. We tussled and I broke away, still clutching the CD. I made for the door, but my path was blocked by a hard object which moved as I made contact with it. There was a smothered squeal. The laughter died on our lips. Jenny stood in the doorframe, rubbing herself as if inflicted with a mortal wound. I developed a sudden urge to use the bathroom, but Jenny was still blocking the entrance, so I was forced to nudge past her. Their voices leaked under the bathroom door.

"Oh God, Jenny, I can't believe it slipped my mind," Jazz said. "We were just listening to some demos and lost track of time."

"You were supposed to meet me there twenty minutes ago. We won't have time for food now."

"Look, we can still make it for the movie. I'll take the car. I just need to throw on some clothes."

Jazz was in the bedroom now. Jenny and I jostled for space at his bedroom door. My shoulder brushed against her temple. I always towered over Jazz's girlfriends; he suffered from a severe dose of small-man syndrome. He pulled a pair of chinos and a T-shirt out of his wardrobe and hopped on one leg as he struggled to put the chinos on.

"Let me get dressed," he grunted. "I'll be out in a minute, I promise."

"Naughty boy, Geoffrey."

I wagged my finger at Jazz, making no attempt to disguise my mirth.

"I'll make myself scarce; leave you two to your domestic."

I retrieved my own clothes in the studio, then went to the kitchen. Jenny lingered in the corridor, twisting her hands, a soul trapped in Hades. At last, Jazz came out. Without a word,

Jenny followed him out of the apartment. The door slammed behind them. By now, I was beginning to feel peckish, so I decided to indulge in one of my favourite post-club delicacies; cold baked beans eaten straight from the tin.

After that, I put the final touches to my set, evening out peaks and troughs, cruising on waves of sound. Through the beats, I heard a key in the lock, then the sound of the studio door being pushed open. I looked up to find Jazz leaning against the doorframe, panting.

"Wow. That was a short film."

"You're still here?"

He sounded punch-drunk.

"Told you I had glitches to sort out."

"We didn't make the movie. She broke up with me."

He dashed his hand across his face.

"Because you forgot about the cinema?"

"You could say that."

His voice shook.

"Bummer. Still, you'll soon find a replacement."

"No, Astrid. I won't be looking for a replacement. Trust me."

Air leaked out of him, in a long, slow hiss. "I have to go out, go to the gym and stuff. I don't think I'll be back when your show finishes."

"Yeah, whatever."

My attention was already claimed by the delicate beats that curled around the studio like smoke.

THINKING ABOUT THE show filled my stomach with a sudden niggling ache. Withdrawal symptoms, nothing more. I checked the phone for a progress report from Jazz. The inbox was empty. I typed, then deleted:

Hp u srvivd putin my sho on d rd.

I hefted myself off the bed, preparing to re-enter the fray. When I reached the bar, they were all sitting at the long table, now rendered almost unrecognisable by a white cloth. Cliona sat at the head of it.

"How's the vision, Cliona?" one of the guides was asking her.

"Oh, you know. The tunnel gets a little darker every year. But I always endeavour to find the light at the end."

She delivered her penny philosophy with a heavy sigh.

Waitresses wearing green and white uniforms were gathering up dinner plates. Johno was surrounded on all sides. Kim stood up to let me slide onto the long couch seat, then perched on the edge of it, beside Cliona's chair. I was sandwiched between him and Mia, my escape route blocked.

"You've missed dinner," Cliona said. "Mia said she tried to call you, but you didn't hear her."

"Surrendered to the arms of Morpheus," I muttered.

"What's that?"

I shrugged, I didn't see the point in elaborating.

"Never mind. I doubt they'll serve you now."

"Reckon they'll spring for a plate of chips?"

"You are wanting chips only, ja?"

The waitress materialised from nowhere.

"Yaw," Johno shouted.

His imitation was far from perfect, but everyone guffawed. Seconds later, the waitress set a plate of chips in front of me. They were a little dried out, but I knew better than to quibble. Cliona embarked on another monologue. The word 'disco' leapt out at me.

"What sort of disco?" I asked.

Cliona gave her short, barking laugh.

"Oh, well I was actually referring to my charity. It's called Disability Cooperative, or DisCo for short. We help visually-challenged people find meaningful social outlets. In fact, we're the ones who spearheaded the trip. We continue to raise the funds each year for the facilities we enjoy when we come."

"It's a brilliant opportunity," Mia said, rubbing her hands hard enough to generate electricity. "You know, to meet other people like me, who understand, like."

"Well, we blindies have to stick together."

I hoped she wasn't including me in that classification. Somewhere in my mind, gates clanged shut. Cliona turned the laser beam of her attention on me.

"What do you do in life, Astrid?" she said.

"International spy."

Mia giggled. Cliona's chin jutted out.

"I won't dignify that with a response."

I decided to take a different conversational tack.

"I read that article about you in the paper. The one describing your epic mountain odyssey."

"Really. And what did you think?"

Her voice quivered in anticipation of plaudits.

"There were seven typographical errors," I said.

She clicked her tongue; the sound was growing familiar.

"And how's the course going, Mia?"

"Oh, great. But it's not important stuff like you're doing," Mia answered dutifully.

Bits of Mia's hair were escaping from her ponytail. She didn't move her head in Cliona's direction. Matthew always drilled me to follow the direction of his voice. *Look at me, Astrid. There's no reason you shouldn't be able to look people in the eye.*

"Well Mia, education is the first step on the road to independence," Cliona stated proudly.

Mia beamed.

"Mia's doing Disability Studies," she explained to me.

Gimptronics. A smirk hovered on my lips. Such a term could be considered cruelty to the blind.

"That's where I began. It's such a wonderful grounding. It helped me to see how important it is to embrace your blindness."

I remembered Cliona pointing me out at the airport and again when I came down for the 'welcome ceremony.' Not the behaviour of a blind person. I tuned out the white noise and attempted to plug into Johno's roared conversation with the Greek Chorus.

"This is me third time here," one of them was saying.

"He dragged me into it."

"You're an awful man altogether," said Johno. "Sure I'm a virgin, you'll have to go easy on me."

They all howled with laughter. I figured the number of beer glasses collected in front of them accounted for much of their mirth. A vodka was in order. I speared my last chip and stood up, squeezed past Kim, and accidentally knocked against Cliona's chair. Her glass wobbled and fizz spilled over the edge. She called after me. I looked over my shoulder.

"Excuse me," I said. "It's very important for the visually challenged to obtain sustenance."

Martin was at the counter with some of the other guides, who were all trading insults at the top of their lungs. The barman approached me.

"Vodka, please."

"You vant I give you Coke with that?" he said.

"No."

I drained the glass. The vodka blazed a trail through my stomach, suffusing me with warmth. The first hit was always the most satisfying.

"You're a hard one, aren't you?" said Martin. "You'll want to go easy on those if you're to be fit for the slopes tomorrow."

I looked past him and ordered another.

✌ Boots & Memories ✌

PERFECTING MY LOOK made me late for breakfast. I began with my hair, slathering on even more gel than usual to ensure that it was immune to the elements. Mia's inane chatter distracted me, despite my best efforts to filter it out.

"I have to ring my mother later," she was saying. "She gets worried. She's been saying prayers for me and all. I was in an incubator when I was born, you see. That's how I..."

She hovered behind me as I inspected my appearance through the black spots in the mirror. I turned around. Her hands hung by her side, her hair fell in a curtain over her face. Her ski suit was in disarray, twisted straps, buttons in the wrong holes. Her zip was suspended in mid-air.

"I can't find my gloves. Or my sunglasses."

She was still in that incubator.

"Here, let me fix your buttons."

I bent over and readjusted the buttons and straps. In order to access her zip, I was forced to kneel in front of her; she was a Lilliputian. There was a clasp at the top of the zip, to keep it in a fixed position. My fingers brushed against her stomach as I felt for it. It was a little too early in the morning for girl-on-girl action.

I rummaged for her gloves and shades while she stood to one side, twisting her hands. The shades were on her locker. The lenses were the colour of cellophane and the frames were similar in texture to the plastic that held beer cans together. Not even authentic knock-offs. The gloves were harder to retrieve; they were obscured by the lid of her suitcase. I thrust them at her.

"You better go down," I said. "I'm going to take about another million years."

Unlike the previous day, the sun was obscured by thick clouds, but its glare still penetrated. Full riot gear was required.

"No, it's okay," she said. "I'd rather..."

Rocks remain impervious to the presence of the limpets that use them for shelter. I turned my attention to my ski suit, which hung in the wardrobe. It was black with flecks of yellow. Almost new. I fancied it gave me an air of menace. The rest of my armour consisted of a Prism baseball cap and a pair of Adidas wraparounds. Not an elegant look, but an unbeatable combination for fending off rays. I plastered on layers of suncream and composed a text to Jazz in my mind, *Armed 4 d slopes*. But as Mia pondered her choice of breakfast, the words evaporated, like steam. She attached herself to my elbow as I pushed open the door, with the grip of someone accustomed to having elbows take her everywhere. I contrasted it with another touch, a touch which landed on my skin with the grace of a butterfly. The strange, niggling ache returned to my stomach; knots began to form.

A BREAKFAST BUFFET ran along one wall. It was almost obscured by a humming swarm of waitresses who hovered around it, selecting choice titbits for the Cabbage Patch Kids. The Greek Chorus sat at the long table, which was strewn with plates. I plonked Mia beside them and a waitress bustled up to her.

The buffet consisted of serried ranks of cheeses punctured with holes and sausage meat of various hues, which glistened up at me. I decided to bypass it; these items were far too random to be eating for breakfast. A pot of coffee stood on a heating plate at a separate table. It produced viscous black liquid that was the consistency of recycled road oil. Just how I liked it.

Johno was now sitting beside Mia, wearing a ski suit in an unfortunate shade of red that clashed with his ruddy complexion. At least all the components of his ensemble were in place. He had no need for a nursemaid, although he was enjoying the attention of a serving wench. The Greek Chorus were explaining that they had enough sight to find their bits and weave their way to the bar. This prompted yet another blast of laughter, setting my teeth on edge. I sat at the other end of the table, giving them a wide berth. My hands laced tight around my cup. The table was scrubbed to a whitish shade; its surface was free of cracks or splinters. The coffee scalded my throat, shocking my system into life.

"All right, Astrid."

I jumped, turning around. Martin stood there, grinning at me. He pulled up a chair and flung himself onto it.

"Hungover, are we?"

Did he have to be so bluff?

"No way. Takes a hell of a lot more than I had last night."

"Nervous then."

"Oh, you figure?"

How did he know?

"Thought you might be, if you're off your grub. Don't worry. I haven't pushed anyone off a cliff yet."

He laughed. A silence fell.

"Right. We need to have a bit of a chat."

He shifted in his seat.

"How much can you see?'

None of your business. Fucksake.

"I know, I know, it's everyone's favourite question."

"Enough."

"Light make everything wonky?'

I nodded. My cheeks prickled.

As we stepped out of the hotel, our feet made contact with puddles of slush and slick pavement. The ground became uncertain. A loose conga line formed, with the Cabbage Patch Kids holding onto the elbows of the guides. We were an expeditionary force, in search of skis and boots. Relieved of my shadow, I decided to make a break for it, stride ahead. But my legs had other ideas. They slid out from under me, made spectacular zig-zagging motions. Martin's arm shot out, a lifebelt offering rescue. I gripped it, letting instinct take over.

"Nice bit of break-dancing, that," he said.

Everyone laughed. I didn't quite grasp the joke.

THE PINK LADIES were our leaders. They were supposed to be called helpers, but I called them pink ladies because they wore soft pink cardigans and had pink faces to match. They wore other colours as well, but most of the time they wore pink. They didn't hold my hand, like Matthew or Mrs O'Brien. Instead, when I walked down steps, or on ground that wobbled, I held on to their elbows.

They gave me glasses to wear, which were gold around the edges. They also gave me sunglasses. When I put the sunglasses on, they turned everything a pinkish-brown colour and made my nose itch. I kept dropping the glasses and sunglasses and the pink ladies always found them and returned them to me, clicking their tongues and saying *Now, now, Astrid.* They were always saying that. The other thing they said was, *Good girl!* When they said it, they sounded surprised. I didn't feel any balloons burst inside me, like when Matthew said it. And they talked a lot about my eyes. I never knew my eyes were so important. They were just there.

The pink ladies were always touching me, giving me hugs and kisses for no reason. They poked at my clothes and brushed my hair and put ribbons in it, like Mrs O'Brien. I didn't want them to touch me. They were too soft; they smothered me in a blanket of slow words and pats. There were a lot of pink ladies, but they were all the same.

Everywhere we walked, there was a pink lady nearby, in the corridors, in the yard and at the top of the table in the dining room. They helped us to dress in the mornings. I wriggled under their fussing hands. But sometimes they took a long time to reach me and I was ready by the time they arrived. I didn't need them to do things for me, like the other girls. I could do things for myself.

I WALKED BESIDE Martin, boxed in by Cabbage Patch Kids. The sound of our feet crunching on the snow was amplified by the empty street. Low beams of sunlight slanted through the clouds, casting a thick yellow glow over the buildings. Hansel and Gretel cottages and quaint shops nestled against the protecting bulk of the mountains. Snow pooled on their curved tiles. Their glowing white walls threw the dirty colour of the snow into sharp relief. The guides gave a droll description of our surroundings.

"We always do this," said Cliona. "It helps us fill the gaps in our vision."

Her voice drilled holes through my skull. The guides gave a précis of the contents in the shop windows. Their words acted as a giant magnifying glass.

The boot shop was situated at the furthest end of the street. As we entered, we were greeted by a blast of warm air, which carried the strong smell of wet material. The conga dispersed in a whirl of activity, as stocky Austrians began plying us with skis and boots. Martin bent in front of me, adjusting the straps on the boots, moving my feet forwards and backwards on the skis. The two orange sticks strapped to my legs were to be my mode of transport over the next few days. They felt precarious.

When my ski fittings were complete, I went over to a set of chairs by the window to practise fastening and unfastening the boots. I wrestled with the straps, trying to imitate Martin's method. When I was finished, I made an attempt to walk. I gimped back and forth, my movements impeded by the cement-bag heaviness of the boots. A white beard flashed in front of me. One of the Greek Chorus. I pitched forward and he put his arms out to steady himself. They landed just below my breasts.

"Watch it," I hissed.

"I'm not trying to cop a feel, love," he said, chuckling.

I wobbled towards one of the chairs and collapsed onto it, covering my face, thinking it fortunate that none of the Cabbage Patch Kids could see me. A thin voice buzzed in my ear; through the gaps in my fingers, I saw my shadow on the chair beside me.

"How old are you?" she asked.

The fastenings were too tight. My fingers fumbled; the grooves that held the fastenings were somewhat bigger than those of a vinyl record.

"Cliona was saying she thought we might be the same age. I'm 26."

My head snapped up. She looked young enough to be carded at Prism. Not that she fit the typical customer profile.

"It's just, there's something familiar about you. Maybe we were in the same class. Did you go to Immaculate Heart?"

"Huh?"

I yanked at my boot, trying to pry it off. The name triggered a faint chime in a dusty corner of my mind.

"You know, the girls' school."

The boot freed itself from my leg with a satisfying glug. My brain dug up the entry for Immaculate Heart. The official name for the pink cage.

"Maybe that's how I know you."

So she was one of the dead-eyed girls, the Cabbage Patch Kids. A taste flooded into my mouth, a half-remembered taste of metal mixed with sugar.

"Doubtful," I snorted.

"Oh really? I could have sworn that's where I knew you from. It's an unusual name, Astrid. You'd remember an Astrid. I was there all the time. It was brilliant craic."

Just then, Mia's guide Kevin came over with her boots and she became preoccupied with learning to strap them up. She was an animal that thrived in captivity.

WHEN THE BROWN lady came, I was dangling upside down on the tree at the bottom of Mrs O'Brien's garden. I loved the tree, with its wide, spreading branches, its solid trunk, its rough bark. The O'Brien boys climbed it like monkeys and I wanted to climb it too.

I knew the lady was coming because Mrs O'Brien and I went to Wexford on the bus to buy a dress. She said I needed a good dress because a visitor was coming. Mrs O'Brien had a lot of visitors. When they came, they sat in Mrs O'Brien's kitchen and talked in low voices. We weren't allowed into the kitchen while they were there.

The dress was light pink, with a darker pink ribbon around the waist. I'd never had a dress before. The skirt stuck out. When I put the dress on, it was hard to move, because the material was stiff and tight. Mrs O'Brien also bought me a ribbon for my hair, which was the same colour as the dress.

When the day came, she helped me put on the dress and tied the ribbon to my hair, at the side of my face. She told me I wasn't allowed to play in the dress. But when I went outside, the boys were hanging from the tree. Before I knew it, I was scrambling up the branches, slipping a lot because I was wearing girl shoes.

"Astrid, don't," said Michael. "Mammy says you've to keep your dress nice for the lady."

"You can't stop me."

The boys reached down and held me steady while I climbed. At last I reached the branch they were on.

"Show me how to hang upside down," I said.

Michael held my hands and Joseph held my legs. As I swung free, my glasses slid off my face. There was a rushing noise in my head, which felt lighter than before. All I could see were clumps of green and yellow. I was at the top of the world. Through my delighted squeals, I heard Mrs O'Brien's voice.

"Merciful hour, child, get down out of there. You'll be killed."

The boys pulled me upright. Hands made a circle around my waist and pulled me down. My feet hit the ground and wobbled. The hands reached out for me again. When I turned around, I saw that they belonged to the brown lady. Mrs O'Brien picked up my glasses and handed them to me. As I put them on, she rubbed leaves and bark off my dress, making sweeping sounds with her hands.

"Look at your nice dress," she clucked. "I told you to keep it clean for the lady."

The brown lady bent down and pressed her face close to mine. Her chin had a point at the end. I took two steps back.

"Hello there, Astrid," she said. "Do you remember me?"

"Where's your clipboard?"

She laughed. I didn't know why.

"Aren't you a clever girl?"

"Why are you here?"

"She just wants to have a little chat with you," said Mrs O'Brien.

"But Matthew isn't here. She only comes when Matthew's here. He shouts at her."

The lady laughed again. Her laugh sounded different this time.

"Come on, we'll go inside," said Mrs O'Brien.

"Don't want to," I said.

The boys were still up in the tree, snorting with laughter.

"It won't take long," the lady said. "Then you can go out and play with your little friends again."

When we reached the house, Mrs O'Brien went to the kitchen. The lady perched on the edge of Mrs O'Brien's chair and asked me questions. It took her a long time to say all the words. I listened to the ticking of the clock on the mantelpiece.

Mrs O'Brien came in with a tray. She always used a tray when the visitors came. Air whooshed out of her mouth as she set it down. There was a teapot, a brown one, not the metal one she used at dinner time. The cups were different too; they were smaller and thinner and stood on saucers. Slices of her sponge cake were arranged on a plate. The milk was in a jug instead of a carton. Mrs O'Brien didn't tell the lady not to sit in her chair. Instead, she sat beside me on the couch. She put a glass of orange liquid in front of me. When I sipped it, bubbles spurted up my nose. It didn't taste like an orange; it tasted of sugar and metal mixed together. I put down the glass and didn't drink any more.

"Astrid, we need to talk to you about where you're going to live for the next little while," the lady said.

"But I live with Matthew. I'm just staying with Mrs O'Brien until he comes back."

"Of course you are," she said. "But your daddy isn't going to be back for a while."

"He said he was coming back."

"Well, he has to rest for a bit longer, you see."

"Why? Isn't his fever gone yet?"

"Oh." She gave a little laugh. "Well, I'm sure he'll be feeling much better soon. And in the mean time, you'll be going to a school in Dublin. It's called Immaculate Heart and there are lots of other little girls there who are just like you."

The taste of the orange drink was still in my mouth, even though I wasn't drinking it. I swallowed, trying to take the taste away.

"You'll love it there; you'll have loads of fun. And lots of little friends to play with."

Her voice went up and down, like a song.

"But when Matthew comes back, he won't know where I am. I'll go to Michael and Joseph's school and then I'll be here when he comes."

"You'll be coming back here on the holidays, pet," said Mrs O'Brien.

She squeezed my hand.

"Your daddy knows where you'll be," said the lady, "and you'll be much happier in the school in Dublin. They can look after you there. We'll be going up in the car next week."

"I only wish you could stay here all the time, but the house is too small," said Mrs O'Brien. "You've only that oul' mattress to sleep on."

I liked sleeping on the mattress. It was on the floor next to Michael and Joseph's bunk-beds and made squeaking sounds when I jumped on it.

"You can go back outside now, pet. We just need to talk about a few things."

The boys weren't in the tree any more. They asked me if I wanted to play football with them, but I said no. Instead,

I sat in the space between the tree and the hedge. The leaves on the ground crunched as I sat down. Matthew was going to come back and find me. The lady's words kept going around in my head. I tried to fit them together, but my head became heavy and dropped onto my knees. Vikings were separated all the time when they went on adventures, but they always found each other again.

ல Rising Steam ல

THE CAFE WAS a heaving mass of bodies. Shrieking Teutonic voices clogged my ears. It was similar in appearance to the hotel, with wood-beamed ceilings and tables covered in pink-and-white check cloths. Warm, thick air blasted into my face, fogging up my shades. I made for a quiet corner, took them off and rubbed them with the sleeve of my ski suit. The crowd blocked out the bulk of the sunlight, but my eyes still began making their traditional escape bid. I slipped my shades back on post haste and squeezed them tight shut. *Calm those eyes of yours* was Matthew's dictum whenever they performed their fluttering dance. Closing them had the desired effect. At least none of them were in a position to witness my little ritual.

"Oh, there you are," said Martin. "Come over and join us. We're getting our kit on. Not off. Just in case you're confused."

He roared with laughter; at least one of us was amused by his wit.

The other Cabbage Patch Kids were clustered at a group of tables by the window. I took a seat at the edge and began the delicate task of inserting my feet into my boots. Johno was beside me, but he was engrossed in the skiing horror stories being related at top volume by the Greek Chorus.

This time, my fingers located the grooves in an instant. I folded the Velcro strap at the top so that both sides were in perfect alignment. All around me, guides knelt before Cabbage-Patch Kids, adjusting their straps. Even Johno was submitting to the treatment. Although Cliona wasn't. She and Kim sat side by side, fastening their boots in silence. As Mia waited for her guide to finish, her body moved back and forth to an inaudible rhythm. It looked eerie. One of the Greek Chorus stood up, his hands flapping from side to side.

"Where's me shades?" he muttered.

One of the guides marched up to him.

"You left these on the bus, mate."

"Thanks," he said. "I was getting worried there for a minute. God, they're awful tight, aren't they, the boots?"

What perception.

"Sure they have to be, so you don't snap your ankles in half," said the other.

"Like the shoes they have for Irish dancing. You could use these for *Riverdance*."

They started thunking their boots off the ground. The noise was thunderous. My jaw clenched, my teeth were set on edge. I ducked my head, in order to dissociate myself.

"Jaysus, could you save the Michael Flatley stuff for the slopes? Me head's killing me," said Johno.

Johno shared Matthew's sentiments. *Best to blend in with your environment. Observe some form of camouflage.* He and I only had time to exchange a grunted, 'Good luck,' before his guide whisked him away. A furry beard came towards me. Martin. I stood up, ready for the off. No need for him to dance attendance.

"Proper speed merchant, aren't you."

"They're all right once you get used to them," I said, with affected nonchalance.

"You're not quite finished kitting up yet though."

"Oh?"

He held out a fluorescent vest trimmed with black. The words 'Blind Skier' were emblazoned on it, above a sick, winking eye.

"Get this on you."

I cleared my throat. Time to establish the ground rules.

"Um, I think there's some confusion here."

"Yeah? Well you'd better clear it up quick then. Snow'll melt at this rate."

"I'm not a stick tapper."

"You what?"

Fucksake, did I have to spell it out?

"I'm not blind," I said, through gritted teeth. "Not even close."

Martin stood in silence for a moment, scratching his beard.

"Well, I have to wear this," he said, holding up another fluorescent vest with the words 'Ski Guide' printed on it. "Matches my green hangover skin."

He laughed. I looked down at my boots and counted the clasps, one two three, one two three.

"Least yours matches your suit. Might as well be in this together then, eh?"

I watched as my hands grasped the offending beast, pulled it over my head and teased the material over my torso. When I looked up, Kim and Cliona were leaving. They were wearing the green uniform too.

"What's he need that for?" I muttered.

"Oh no, he's got a guide one. He takes Cliona down every year," Martin said, following my gaze. "He's been skiing since he was knee-high."

"His-n-hers skiing vests."

Martin laughed.

"That's it."

"Guess they're the fashion must-have of the season."

He was right; it highlighted the flecks of yellow and green on my suit.

ONE DAY I didn't go to school. Instead, I went to a big room full of toys and played games while people watched. Some of the games were the same as the ones in the clinic, but some of them were different. The people threw coloured balls that were never where I expected them to be. When they asked me to draw, I didn't know what my pencil was supposed to do and it made a hole in the paper. They said it didn't matter. My mouth became filled with the taste of orange-drink. It did matter. It mattered to me and to Matthew.

The games lasted for a long time. It felt strange to play them without Matthew there to watch. But I listened to his voice in my head, giving instructions as I wrote my name, read lists of words and stacked coloured blocks with numbers written on them. When the pink ladies said, 'Good girl,' I heard him say, 'That'll do.' It was easier to listen to him.

When the games were over, one of the pink ladies brought me to a clinic, like the one at home. We drove there in a car, because it was far away. When we arrived, we went to a room with a lot of machines in it. The pink lady sat on a soft chair in the centre of the room and held me in her lap. Her grip was soft, but too tight to escape from. She gave me a sweet with pink and yellow swirls. I held it close to my face and examined it, pressing my fingers into the swirls and squashing them flat. When I licked it, sugar stuck to my tongue. Another lady came in. She wore a white coat and held a small stick in her hand. There was a black and red dot at the top of the stick. When she held it close, I saw that it was a mouse, with round ears and a pointed nose. It wore a red dress. I knew the mouse wasn't real, because real mice didn't wear clothes. She moved it backwards and forwards; it was there and then it was gone. I swivelled my head in time to the movements. Then she asked me if I could follow the stick without moving my head and I couldn't see it any more. She put the stick away and asked me to read letters at the other side of the room. But I could only read the biggest one.

After that, a man came in, with a lady who wore a white dress. The man wore a white coat, like the first lady. He took out a box with metal rings on it and put them on my eyes. His hands were cold and the rings were cold as well. The lady in the white dress told me she was going to put liquid into my eyes. The people in the clinic never did that. The liquid stung my eyes and I whimpered.

"You're alright, lovie," the pink lady said.

I stopped wriggling. In my head, Matthew was telling me to be a brave little Viking.

Then the bright lights came on. My eyes kept jumping up and down. They always did that when the lights shone on me. They were trying to pop out of my head. I wriggled, but I didn't make any noise. When they turned the lights off, black spots appeared in front of their faces. The pink lady clucked when she saw that I was still holding the sweet. She covered it with a tissue and took it away, but bits of it were still stuck to my hand, so she took me to the toilet to wash it off. When I looked in the mirror, I saw huge black holes where my eyes were supposed to be. In the car on the way back to the school, I held my fingers up to my face. They blurred into each other. I closed my eyes. Matthew's voice was still there, he was telling me that I could be whatever I wanted.

MARTIN AND I spent the rest of the day on the patch of snow outside the ski cafe, as I followed the traditional recipe for learning to ski: start, stop, turn, fall over. Rinse and repeat. It wasn't too taxing; I only ever moved six feet or so in each direction from my original spot. Yet even that minimal effort was enough to mangle my limbs. The sun never emerged from behind the clouds, but my eyes still burned. As dusk fell, I tottered towards the bus, my legs struggling to hold me up, my ears still ringing from Martin's avalanche-inducing yells. The back of the bus was open and the Greek Chorus sat on the edge, taking off their boots.

"Ahhh," they sighed in unison as the boots slid off.

"It's like an orgasm, isn't it?"

"How would you know?"

When I took off my own boots, I was inclined to echo their sentiments.

The bus was driven by Kevin, Mia's guide. He drove round hairpin bends at speed, the radio playing in the background. The music was a palatable mush, Complan for the ears. Cliona was in full flight, describing the minutiae of her skiing technique and giving a thorough evaluation of her own performance. Johno was describing his falls in detail to Mia; each spillage was more dramatic than the last. She herself contributed little to the conversation, other than helium-balloon giggles. I switched on my phone. The screen taunted me with its resolute blankness. I filled it with the words,

```
Ges who cn ski.
```

Then rendered it blank again.

The windows were covered in condensation. I traced words on the steam, the Latin names of all the muscles I believed were hurting me at that moment. As Cliona's monologue reached its climax, I wrote the words *Stercus pro cerebrus*. Shit for brains. That was the good thing about Latin. It enabled me to deliver stealthy blows.

"Oi, Astrid, you're writing filthy words on the window," Kevin yelled over his shoulder.

Nuts.

"Just random observations," I muttered.

"G'wan, tell us," said Johno.

Anything to reel him in.

"Sort of posh swear words."

"Like what?"

Words flashed across my mind; my eyes oscillated in tandem with my thoughts.

"You ever hear of onanism?" I asked Johno.

"What's that?" Kevin asked.

"Sort of biblical masturbation."

"Ooh, kinky," said the Greek Chorus.

Mia giggled with her hand over her mouth. Cliona and Kim carried on with their own conversation, their voices lowered to prevent words from escaping.

"I could do with expanding me vocabulary," said Johno. "You'll have to give us a posh swear word every day."

This was an encouraging development, a strong tug on the line.

∓ Pictures at an ∓ Exhibition

THE CHURCH WAS almost full. Matthew's heavy footsteps drowned out the clamour of voices. We claimed our usual places near the front, at the edge of one of the long church seats. Beams of sunlight poured through the windows. Dust danced in the air. I kept my shades on, but put my straw hat on the floor, under my feet. As I straightened up, a shadow floated in front of me.

"Excuse me," said a soft voice.

Matthew grabbed my arm and pulled me upright.

"She needs to get past," he hissed.

The woman stepped over our feet and sat down with a plop on Matthew's other side.

"So sorry," she muttered, as she settled herself in.

I sat with my hands folded in my lap. My plaits were threatening to unravel. Mrs O'Brien showed me how to make plaits before she moved away, but mine never stayed tight like hers. I tilted my head so it perched on my shoulders. Figures moved around, wearing black and white suits like the one Matthew wore when he went to Dublin. Some of them carried violins which gleamed in the sunlight. Matthew nudged me.

"What have I told you about sitting like that?" he said.

I straightened up and the musicians swam out of focus. He read to me from the programme. This time, the concert featured a performance of *The Four Seasons*, by Antonio Vivaldi.

The music began; as I listened to the procession of notes, my mind stood still. My head slipped back onto my shoulders, but Matthew was too immersed in the music to notice.

Afterwards, there was tea and sandwiches in the garden behind the church, because it was the last concert of the season. First, we queued up to buy a cassette for the car. Our concert neighbour was now ahead of us in the queue. She was small and round, with a mass of curly brown hair that hid her face. The sunlight transformed her into a shimmering purple haze. A gust of wind blew her scarf to the ground. It was much thinner than the ones I wore in winter. Matthew bent to pick it up.

"Oh, thank you," she said. "Excuse me; I must pay for my tape."

There was also a big queue for the tea and sandwiches. The woman wasn't in it. Ladies wearing large hats and soft cardigans admired my sailor dress and remarked on how attentive I was during the concert. They said the same things every week. I tried not to squirm as they patted my head with their gloved hands and compared my hair to silk.

Matthew took a plate of sandwiches and a cup of coffee to a table. I followed behind with my cup of water, careful not to spill it.

"I can procure you some refreshments if you wish," Matthew said.

I was about to remind him that we already had sandwiches when I realised he was talking to the purple woman, who was standing behind us. Matthew never talked to the people at the concerts, even though they always wanted to talk to him.

"Oh no. There's no need to go to any trouble. I've already had lunch. Anyway, they have so many people to serve."

"Nonsense. They have nothing better to do."

He turned back towards the refreshments table. I adjusted my hat, which was slipping over my eyes. It was always doing that.

"My name is Astrid," I said to the woman, to fill the space left by Matthew.

"Nice to meet you, Astrid."

I waited for her to pat my head, but she shook my hand instead.

"What's your name?"

"I'm Ora."

"Is that spelt A-u-r-a?"

She laughed. Her laugh tinkled.

"Not quite. It begins with an 'O'."

Matthew came back with the refreshments and gave them to the woman. The plate and cup wobbled in her hands.

"The hungry masses are thinning out, so it wasn't too difficult to obtain these."

The woman smiled and thanked him, but then she put the plate and cup down on the table and didn't touch them. For a moment, nobody said anything, then Ora broke the silence.

"Maybe you could tell me your name, since you went to the trouble of getting me all this food."

"Dr Matthew Johnson. Pleased to meet you."

He shook her hand. Then he reached for his cup and drank most of the coffee in one gulp.

"So how old are you, Astrid?" Ora asked.

"Nine and five-sixths," I told her with a flourish.

She laughed again. I didn't know why. It was my age after all.

"Ten in November," Matthew added.

There was a frog in his throat.

"Aren't you lucky you didn't have to start school today?"

"Don't go to school."

"Oh! Don't you?"

"I educate her," Matthew said, before I could reply.

"Goodness. That's wonderful."

"Yes, this concert is part of our educational programme. We've been to all the concerts in the series. I take it this is your first one?"

"Yes. I'm not from here, you see. I was in the area. It was such a lovely surprise to find out it was on. Did you enjoy it?"

"Vivaldi is tolerable, I suppose. Are you familiar with the works of J.S. Bach?"

Matthew started talking about the Bach pieces on the tape. The woman fiddled with the end of her scarf. He talked for a long time and my legs became restless.

"Matthew, I want to listen to the tape," I said, tugging his sleeve.

"Oh," he said, in the voice he used when I interrupted his sample collecting. "Right. Yes."

He rummaged in his pocket. The car keys jangled. He thrust the keys and tape at me.

"You remember where the car is?"

"Yes."

"All right. I won't be long."

He started talking to the woman again, in a voice too low for me to catch the words.

THE CAR WAS warm from the sun. I slid the tape into the machine and lay down on the back seat. I recognised the music from the records we listened to in the evenings, on the record player that Matthew said was an antique. Matthew said Bach was good for my brain. He didn't like any other music. The soothing sounds washed over me. My eyes grew heavy and I let them rest.

A hand touched my shoulder. Laughter floated towards me from a distance: Matthew's rumbling laugh and a gentle, tinkling laugh. The purple woman's laugh. Aura spelt with an 'O.' She was standing beside Matthew, peering into the back seat. Keeping my eyes shut, I fumbled for my shades, which were on the floor.

"Sorry we were so long," Ora said. "We were walking in the garden. Matthew was showing me all the plants. He knew all their proper names; it was amazing."

Matthew didn't like it when people called him by his first name. I waited for him to correct Ora. But he didn't.

"Pity you missed it," she went on.

"Doesn't matter. I've already seen the garden lots of times."

She smiled.

"I suppose you have."

Ora gave Matthew a piece of paper, which he put in the space between the seats.

"It's not going to be at four on the dot," she said, as Matthew and I put on our safety belts. "There'll be a speech at 4.30pm. But there'll be refreshments and you can look around."

"I have various work commitments to attend to next week."

"Well, if you wanted to come, you know…"

Her hair hid her voice.

"Yes. Thank you. Goodbye."

Matthew started the car. The gears groaned in protest as it shot forward. He held tight to the steering wheel.

"What does she mean, not at four on the dot?" I asked Matthew.

"Her photographic exhibition is opening next Tuesday week in the municipal library. She thought we might like to go to it."

"Could we?"

"We may be in Dublin next week."

I didn't say anything more. Matthew liked to concentrate when he was driving.

"I'll be postponing your introduction to the Latin tongue," Matthew said, as we ate our lunchtime stew. "We'll be going to the library instead."

"Why?"

Matthew always said that routine greased the wheels of life. A change to our lesson plan was an unexpected treat.

"I've heard they've made some interesting acquisitions in their wildlife section."

"But you said their book collection was paltry."

"Yes, well I have it on good authority that they've received some interesting papers from the Wexford Birdwatching Society. They might be worth a look."

As I brought my plate to the sink, a piece of paper fluttered to the ground. It was covered in stew marks. The writing was big, so it was easy to read.

"Look, Matthew, it's the concert lady's exhibition. We can go and see it after all."

Matthew cleared his throat.

"Oh yes. We may look in," he said.

After lunch, Matthew told me to wait for him in the car. When he came out, he was wearing his Dublin suit, the black one with shiny patches on the material. He wore his white shirt underneath. His hair looked different too. It was pushed back from his forehead and it glistened. He smelled of chemicals; the smell tickled my nostrils.

THE PICTURES WERE hanging on the brick walls in the library's exhibition area. Ora was already there, surrounded by a cluster of people. Most were women wearing scarves that fluttered like hers. They buzzed around her in a swarm. Matthew didn't go over to her. He handed me a plastic cup filled with water and took one for himself. We stood in front of each picture while Matthew scrutinised them. I craned my neck and tried to look at them too, but they were hung too high, the colours and shapes danced out of reach. So Matthew described them to me instead. All the pictures were of children playing on beaches, on patches of waste ground, by busy roads. There were colours everywhere. The last picture was of a little girl who stared in wonder at a rainbow in a puddle. Matthew explained that the rainbow effect was caused by contact between car oil and water. As he spoke, the hum of voices stilled. All I heard was the sound of footsteps. Matthew carried on talking, but I turned around. Ora was standing there.

"Hello there. I wasn't expecting to see you," she said.

Matthew stopped mid-sentence and whipped his head around.

"Oh, it's you," he said. "Well, we happened to be doing some research in the library, so we were in the vicinity."

"I'm so glad you could come."

She smiled. Little dimples appeared at the sides of her mouth.

"What do you think of them?"

"Well, I don't profess myself to be an expert in photography, but the juxtaposition between subject and location is interesting. You appear to have a gift for catching people at unguarded moments."

"I like the rainbow made out of car oil," I said.

She laughed. Then she made a loud swallowing sound.

"I hate to disturb you, but we're trying to start the speeches."

"Oh. Forgive me. I didn't mean to interrupt proceedings."

I was surprised to hear Matthew apologising. He didn't like being told what to do. And he didn't like speeches either. We stood at the back of the room while they were being given. As soon as they were over, Matthew strode towards the double doors at the entrance to the library. He moved so fast that I had to run to catch up with him. There was a noticeboard on the wall near the doors. As I reached it, I felt a hand on my shoulder.

"Just a moment."

It was Ora. Matthew was already at the second set of double doors.

"Hurry up, Astrid, you know I despise malingerers."

"Matthew, Ora wants to talk to us."

Matthew paused, leaning on the door handle. His breath was loud, even though he wasn't running. He turned and walked back towards us.

"I won't keep you, Matthew. I just thought..." Ora took a deep breath. "I could show the prints of the photographs to Astrid. She might find it easier, you know. She could get a better look."

"I suppose they were a little out of her reach," said Matthew.

"Now?" I asked.

"Of course not now," said Matthew. "Come for lunch. Next week. If you're in the area, of course."

My jaw gaped open. No one came to our house except for Mrs O'Brien and she was gone now.

"I'll be delivering photos on Monday morning. Maybe after that, if it's all right."

"Very good."

Matthew rummaged in his briefcase and produced a

torn-up piece of paper and a pen. He wrote on the paper. When I bent over to look at the paper, I saw our telephone number. Matthew never gave our telephone number to strangers. As he handed her the paper, it fell on the ground. They both reached down to get it and their hands bumped against each other.

"Let us know what time you'll be arriving," he said.

"I'll do that. Thank you so much. I must go."

She returned to the throng, her purple scarf streaming behind her. Matthew didn't leave straight away. He turned back towards the doors and stood very still, the way he did when he was observing fish in the rockpools.

THE SUNNY WEATHER was gone now. Clouds dripped warm rain in a constant stream. The heavy air made my brain sluggish, as I toiled over unyielding fractions. It took longer than usual to finish the questions. I expected Matthew to be impatient with my efforts, but he just looked at my paper and put it down.

"We'll tackle this later. Let's work on those samples instead."

Delighted with the reprieve, I went to get the silver bucket, where the seaweeds awaited inspection. They were almost dry now. I brought them into the kitchen and let them spill onto the table. As always, I was tempted to burst the pods that lurked underneath the fronds. But now I knew the reason why it made Matthew cross; it destroyed the sample. Matthew was on the telephone. He was saying Ora's name. I remembered that she was coming for lunch. There was a frog in his throat again. When he finished, he came into the kitchens.

"Begin the sorting process. I have to start lunch."

Matthew always gave me work to do while he was making the stew. The task of sorting the samples absorbed my attention. Matthew was teaching me the Latin names for the seaweeds. As I worked, I recited them, relishing their twists and turns, the shapes my tongue made. Matthew's spoon stabbed the bottom of the saucepan as he stirred the stew. When I finished, I brought the silver bucket out to the small room where the washing machine was kept. As I set it down, I heard a faint thump. It came from the front of the house. I went back into the kitchen.

"Matthew, did you hear that noise?"

"Astrid, please don't distract me while I'm cooking."

There was another thump, louder this time, loud enough for Matthew to hear it too. Someone was knocking at our front door.

"Ah. You're right. Our guest has arrived."

Matthew wiped his hands. Then he ran them through his hair, which was sticking up at the front.

"I didn't realise it was so late. Go and answer it."

I had to pull hard at the front door to open it because it was stiff. By the time I managed to open it, Matthew was standing behind me. He was wearing different clothes, a white shirt and a pair of grey pants. He smelled of chemicals again. His hair didn't stick up any more.

"You're most welcome to our home," he said.

He stood aside to let Ora pass, pulling me with him. Damp trails of hair clung to her face. She carried a lot of paper bags, which were covered in large splodges of rain. Matthew reached over to take them from her.

"Find the way all right?" he said. "I hope my instructions weren't too labyrinthine."

"No. I asked in the village. All I had to do was mention the road and they knew it was your house."

"I have no doubt they did."

In the kitchen, she opened the bags. They contained a plant with purple flowers which matched her scarf, a hunk of cheese which smelled of old socks and a folder which I guessed contained the photographs. Matthew put the plant on the window. As he placed the cheese on the top shelf of the fridge, Ora reached over and took it out.

"I'm so sorry, it's just it'll lose its consistency in the fridge. Have you got a press to put it in?"

"Oh, yes of course. Astrid, put it in our food drawer. I didn't realise."

"I was a caterer before, you see."

"Then I'll bow to your expertise on this matter. We should eat. This thing is as ready as it's likely to be."

I took out plates and knives. Ora sat beside Matthew at the table and I faced them. There was less space at the table than usual. The seaweed lay in neat piles at the other end, waiting for Matthew's scrutiny. We ate our stew and washed it down with water. Ora said she liked the stew. She ate all of it except for the lumps, which she stacked in a neat pile at the side of the plate. Matthew talked all the way through the meal, about the samples he was collecting and our lessons. Ora kept asking him questions. She sounded confused, because Matthew was using all the long words he used when he talked to the people in Dublin. He appeared not to hear her. At last, he stopped. We all stared down at our empty plates.

"Did you partake in any interesting activities at the weekend?" Matthew asked.

"Well, my son came home. It was his first weekend home."

"Home from where?" I asked.

"He's away at school," she said. "He comes home every second weekend."

"That must have been pleasant for you," said Matthew.

"Oh, it was lovely. But it was hard, you know, dropping him back."

Her hair fell in front of her face. She sniffed and fumbled in her handbag.

"Have you got a cold?" I asked her.

Matthew reached in his pocket and took out his handkerchief. He put it on the table in front of her and began gathering the plates, clattering the knives and forks together.

"Astrid, help me with these," he said, his voice louder than usual. "Then go inside and look at those pictures Ora was kind enough to bring for you. We'll follow you."

I sat in a chair by the fireplace, Ora's folder in my lap. I opened it and flicked through the pictures. Without Matthew's narrative skills, they failed to hold my attention. I waited for

Matthew and Ora to come in, but they didn't. The murmur of their voices drifted towards me. I set the folder down at my feet and stole an opportunity to immerse myself in *Treasure Island*, which I was only allowed to read at night, after all our work was done. I finished two chapters before Matthew and Ora came back in.

"Goodness, we didn't even notice the time passing," said Ora. "Hope you enjoyed the photographs."

I snatched up the folder and covered the book with it.

"Oh yes," I said. "They were very interesting."

"I dabbled in a little photography during my time in Africa," said Matthew. "My efforts were somewhat amateurish, but I'm going to make the bold assumption that they may be of interest to you."

"Oh, I'd love to see them," said Ora.

Matthew started to rustle through one of his tattered folders. Ora walked around the room. She picked up some of the books and put them down again.

"So many books," she said. "Have you read all of them?"

"Of course I have," said Matthew. "I don't keep them for decoration."

Ora didn't reply. She fingered one of the tapestries, the one of Tutankhamun in his gold armour, which was my favourite.

"This is beautiful," she said. "So much attention to detail. Who did them?"

"Astrid's mother," said Matthew.

Matthew had never told me that. I wanted to ask him about it, but he whipped his head away from the tapestry and spread the photographs out on the coffee table.

Ora picked up one of Matthew's photographs. When she was finished looking at that one, Matthew passed the others to her, one at a time. She examined them for a long time. The clock on the mantelpiece marked each minute. My legs kicked against the chair. Matthew and Ora talked with their heads close together, so I couldn't hear what they were saying. When they stopped talking, I went over to them.

"Matthew, could we go outside now? It's stopped raining."

"So it has. Would you like to get some air?"

"That's a lovely idea," said Ora.

We didn't go to the beach, because Ora wasn't wearing the right sort of shoes. Their pointed heels dug into the ground. When we walked in the garden, she stumbled and Matthew caught her arm. She didn't fall, but Matthew forgot to let go. They kept stopping to examine the flowers, which strained against the wind. I was able to pass Matthew out.

"I'm afraid these are rather shabby efforts at horticulture," he said. "Astrid's mother was the gardener in the family."

Ora caused Matthew to say the most surprising things.

"Oh, I meant to tell you. I've been offered some work," Ora said. "It's quite a big project too. A brochure promoting tourism in Wexford. It'll be out next year."

"That's quite a coup, for such a recent photography graduate." said Matthew. "Wexford has a great many hidden wonders. We could bring you to them, couldn't we, Astrid?"

"Yes." I turned to face them and started walking backwards. "We know lots and lots of places. From our field trips."

"Well, I was kind of planning to start taking interior shots next week."

"Excellent," said Matthew. "We should be able to fit you into our schedule."

"That's great. I'll look forward to that. Now I'm afraid I have to go. I've to deliver some more photographs on my way back to Wicklow."

We walked with her to the front of the house, where her car was parked.

"Ring me. We'll decide on a venue," said Matthew.

"Thanks for the lovely afternoon."

Matthew leaned over and kissed her cheek. He had to bend over to do it and his lips made a loud smacking sound. Then he spun around and walked back to the house. I stayed where I was and waved until she was gone.

ORA CAME ON all our field trips after that. We went on a lot more field trips than before, which I loved, because it meant I had less homework to do. Ora enjoyed them too. She smiled and laughed a lot. She was always asking if everything was all right. I didn't know why she asked so much, because the answer was always yes. Ora was the most colourful person I knew. Her clothes floated around her. She looked like a bird of paradise, with her plumage of red, yellow, purple and blue. When I told her that, she laughed, which puzzled me. It wasn't supposed to be funny.

We drove all around Wexford, along rough, twisty roads. When the days were clear and bright, we took her to Viking burial sites and places where unusual flowers grew. On wet days, she did her interior shots in big old houses which were hidden from the road by trees. I liked the sound of the gravel crunching under our feet as we walked up the avenues. Ora wanted to take pictures of us, but Matthew said no, which was a relief. Having my photograph taken was a tedious experience.

On each field trip, Matthew delivered monologues about the history and wildlife of the area. I regaled her with stories about the things I had learned during our lessons. She talked to me in a grown up way, which I liked.

Ora brought picnics in a big wooden basket. The bread she brought was different from ours. It was softer and there were little nuts on the crusts which crunched when I bit into them. She always brought a flask of coffee, but Matthew was the only one who drank from it. He let me have a little and I grew to savour its fragrant tang. Ora drank tea. It didn't smell like Mrs O'Brien's tea; it smelt of flowers.

When we weren't on field trips, Matthew and I came up with plans for the next one. He grumbled about the time we were wasting, but I knew he enjoyed them, because he smiled a lot too. Sometimes he threw back his head and laughter boomed out of his open mouth. He talked a lot more than usual, stumbling over the words. There were times when he forgot to stop talking and I had to tug his sleeve to remind him that it was time to go home.

MATTHEW AND I always went on a special field trip for my birthday. When she heard it was my birthday, Ora offered to cancel, but Matthew told her not to be silly.

"I'll bring something nice to eat for dinner afterwards. What kind of food do you eat, Astrid?"

"I'm an omnivore. That means I eat everything."

She smiled.

"That's handy," she said. "You're easy to please."

MATTHEW ALWAYS GAVE me books for my birthday. But this year, Matthew presented me with a copy of a magazine called *National Geographic*, with a note saying that I was to receive a copy of it every month for a year. It was full of information about wildlife, bones and distant tribes. I was sitting at the window seat leafing through its crisp, shiny pages when Ora arrived. The window seat was a nice place to read, because the sun never came into the kitchen until the early evening, so the light was soft. She looked over my shoulder at a bird perched on a slender branch.

"Oh, aren't those pictures stunning," she said.

I swung my legs around to make room for her on the windowseat and handed her the magazine.

"Goodness, that's *National Geographic*. I always stole my brothers' copies when I was young. The photographs were so beautiful. Aren't you lucky to have one of your own?"

"Why didn't your parents give one to you?"

Ora's face turned pink.

"Oh, I don't know. I never thought of asking."

"Maybe someone will give it to you for your birthday. Matthew gave it to me for mine."

"Well actually." She rummaged in her enormous leather handbag, "I got you something too."

No one ever gave me presents except Matthew.

"Why?"

"I believe the correct response is thank you, Astrid," Matthew said, as he walked into the room.

"Oh, here it is," Ora said.

She handed me a parcel covered in stiff paper that

crackled when I touched it. It was a treasure chest waiting to be unlocked. Matthew's presents were never wrapped in layers like this. The folds of paper came away to reveal a black cap with the word Yankees written in white letters. There was a visor at the front of it.

"Why does it say Yankees on it? Does it come from America?"

"I think it's the name of a baseball team. You know, because it's a baseball cap."

She cleared her throat.

"Why don't you try it on?"

I went to the mirror by the window. When I put it on, I looked different, sleek and grown-up. The visor was better at blocking out the sunlight than my straw hat and it fit me better too, because there was a plastic clip at the back which I could adjust to fit the shape of my head.

Our field trip that day was long. They were often long now. When we came back, Ora took pieces of meat, onions and potatoes out of a bag. She cut them up and put them all in a frying pan, until the potatoes were brown and the onion was soft and sweet. The meat was dark and crisp at the edges, but it was soft in the middle, softer than the meat in the stew. She said it was called steak. As we ate, the rain blew against the windows. Matthew said the weather was too bad for Ora to drive back to Wicklow, so she could stay the night. It was lucky that we had a spare room for her.

ONE MORNING, ORA came up to me as I was reading on the window seat. My hair was still damp from my swim. I didn't have to do any lessons after swimming because it was a Sunday. Even though Matthew didn't believe in God, he still thought we deserved a day of rest. Ora was staying the night again. She always did that now when our field trips were long. I jumped as she touched on my shoulder. The *Swiss Family Robinson* fell to the ground.

"Sorry. I didn't mean to give you a fright. I've just been taking some views of the beach from the bottom of the garden. The light is so soft this morning."

I shrugged. She was always taking photographs.

"Well, you see, the thing is." She took a deep, gulping breath. "I ended up taking a picture of you. It just sort of happened; I swung the camera around and you were there. I hope you don't mind."

I had a vague recollection of a click and a whirr, camouflaged among the wildlife sounds.

"Doesn't matter."

I reached down for my book, anxious to return to the desert-island paradise.

"It's just that I wanted to give it to Matthew for Christmas. Is that all right?"

"We don't celebrate Christmas. We're humanists."

"Oh, I didn't realise." Her voice was faint. "It was just an idea.

She moved away, her feet dragging along the ground.

"But he likes your pictures. He says you have an eye. I don't know why he says that, because you have two eyes."

She laughed. Her cheeks were pink.

"It's just an expression."

She turned back to face me.

"So you don't mind if I give it to him?"

I shrugged again. It was only a picture.

ORA VISITED US once more before Christmas. As always, she came laden, but this time one of her parcels was a flat package, wrapped in gaudy paper.

"It's just a token," she said, as she handed it to Matthew.

"That was unnecessary," he said. "We don't subscribe to that sort of nonsense."

"I know. It's just something small."

The paper crackled as he tore at it. It fell to the ground. I picked it up and crunched it into a ball.

"Must you make such a noise?" said Matthew

He was staring at the object inside the package. It was a photo frame.

"Let me see," I said.

I inserted my head in the crook of Matthew's elbow. The picture was covered in splodges of grey and there was a girl at the centre, silhouetted against the sky. The grass she was standing on looked familiar, but it still took a moment to realise that the girl was me. Matthew shook me away.

"In a moment," he said.

He held it at arm's length. The kitchen clock marked the seconds. Ora broke the silence.

"Don't you like it?"

"You've captured her," he said.

The frog was back in his throat. He took his handkerchief out of his pocket and blew into it.

After Ora left, I went to fetch Matthew in his study, to tell him it was time for tea. He didn't hear me knock, so I pushed open the door. He was holding the photograph in his hands. I didn't know why the photograph fascinated him so much. He already knew what I looked like.

❧ Back to Black ❧

I COLLAPSED ON the bed with a plop; my whole body sighed with relief. The curtains were drawn. After the brilliant brightness of the slopes, the relative darkness of the room was blissful. I was wearing only a towel; it was difficult to summon up the energy to dress. My skin tingled from my shower and the exertion of the day. Mia's suitcase was propped up against the bed. She made no effort to lift it.

"Aren't you going to choose your evening attire?" I asked.

"My what?"

"Your clothes." Was I required to dress her?

"It's just my suitcase; it's kind of heavy. Can you give me a hand lifting it?"

I didn't move.

"Why did you bring such a heavy case if you find it difficult to lift?"

The flawless logic of my question silenced her. She began to make vague tugs at the suitcase and it thunked onto her bed, causing my own bed to vibrate a little. Rather than choose an item of clothing, she burbled about her day's skiing and how wonderful her guide was. I closed my eyes and let my hand travel towards the bedside locker. It brushed past my glasses and phone before it landed on my iPod. Without opening my eyes, I began making my selection. Air's *Moon Safari* was number three on my French electro album playlist. I was in the mood for retro. The wheel wobbled for a moment, but soon, the familiar beats caressed my ears and drowned Mia out. I fast-forwarded to *Sexy Boy*, which provided an ideal backdrop to thoughts of Johno. I summoned up images of his arms, my hands tracing their protruding veins. But other arms kept obscuring my view, chunky arms with muscles that rippled.

THEY DON'T HAPPEN very often now, these interludes. Maybe once or twice a year, when neither of us are hooked up and I end up back at Jazz's after the club. I just follow Jazz into his room instead of sleeping on the couch. His bed waits for us, with its vast expanse of duvet, mountain of pillows and burnished-steel bedstead. We lie naked in the bed, spooning each other, flesh against flesh. The mattress moulds our bodies. Our hands wander everywhere. Then we fall asleep, our arms interlocked. We never face each other, never speak.

I REACHED FOR my phone and typed:

```
Hot guy here. Taller dan u. Skinnier dan

u.
```

Always aim for the Achilles heel. I punched in the number. Jazz looked back at me, his buzz-cut hair accentuating the planes of his face. I erased the message, dropped the phone back on the bedside locker. There were far more important things to consider. Like the next stage in my campaign to lure Johno. After a day of being separated by a wall of Cabbage Patch Kids, serious spadework needed to be done.

When I took off my headphones, Mia was still delivering her stream of consciousness monologue. I peeled myself off the bed and wrapped my towel tight around me. Mia's insistent woodpecker touch landed on my shoulder. She stood by the bed, her hands flapping. She was already dressed, in a long denim skirt and a pink shirt adorned with frills. She was a nifty mover when it suited her.

"Astrid?"

"In a minute."

I went over to the wardrobe and selected a black silk shirt and denim hotpants. I tied the shirt under my breastbone so that my taut midriff was exposed. Given the gloom of the bar, the need for shades wasn't pressing, but I decided to wear my Miss Sixtys with the jagged bolts of lightening running along the arms. It never hurt to make a statement. My hair was free of gel after my shower, so I combed it into a soft flip.

"You ready?" I asked Mia.

"No."

Her voice shook, stopping me in my tracks.

"Can you help me find my earrings?" she whispered.

Her bed was strewn with detritus.

"How do you expect me to find them?"

"Well, you see, they were a birthday present from my parents. I don't want to lose them."

She had that little-girl-lost act down; even I was sucked in. I bent over her bed and ran my hand up and down the duvet with angry sweeps. Something hit the ground with a tinkle. I crouched down and inched my hand along the ground until it made contact with a small, hard object, camouflaged by the wooden flooring. The second earring was easier to locate. As I straightened up, I saw a gleam of gold next to the handle of her suitcase. I pressed the earrings into Mia's outstretched hands.

"Here. Guess we're ready to roll."

While Mia inserted the earrings, I examined my reflection through the black spots of the mirror. Hot, in a mellow way. Not an ounce of superfluous flesh. Of course, there was the small problem of Johno not being able to see me, but I planned to circumvent that by inviting him to lay his hand on my shirt sleeve, to feel the soft silkiness of the material.

WHEN I OPENED the door, Kim was standing there, poised to knock. He was wearing a purple shirt and tight jeans. Naff in the extreme. Cliona stood beside him.

"What do you want?" I said.

"We were just on our way down for dinner," said Cliona. "I see you're wearing black this evening."

I see your eyes are working well this evening.

"Are you not worried it'll make you look washed out?" she asked.

"Not especially."

I looked shit hot in these clothes.

"You need to be careful how you dress, you know. Seeing as you look a little different."

Cliona wore a pair of sagging jeans and a white T-shirt that billowed outwards, masking her figure.

"Perhaps you should attend to your own wardrobe."

I jostled past them and clattered down the stairs, pulling Mia in my slipstream. The stairs were familiar to me now, so it was easy to make a quick getaway. But I still heard Cliona's tongue-click from halfway down.

IN THE CLASSROOM, time stood still and dry air stuck to my cheeks. Brown tiles criss-crossed the floor. The walls were made with white bricks. Shelves stretched the whole way round the room. They were filled with books and colourful objects.

A woman stood at the top of the classroom. She was fat with curly hair, like Mrs O'Brien. She was just like all the other pink ladies, except that she gave us lessons. I told her Matthew was my teacher, but she said she was my teacher while I was here.

There were seven other girls in the classroom. We sat at a big brown table made out of little tables that were pushed together. It was covered in pieces of paper, like the table in Matthew's study. Some of the pieces of paper were covered in bumps. The teacher said that the bumps were for the girls who couldn't see; to help them read words with their fingers. The bumps were made with machines which sat beside the girls on the table and made strange crunching sounds. We sat so close together that the chairs bumped into each other. The blue paint on the legs of the chairs was full of ridges and holes. I dug my fingers into them and the paint flaked off. The teacher told me to stop doing it because it made paint go all over the floor. But I still did it when she was busy with the others. It felt good.

The lessons lasted a long time. There were no trips to Africa, no samples to sort, no bones to examine. There were just letters and numbers, all day, letters and numbers. The teacher wrote them out on a blackboard with a stick of chalk. She made the writing big, so we could see it. I didn't read the paper with bumps on it. Instead, I read books with big black letters, like the ones I read to Matthew. Some of the other girls read those books too. They were books without stories, only words. *Ann is in the garden. Barry is in the garden.* The teacher spent a long time teaching us to say the words. But I already knew them, even the bigger ones.

Afterwards, we wrote the words that we read in the books. We didn't have to write for as long as I did with Matthew, but my head still kept landing on my pencil. My letters always wobbled, but the teacher said it didn't matter if they wobbled and that I was a good girl. When she said it, I tasted orange drink in my mouth. I wanted to show Matthew that I could do neat letters. So I kept going until the bad taste was gone and my eyes started to close from tiredness.

Sometimes I finished before the others and asked the teacher questions, but she told me I was disturbing the others and had to be quiet until they were finished. I didn't know why my questions annoyed her so much. Matthew was always telling me to ask questions. He said they were a sign of an enquiring mind. I didn't know what that meant, but at least he always answered my questions.

After a while, I stopped asking the teacher questions. Instead, I examined the objects on the shelves. The other girls threw them at each other, or pretended they were something else. I picked them up one by one, looked at them, felt them, then put them down, like Matthew did when he was examining samples on the beach. They were all the colours of the rainbow: green, orange, yellow, blue. And pink, lots of pink. I liked touching the objects, squashing them into a ball, or bouncing them up and down. Sometimes my fingers left holes on the surface of the objects, like the holes in a piece of cheese. Some of the objects made noises, rattles, squeaks, even musical sounds. At first, the sounds startled me, but then I began to enjoy them and kept making noises until the teacher told me to stop. While I examined the objects, I recited everything I knew from Matthew's lessons. My lips moved, but I didn't make any noise. I named rocks, plants and animals, spelt words, added and subtracted numbers, told myself stories. And I stored up all my questions. I didn't want to forget.

The globe stood in a corner of the room. It was my favourite thing in the classroom and I always saved it till last. It was big, too big for me to hold in my hand. A ring of plastic surrounded it. The countries were painted in glowing colours. Their names were printed in wide, bold letters. They floated on dark blue seas. The globe was covered in little bumps, like the ones on the pieces of paper. Thick black lines divided the countries from each other and from the sea. The globe was easier to see than the atlas; I didn't have to use a magnifying glass to look at it. Sometimes I spun it fast so it looked like it was flying and I pretended I was flying with it. Other times, I traced the outline of the countries and mouthed their names, pronouncing them as best I could. The names of the African countries in Matthew's stories were warm and familiar. I travelled to them. Hot dust blew onto my face and strange words were spoken. The people wore colourful clothes and had dark skin. I travelled to other countries where there was ice and snow and people lived in houses made of ice. They wore the skins of bears and cooked their food on big fires. I set off on my travels with a cloth bag on my back, escaping from the classroom, from the school itself.

JOHNO WAS ENJOYING an exalted position at the head of the long wooden table. The lurid yellow colour of his shirt made me grateful for the protection offered by my shades, but his god-like appearance was undiminished. There were spaces on either side of him. Mia began the laborious process of arranging herself on the green couch. I considered the chair to be a better vantage point, giving me opportunities for my leg to brush against his. Mia's guide Kevin came over with a glass of beer and placed it in front of her, guiding her hand to the glass. Johno reached for his beer at the same time and his fingers made contact with the sleeve of her blouse.

"Oh look, you've all these little frills on yer shirt," he said to her. "Like me granny's lampshade."

"Well, it's my frilly shirt," she said, her voice breathy.

"God, you're such a girl."

The admiration in his voice was a little alarming.

"If you like the feel of that, wait till you try mine," I said.

"Is that an invite?"

"Could be."

I reached over and placed his hand on my sleeve.

"Is that real silk?"

I knew then that he was a no-frills man.

"You're a lucky yoke, sitting between the girls," shouted one of the Greek Chorus from the other end of the table.

They wore identikit brown jumpers and shiny trousers that rode upwards to reveal white socks. Their outfits indicated a high level of maternal interference.

"Ah yeah. Blessed am I among women. Gettin hungry now though. Where's the grub?"

I picked up the menu. Realised with a jolt that my monocle was upstairs.

"There are many delectations on offer," I said.

"What? Speak English," Johno said.

"At least you're in good time to enjoy your food tonight, Astrid," said Cliona.

A well-timed Exocet. I pictured her sitting on a black horse at the Circus Maximus, her stolid frame encased in armour, fighting to the death.

The words on the menu were crammed together. I inched it closer.

"You all right with that, Astrid," Martin yelled from the next table.

"Yeah, I'm good."

Reading without my visual aid always invited well-meaning scrutiny.

"Let's see," I said. "Sausages, sausages and more sausages."

"You'll have to give a little more feedback than that, Astrid," said Cliona.

Beside her, Kim was providing a laborious description of every dish on the menu, for the benefit of the Greek Chorus.

"And a few chips," I continued.

Johno gurgled.

"Any steak?"

"I have no doubt there is."

A suitable dish for a red-blooded male.

"Mint."

Johno rubbed his hands together.

"Excellent choice. I'll have the same."

"Girl after me own heart."

The waitress came around and we ordered.

"Is there anything vegetarian?" Mia said, her words directed at the table.

The waitress frowned. Mia didn't bother to qualify her statement.

"*Vegetarier,*" Kevin said.

"Ah, *vegetarier.* Yes. We have garden salad, potato salad."

Mia selected a garden salad.

"Not a meat muncher then, Mia?" Kevin asked.

"I just think it's cruel. They force pigs into pens and kill them for meat."

Johno let out a squeal, a rather authentic rendering of a pig's last gasp. Laughter ran around the table like an electric current. I smirked. Strike one for me. Our steaks arrived. I bent over it and made a careful incision, to avoid staining my clothes with juice. Following the grains of the meat required dexterity. Johno jabbed at his steak with gusto, handling the knife with remarkable skill for someone who couldn't see what he was doing.

"Ah, that's the stuff," he said.

His shirt was now decorated with gravy, but I sensed he was unlikely to be troubled by that.

I WAS IN a cage with pink bars. A lot of people were squashed into the cage, talking all at once. They wore pink clothes. There was nowhere for their voices to escape to, so they bounced off the roof of the cage and pressed against my ears. I shoved through the crowd until I was at the edge of the cage and pushed against the bars, but even though they were soft, they didn't yield.

There were wide spaces between the bars, but when I tried to squeeze through, the space narrowed. The bars pressed into me, smothering me in a soft embrace. My mouth formed a soundless oh and I kicked against the bars with my legs and arms, but their hold grew tighter.

The darkness was total. My blanket was twisted around my limbs. I reached down to straighten it. The only sound was Mia's heavy breathing. The dreams were an infrequent occurrence these days, but I could never sleep after they came. I risked switching on the lamp and attempted to banish the lingering traces of the dream with my Sherlock Holmes book. At least Mia couldn't see the light.

THE DARKNESS IN the dormitory was orange. It never went all black; there was a glow all the time. The air was always warm and sticky, not like at home where the wind was cold and tasted of salt. When I went to sleep, instead of listening to the sounds of the sea, or the wind rattling my window, I listened to the sounds of breathing. Noisy breathing, sucking sounds, sighs, mumbled words, giggles and cries. The sounds rose upwards, through cracks in the wooden partitions that divided the dormitory into little pieces. Whenever someone moved, their bed squeaked. The floorboards made creaking sounds when someone stepped on them. The pink ladies walked up and down, their steps heavy. Sometimes they came over and tightened our blankets. When they did that, I couldn't move my legs and arms. Because of the orange glow, my eyes refused to close all the way. Sometimes the glow became very bright, when the door creaked open and footsteps went through it. The sudden piercing of light sent me under my blanket, where I curled up in a ball and listened to the squeak of my bed. There was a place where the mattress sank in the middle and the springs poked through. I buried myself in it. Sometimes the pink ladies found me there in the morning.

The Good, the Bad, & the Not-So-Ugly

MY BOOTS WERE being less cooperative this morning. The Velcro strap refused to align itself, despite a lot of patient tweaking. The sound of the others slurping drinks reminded me of my dire need for a caffeine hit. As I straightened up, Martin appeared in front of me.

"Ready to conquer the slopes?" he said, rubbing his hands.

"Suppose you won't give me a chance to have some coffee?"

I wasn't about to enter the battlefield without reinforcements.

"I can go one better," he said.

Two cups of coffee appeared in front of us. He pulled out a tiny silver flask and poured a thin brown stream of liquid into his cup, then mine.

"Little Austrian trick, add a bit of rocket fuel to your coffee. I know you're a vodka girl, but brandy's just the thing to keep you going on the slopes."

"Why do I need that?"

"Well, you did so good yesterday, I'm going to let you join the big boys on the main slope."

I tasted the coffee. The brandy warmed my throat. Now I knew why Matthew drank brandy on cold evenings. A knot loosened in my stomach; I never realised it was there.

"We'll start off at the baby slope, see if you can remember what I taught you, then we'll crack the main slope. Sound good?"

I nodded.

"All right. How d'you want to be guided?"

There were options?

"I can order you about the place, tell you when to turn left and right. You might've noticed; I can yell pretty loud."

I squirmed.

"Not keen? Well, Cliona's got a good routine going, following Kim down. You could do that. That suit you?"

This conversation was becoming tedious. I gathered my gloves and shades.

"Take it that's a yes then. All right. Let's get to it."

Walking in the boots was still a precarious business; layers of polish turned the floor of the cafe into an ice rink. Martin turned around and held out his elbow.

"Want to hook on?" he said.

I just stepped around him and made my way out the door, a satisfied smirk on my face. No point in him guiding me before he had to.

FOR A WHILE, I strutted my stuff on the small slope outside the cafe.

"This is getting too easy, isn't it," Martin said. "Time for a real challenge."

He came over and took off my skis in two quick moves. Then he made to put them on his shoulders. I snatched them back.

"Don't need a butler service," I said, balancing them on my left shoulder.

"Should have known. Bit of a warrior, aren't you?"

He turned away, towards the vast expanse of the main slope. I followed him, keeping a firm grip on my skis to prevent them from separating. His body began to shrink, as he descended a grey column of steps. The steps blended into each other, landmines waiting to explode. I edged forward, testing the water. Ice crunched under my feet. My legs wobbled.

"Steady on there," said Martin, who was at the bottom of the steps by now. "We don't want you to start breakdancing again, do we?"

His use of the first person plural was somewhat redundant. He placed his skis on the slope and vaulted up the steps. Again, he proffered his elbow. This time I succumbed, though I still kept my skis on my left shoulder.

As we set off, I noticed a familiar looking wire overhead. My stomach lurched. I lowered my eyes and concentrated on negotiating this uncharted territory, Martin's vest was a reassuring beacon. It was only after we stopped that I saw the ropes hanging from the wire, with horizontal bars attached to them. Skiers balanced on the bars and allowed themselves to be hauled upwards by the ropes. This was indeed an alarming development. The bars were ghosts, taunting me. *Remember us? We're going to get you.* I tried to shove the memories downwards, into the ice fortress, but it was no use. My breath came out in ragged gasps.

"These are the T-bars," Martin said, from far away. "That's how we'll be getting to the top. I'll show you what to do."

"I hate those things," I muttered.

"Thought you never skied before."

Bang on target. Right in the solar plexus. He was an excellent marksman.

"Not so you'd notice."

"Then how come you're doing those antenatal exercises?"

"What on earth are you talking about?"

"Huffin' and puffin' like a woman in labour, you are. Never mind, we'll make this as painless as possible."

THE TRIP WAS to Livigno. Some of Jazz's friends were organising it and there was a last-minute cancellation. I jumped at the opportunity, anticipating a week of thrills and spills. But I didn't bargain on the light, which cut through even the strongest shades, robbing the world of definition and dimensions.

We blew off ski school after the first day. While the others scaled the heights, I floundered. The lifts danced away from me; lumps of snow caught me unawares. I kept grinding to a halt in the middle of the slope, as figures swooped in front of me without warning.

The incident occurred as the day was drawing to a close. As I trundled down the centre of the slope, a red figure flashed before my eyes, too near for me to swerve. Bone crunched against bone as our bodies fell in a tangle onto the snow. A stream of Italian curses assailed my ears as I shook myself off. When I tried to apologise, he declared in perfect English that I was a menace to the slopes and wasn't fit to wear skis. I was inclined to agree with him.

For the rest of the week, I retreated into darkness, into shuttered bedrooms and cavernous clubs with a selection of Carlos. I came up with various plausible excuses for my absence from the slopes and mooched around coffee shops, drinking endless cups of coffee laced with vodka from a small bottle I kept in my pocket.

When I went down to Wexford a week after my return, I regaled Matthew and Ora with tales of derring-do. Matthew made clear his views about the pointlessness of hurling oneself down a mountainside on two sticks, but I knew he approved.

The next day, after our morning walk, I told Matthew I wanted to walk for a little longer. I pounded the beach for a second time, trying to drive the sour taste from my mouth. Before going back to the house, I decided to rest on the flat rock at the bottom of the cliff path, in order to brace myself for the next onslaught. My legs were bent; my head rested on my knees. A hand brushed my back. I looked up. Ora was standing there. Her pumps were covered in sand. She never wore the right shoes for the beach. I made a slight feint to the right. Her knees creaked as she lowered herself down.

"Goodness, I must be getting old," she said, with a little laugh. "I'll be lucky if I get up again."

She twirled a strand of hair around her finger.

"Come on Astrid. How was it really?"

My midnight-black Ray-Bans obscured the bright sheen on my eyes.

"Said I enjoyed it, didn't I?"

The waves sucked and surged.

"Did Jazz say something?"

"He didn't have to."

"There was just too much light there," I muttered, the words muffled by my knees.

I slotted my index fingers into the space behind my shades and rubbed my eyes. Her arm snaked around my shoulders. I didn't move or turn around. But I didn't shrug her away either.

BEFORE I KNEW it, I was being manoeuvred past gangs of Teutonic schoolchildren, towards the ticket machines. My body was pressed against a metal bar. Martin told me to wave my arm at the machine and the bar gave way. I felt a gentle tug at my elbow and realised we were on a rutted path. A moment later, Martin told me to stop and face forward. His arm shot out and grabbed one of the ropes as it floated past. Something hard landed under my posterior. I was propelled forward with a sickening lurch. A weight settled on my chest. Martin's arm was on my waist, steadying me.

"Don't sit on it, Astrid. Lean into me, nothing like a bit of up-close and personal. There, you've cracked it. Wasn't so bad after all, was it?"

Relief surged through me; my head spun. Martin began spewing out a monologue, to the accompaniment of whoops and yells from the Teutonic schoolchildren. It could have been a discourse on the merits of Socratic versus Platonic debating techniques for all the attention I paid to it. My body was coiled, as the ground threatened to slip away from me.

"Don't say much, do you?" Martin said.

What did he expect? I wasn't in the most comfortable position for sparkling repartee. Minutes stretched out, civilisations rose and fell. Martin's arm was still around my waist. I preferred my tactile stimulation to take place under cover of darkness, but I couldn't summon up the nerve to remove his arm. Again, a memory of another arm bobbed to the surface, a warm weight encircling my body. When we reached the top, Martin told me to turn left. As I turned, my legs wobbled and collapsed with relief. Martin yanked me to my feet.

"Get going, you lazy git," he said, laughing with enough volume to trigger an avalanche.

Up here, the sun's laser beam was even stronger and there were no clouds to block it out. Martin swung his skis around so he was in front of me.

"Right, remember what we agreed. Follow my beautiful green vest. We'll take it nice and slow. Got that?"

I nodded. He set off. The trees at the top of the slope provided some shelter from the sunlight. Their branches cast long shadows on the snow. My legs obeyed my commands. I was Queen of Cabbage Patch Land. An electric pulse surged through me. I took a sharp turn and almost passed Martin out.

"You're too good for me," he said. "Have pity on my old bones."

I knew I could blow him off.

After the next turn, the trees disappeared. A flat white expanse stretched in front of me. The snow glittered with tiny crystals. Martin was now a shadow, a yeti. My eyes burned. I forced myself to keep going, towards the next batch of trees. The weight returned to my chest; breathing became a struggle. I didn't turn, just kept going in a straight line, my skis moving fast enough for me to wonder if they might detach themselves from my legs. But there was no escape from the light. *Fucksake*, I muttered.

"Oi," Martin yelled as I shot past him.

My skis juddered against a bank of snow. I tried to force them onwards, but they intersected. The fall happened in slow motion, the air leaving my body as I hit the ground with a crunch.

I heard the swish of skis and Martin appeared in front of me.

"You all right?"

The taste of orange drink filled all the space in my mouth, rendering speech impossible. The weight in my chest became heavier, spread to my arms and legs.

"Occupational hazard I'm afraid," he said, laughing.

I batted away his outstretched hand and forced myself to stand back up.

"Glad you find this so amusing."

"Nothing wrong with your tongue anyway. Let's crack on then, shall we."

This time, my pace was more moderate. Martin's vest was a more useful marker than I cared to admit, but the weight refused to lift from my chest. It trapped all the air inside. The trees cut in and out, tantalising me. There was only the feel of the ground under my skis to guide me as I navigated the white expanse. The slope was never-ending. Every muscle in my body strained in an effort to keep Martin in my line of vision, even though he was only a turn away. His green vest was now a sludgy colour.

"Nearly there," he yelled back to me.

Just as I permitted myself to hope that I could escape this ordeal unscathed, a figure appeared from nowhere. In a reprise of the Livigno incident, my body crunched against his and our limbs became entangled. My skis detached themselves. An engorged red face hovered above me, emitting a stream of curses, German ones this time. Martin approached the man, pointing to me and gesticulating. I tried to rustle up words of apology, but the weight was in my throat now, blocking my vocal chords. My skin prickled all over. Beads of sweat formed on my forehead, under my armpits. I pulled my legs towards me and rested my head against my knees, zoning out, searching for my ice fortress. But Jazz blocked my path. *You pretty much are one.* My head pounded. Martin edged towards me, but I didn't look up.

"Thought World War II was over," he said.

"Thought you should know. It's not going to work. I'm calling it a day."

The shake in my voice enraged me. It resembled Mia's.

"Oh no you're not," he said.

His gentle tone belied his words. My eyes stung.

"Honest, it's the only way."

I remained hunched, my head buried in my knees.

"Wasn't your fault, Astrid. That Fritz came out of nowhere. I should have stayed closer to you, headed him off. That's my job. Bloody ignorant, most of 'em. Vest doesn't seem to stop 'em."

He helped me to my feet. I put my hand on his shoulder for balance as I clipped on my skis. His shoulder was broad. Like Matthew's. Like Jazz's.

"We're nearly there anyway. Two more turns and we'll be at the caff. You'll be all right after a breather."

I planned to get toasted.

"And then we'll go out again. Only this time, we'll do it like the others do it. I'll go behind you and yell myself hoarse. Take the stress out of it for you."

I opened my mouth to voice my protest, but couldn't form the words fast enough.

"I know you think you don't need it. But it'll make life easier for you. That's not a bad thing, is it?"

You always have to turn everything into a fight.

"Fine. If you insist."

MY PATH WAS blocked by a phalanx of Austrians, all with huge shoulders. The voices of the Cabbage Patch Kids were still audible through the roar of the crowd. I prepared to adopt my usual battering-ram mechanism for dealing with crowds, but a hand restrained me.

"All right Astrid, I've got you," Martin said.

He weaved me through the throng, which parted like the Red Sea. Jazz had a similar effect on crowds at concerts and nightclubs.

"Johno mate, got room for a tall one?" Martin yelled as we reached the table.

I registered the empty chair next to Johno, but was too tired to care.

"Plonk yourself down there girlie," Martin said to me.

I wedged into the chair and gazed down at the plastic-topped table. Opposite us, the Greek Chorus were carrying out a noisy comparison of war wounds.

"I'm after banjaxing my knee."

"I think I've a hamstring injury," said the other. "A bit like a footballer."

No doubt the entire cafe was now aware of their injuries.

I studied Johno's battered, lived-in face. It was close enough for me to discern the layer of stubble covering his cheeks.

Jazz's skin was always at its most pleasing after a shave, smooth, fragrant with his lingering citrus odour.

"Does he even know where the hamstring is?" I whispered.

"Probably thinks it's near his elbow. Did you have a good time out there?"

A little censoring was in order.

"Oh, I killed it. You?"

"Brutal. Me hole is killing me from landing on it."

Least I wasn't the only one. Odd how he gloried in his humiliation, viewed falling as a badge of honour.

"Were you on the big slope?"

I jumped when I heard the helium voice. Mia was sitting opposite us, dwarfed by the crowd.

"Yes I was."

My equilibrium was beginning to restore itself.

"I was just on the little one."

"But you did really well, didn't you?" said Kevin.

"I only fell over once."

Kevin put his arm around her shoulders. She beamed, thriving on the incidental touches the guides were so fond of bestowing.

"Jaysus, the little one's bad enough," said Johno.

No contenders for my throne here.

As Mia and Kevin began reliving the morning's skiing, a waitress bore down on us. She was blonde and wore traditional garb, a wide check skirt with an apron and a white blouse with puffed sleeves. Several buttons of the blouse were undone, exposing acres of bare skin. She took the Greek Chorus's order first.

"Aren't you a lovely girl," one of them said to her.

He reached out to touch the fabric of her dress, his hand perilously close to the mounds of flesh underneath.

"Sorry love," he piped up. "Didn't see you there."

This prompted much chortling.

"Who let the dogs out," I muttered.

"Is he getting excited," Johno said, gurgling.

"You could say that. Although I suppose he has reason. She is exposing rather a lot of flesh."

"Yeah? Enough to make the blind see, what?"

His gurgle was less endearing than before; it set my teeth on edge. Mia and Kevin gave their orders, then returned to their conversation. The waitress was still hovering. I only hoped she couldn't speak English.

THE LADY WAS wrong. I wasn't like the other girls. They were aliens. When I was around them, my flesh itched and became tight. They clutched dolls which wore pink dresses. The dolls had soft bodies, but their faces were made of plastic. They had round cheeks and they smiled for no reason. The girls called the dolls Cabbage Patch Kids and asked me if I wanted to hold one. But I didn't. The dolls had dead eyes, just like theirs.

I PICKED UP a menu, so we could give the good Frau our verdict.

"Well there's chips anyway. I'll have those. And a couple of those huge sausages. With some sparkling mineral water to wash it down."

"Me too. And coffee with some of that lovely mother's milk," said Johno.

Up close, his six-pack was visible. Pity his hands were so rough. But his fingers were long and tapered; a very good sign. Jazz's fingers were rounded and soft at the tips, the ideal shape for working a mixer. Made for sucking on.

"I'll have that afterwards. For now, I'll stick with good old fashioned *aqua vitae*."

"What? That some sort of yuppie drink?"

I was willing to overlook his lack of intellectual acumen.

"Nope. Water by an other name."

My earlier humiliation was a distant memory; the bubbles in the water brought my mouth back to life. I was beginning to enjoy this unparalleled access to my quarry, even though his attention was diverted by his food, which he attacked with vigour, a pig slurping swill from a trough.

I WAS SPEARING my last chip when Martin came to reclaim me. My legs were splayed out, to give my muscles a chance to relax. I patted my stomach in satisfaction. Johno's hand rested next to mine. The temptation to lift it up and place it on my stomach was almost unbearable. Martin's bellow shattered the dream.

"Get a move on, girlie. Have to work off that lunch."

"Bet you've some job keeping her in line," Johno said to him.

"You're telling me, mate. Bloody hard work, she is."

"I don't envy you."

I grinned.

"Wait'll I start on you," I said.

"Wha?" Johno muttered as I heaved myself out of my seat.

Sometimes I liked to keep them guessing.

ON THE SECOND lift run, Martin decided I was stable enough for some light interrogation.

"So what do you do for a crust, then?"

"What?"

"You know, for a living?"

"Oh. Freelance proofreader."

"What's that when it's at home?"

His attention was a laser beam. Too much light at once.

"I doubt it's of interest to you."

"You'd be surprised."

"Looking over books and papers before publication to check that there are no errors."

That was sure to sate him.

"Sounds all right. Any blockbusters?"

"No. Medical and scientific books."

"Manage all right with that? You know, with your eyes."

"Yes of course."

I saw myself at Jazz's kitchen table, my head resting on my closed fist, reading faint lines of text which blurred into each other. Grit filled my eyes; my eyelids were pulled downwards by an invisible force. Jazz came over to me and touched my shoulder. *I didn't know you could read with your eyes closed.*

Such incidents only occurred when there was a tight turnaround time on a document and I couldn't take my usual breaks.

THE TOP OF the lift beckoned. This time, my legs didn't collapse. I fiddled with my gloves and my shades.

"Come on, stop faffing about," said Martin.

I tucked my poles under my armpits and propelled myself forward.

"Right, point your skis downhill... give yourself a bit of speed. And we're off. Swing to the right... check your speed... left... get that leg round... right... relax now... let your skis run straight... build up some speed through the flat bit."

There was no time to think, no time for the weight to build in my chest. The sound of Martin's voice filled up all the space in my mind. It cut through the dazzling whiteness, acting as both safety net and spur. I was flying.

"Little left... not too much... big right... get round these schoolkids. Keep it running... that's the way. Little turns here... left... right. Eh, you're going fast here, girlie, you going for the Winter Olympics or what? Check your speed, bit more of a plough... and stop."

I jerked to a halt, spinning around and almost crashing into him. It was over already. My head spun. I leaned on my ski poles for support.

"How was that for you then, girlie?" he asked, chortling.

I looked down at my boots.

"Fine. No big deal."

But a grin leaked across my face. Bolts of electricity coursed through me, shocking but not unpleasant. This was how it felt to meld two pieces of music into each other, until it was hard to tell where one ended and the other began.

"I'm guessing you enjoyed it then. You up for more punishment?"

"Bring it on."

We blasted down the slope several more times, each run more successful than the last. His voice gave me wings.

❧ The DJ Shack ❧

MY COMPOSITION LAY on the table in front of Matthew. It was my first typed composition and I was eager for Matthew's verdict. He was teaching me to type, because handwriting was still a Herculean labour for me. I used his old typewriter from university. It was cumbersome and made a lot of noise, but the speed with which it produced letters mesmerised me.

Matthew gave my efforts only a cursory glance.

"I have some important information to impart," he said. "Ora will be visiting us at the weekend."

He was always more lenient about my work in the days before Ora's visits.

"That's not a newsworthy event."

"Well on this occasion it is. She will be staying for the entire weekend. And she will be bringing her son Geoffrey with her. He was due to come last weekend, but he was celebrating his thirteenth birthday."

That was indeed interesting. Ora talked about her son often; she gave him the status of a demigod.

VOICES FLOATED TOWARDS me from the washroom; they were early. Ora burst into the kitchen, trailing bags, a familiar enough visitor by now to not feel the need to announce her presence. I carried on reading my *National Geographic*, determined to finish my article. At the sound of a second set of footsteps, I lowered the magazine a couple of inches. A plump boy stood by the door, clutching a sports bag and a long, grey object which I couldn't identify. His shoes squeaked as he scuffed his feet against the tiles. Ora placed her parcels on the table.

"Astrid, come and meet my son Geoff," she said.

I slid off the windowseat and stood in front of the boy. His face was soft and round. It was framed by a cap of dark hair. He wore a blue jumper with a logo on it, a white shirt, a blue tie and grey pants. I guessed it was the uniform for his school. The fabric of the jumper stretched over a round belly. He placed the objects on the ground with care, treating them as delicate samples. Then he shook my hand. His hand was soft and damp. His thick glasses mirrored mine.

"Hello," he said, his voice directed at the floor.

"What's that?" I said, pointing to the long, grey object.

He picked it up and held it out for me to inspect. It was covered in small round knobs. A long silver pole poked out at the top.

"It's a ghetto blaster. He got it for his birthday last week," said Ora.

"What does it do?"

"It's for music," he said. "It's got a radio and it plays tapes and stuff."

"Why did you bring a radio? We have radios here too, you know."

"Geoff, come and help me with this food," Ora said.

Matthew came in as they finished putting the parcels in the cupboards.

"There you are," he said, his voice reverberating around the kitchen. "Never heard you arrive. Apologies for that."

He strode over to the boy and pumped his hand.

"Pleased to meet you, Geoffrey. I'm Dr Johnson. Not to be confused with the lexicographer."

The boy opened his mouth, but no sound came out.

"Don't you know what a lexicographer is?" I asked him.

"Why don't we show Geoff the beach," said Ora.

"Splendid idea," said Matthew. "The evenings are beginning to lengthen. There should be time for a short walk."

"Geoff, why don't you get changed," said Ora. "I'll show you your room."

When the boy came downstairs, he was wearing brown leather shoes with laces on them, jeans and a red jumper which billowed outwards, concealing his belly.

"I'M ALWAYS AMAZED she never hurts herself," Ora said as I began my flight down the cliff path.

There was a mixture of awe and fear in her voice. Ora was easy to impress.

"Well, we do use it to access the beach on a daily basis," said Matthew. "It's your child who is struggling."

The boy took a long time to reach the bottom. His face was the same colour as his jumper. We had to wait for him to catch his breath before we began our walk. I picked up rocks and seaweed and recited their names with pride, giving them their correct classifications. Ora exclaimed over them.

"I don't know how you remember all those names. It's amazing, isn't it?" she said to the boy.

The boy yawned and put his hands in his pockets. Matthew grunted.

"Glad to see my education is producing some results."

THAT NIGHT, THE boy slept in the room to the left of mine. Ora slept with Matthew, because there weren't any other bedrooms and Matthew's bed was big enough for two people.

IT TOOK A long time for the boy to come out of his room the next morning. Ora said it was because he was doing his homework. He only came downstairs when we were eating our lunch.

"Matthew's offered to drive us around the coast," Ora said to him when we finished. "That'll be fun, won't it?"

The boy nodded and brought his hand to his mouth to cover a yawn.

"We'd better press on," said Matthew. "We have lots of things to show Geoffrey this afternoon, don't we, Astrid?"

"Yes," I said. "Wexford is full of delights."

The boy made a strange sound at the back of his throat, a sort of gagging noise.

IN THE CAR, the boy and I sat as far apart as possible, our bodies pressed against the doors. We drove along narrow country roads and stopped whenever we saw an interesting landmark or geographical feature. Ora took photographs. Matthew talked about the history of the area and I chipped in.

On the way home, we went to Hook Head to look at the lighthouse. Despite the brightness of the day, it was cold. The water around the cliffs was white; it foamed and hissed as it landed on the rocks.

"Well Geoffrey, one could argue that this is indeed God's country, if one was so inclined. Don't you agree?"

"It's okay," the boy muttered.

Matthew snorted, one of the explosive snorts he reserved for remarks he thought foolish.

"If you say so. Come on, we'll walk around the lighthouse."

Matthew strode off over the springy green grass. The lighthouse was surrounded by ridged grey rocks. Since we were frequent visitors there, Matthew was satisfied that I could reach the other side unaided. But it always took a long time; the rocks required some negotiation. I fell into a groove, searching for clefts in the rock, then inching forward. My progress was steady; only the occasional wobble impeded it. The boy was a little ahead. He took sluggish steps, his hands in his pockets. I stayed close to the lighthouse, but its solid surface was beyond my reach. Ora fell into step beside me.

"How are you going there?"

"Fine."

I didn't look around or say anything more; the task of putting one foot in front of the other took up all the space in my head.

"Well, I don't know about you, but it's quite rough, isn't it?"

I shrugged; my gaze was directed at the ground.

"Maybe we'd be a bit faster if we went together. We could beat the boys to the other side."

I looked up. She was holding out her elbow. Without looking at her, I took it. We walked around the rest of the lighthouse without saying a word. I was able to count the stark black and white lines painted on the lighthouse and gaze out at the snowcapped waves that surrounded it.

IT WAS TWILIGHT when we arrived home. The boy went into the kitchen to help Ora cook dinner.

"Why can't they help?" I heard him whisper as they went in.

"They've got work to do too," Ora replied.

I followed Matthew into his study and we immersed ourselves in the *National Geographic* pullout, which depicted the skeletons of primitive cavemen. Time disappeared as we held the pictures up to Matthew's skeleton. Matthew positioned my hands on the skeleton, as we compared the modern and ancient bones. The modern bones were longer and denser. A knock on the door jolted me back to the present.

"Yes, who is it?" Matthew barked.

"It's me," said Ora. "I hate to disturb you, but dinner's ready."

"All right, we're coming."

"But I'm not hungry," I whispered.

"Well, she's been fussing in that kitchen for hours," said Matthew. "We'd better do what we're told, for once."

In the kitchen, I rummaged for cutlery to set the table. The boy brought saucepans to the counter. Matthew pulled a bottle of wine out of the fridge.

"I unearthed this specimen. Hope it will complement our food tonight. Some local woman brewed it up."

He held the bottle out to Ora, who wiped it with a cloth and examined it.

"Elderflower wine. Lovely! But don't you want to save it for a special occasion?"

"You've brought your son to visit; that's occasion enough."

His voice was gruff. There was a pink flush on Ora's cheeks.

"You hear that, Geoff?" Ora said.

The boy didn't say anything. He fiddled with one of the saucepan lids.

I sat at my place and the boy put a plate in front of me. It was covered in long tubes, which were smeared with sludge-green paste. I poked at the paste with my fork. A piece of chicken revealed itself.

"Ora, what on earth is this?" asked Matthew.

"It's chicken pesto."

Ora came to the table and put plates of food in front of Matthew and herself.

"Why's it so green?" I asked. "Is it mould?"

Ora made a gulping noise.

"It does look rather unorthodox," said Matthew, "but it's a shame to waste food."

He poked at the paste too, then took a bite. The boy was shovelling food into his mouth. There was already a dent in the mound on his plate.

"I think it's lovely," he said.

For the first time since his arrival, there was animation in his voice. I scraped the paste off the chicken and ate it piece by piece. I didn't touch the tubes; they had the same texture as rubber. Halfway through the meal, Matthew jumped up and left the room, saying he needed to use the bathroom. He was gone for a long time.

"I hope it didn't upset your stomach," said Ora, when he returned. "I suppose it's a bit richer than you're used to."

"That's what bouts of amoebic dysentery will do to you."

"Oh. I'm sorry. I just wanted to make something nice."

Ora's voice wobbled.

"I daresay you did. But we're more accustomed to campfire cuisine."

The boy asked for a second helping and Ora jumped up to get it.

"There you are," she said.

The wobble was gone from her voice.

"You'll get indigestion if you eat too much," I informed the boy.

He didn't reply, just kept eating. His slurping sounds filled the room.

AFTER DINNER, WE went into the living room.

"Where's your telly?" the boy asked.

I knew that telly was short for television.

"We don't have one," I said.

The boy's mouth formed an 'O.'

"Do you not get bored?"

"No."

"There's a quaint pastime we like to indulge in," said Matthew. "It's called reading."

He gave a dry chuckle. The boy looked at the ground. I wondered what he saw there that was so interesting.

"Didn't you say we were going to listen to some music, Matthew?" said Ora.

Matthew went to the antique record player and placed *The Well-Tempered Clavier* on the turntable. I went to sit in the armchair to the left of the fireplace. The boy sat on the stool near the window, behind the table Matthew and I used for our evening chess games. The board obscured his face, as it waited for our next move.

"You love Bach, don't you," said Ora.

"Music reached perfection with J.S. Bach," Matthew said. "He has no equal."

As Matthew slipped the needle into the groove, the boy got up and moved around the couch, towards the record player.

"That's gorgeous," he said. "It's vintage."

His voice was peculiar; it spanned several octaves within the same sentence, sometimes squeaking, sometimes growling. His hand hovered above the record player's gleaming mahogany surface.

"You can't touch it," I said, folding my arms. "Only Matthew's allowed to touch it."

"I wasn't going to."

The record made strange scratching noises. Matthew fiddled with the needle, muttering under his breath. The boy was still standing by the record player, watching Matthew.

"Sir, if you want, I think I know what..."

He reached over and touched the needle, before Matthew could stop him. I waited for Matthew's roar of retribution. But the record sounded normal again.

"Thank you, Geoffrey," said Matthew. "It's useful to have someone with a technical bent in the house."

The boy's mouth opened and shut. Again, no sound came out. His face was red, like before on the beach. He retreated to his chair.

"Why don't you say anything when Matthew talks to you?" I asked.

"Leave him be, Astrid," said Matthew.

I didn't know why Matthew was cross with me. He was the one who told me that it was important to have an enquiring mind.

We listened to the music in silence. Matthew went over to the couch to sit beside Ora and she rested her head on his shoulder. I guessed that she was tired after all the cooking.

IT WAS SUNNY again the next day. Matthew set an even faster pace than usual during our morning walk; I had to run to keep up with him. He left the beach before I did. This always happened when Ora visited. He said it was because he didn't want to leave her on her own for too long. I wandered among the sand dunes, tweaking at pieces of dry grass, letting sand run through my fingers. The sand was thick with the fragments of shells. I picked some of them up and examined them. The beach was empty; it stretched into infinity.

As I reached the top of the cliff path, a tinny sound crept out of the shed at the bottom of the garden. I closed the garden gate and ran over to it. The door was ajar; I pushed it open. There were no windows in the shed; the light was dim. A figure sat at the other end of the shed. It was the boy. He sat in a sagging deck chair, his back to me. His radio was perched on top of two metal buckets that Matthew used for the garden. He didn't turn as I came over to stand beside him.

"Haven't you heard of knocking?"

A storm brewed in his voice, rain clouds gathered.

"Well it is our shed," I said. "What are you listening to?"

"Nothing you'd be interested in. So you can either shut up or get out."

The boy twiddled with various buttons. The radio began to produce a disjointed series of sounds, a drum beat, scratching, the tinkle of bells, a droning sound which grew into a swirling melody, a piano. The sounds began to form layers. There were voices too; first a male voice made incoherent sounds, then a female voice sang about a day without a night and a body without a heart. The words didn't make much sense, but they were filled with yearning. At intervals, another female voice, fainter than the first, repeated the word 'hey.' The sounds fused together and formed a current which carried me along, took me far away. I was a shooting star, travelling through the galaxies. A tingling sensation spread outwards from my chest, through my veins. Towards the end, the rhythm started to slow and the other sounds began to fall away, to fade into silence. The boy pressed another button, which made a whirring sound.

"What was that?" I asked him.

"*Unfinished Sympathy* by Massive Attack."

"*Unfinished Symphony*? Like Schubert?"

"No. Just *Unfinished Sympathy*."

He spoke with exaggerated slowness.

"What instruments do they use?"

"They don't use any. The sounds're generated by electronics."

There were no longer any peaks or troughs in his voice. It carried the same note of authority as Matthew's did when he talked about his samples.

"Could you play it again?" I asked.

"Okay. If you want."

He sounded surprised. As we listened, he pressed his fists against his cheeks. His skin puffed out over his fingers. This time, I began to discern a pattern in the tinkling of the bells. Two, two, two, three. I was able to sift through the layers of sound, separate them. As the beats died away, I said,

"I think that's the most extraordinary thing I've ever heard."

"It's okay," the boy said.

"That's not the right word. It's exhilarating."

"I prefer harder stuff. You know, faster. But it's good. Yeah."

He took his fists away from his cheeks. His skin was covered in little white marks, from the pressure of his knuckles.

"Did you know there are nine bell sounds?"

"No."

"It's a pattern; it keeps repeating. Listen out for it."

"Yes, teacher," the boy muttered.

Over and over, the tinkling bells and soaring melodies filled the shed. The music hypnotised us, made everything outside the shed disappear. In the distance, we heard Ora calling the boy's name. He pressed another button and the music stopped.

"They call me Not So Jazzy at school," he blurted into the sudden silence.

"What does that mean?"

"Like the DJ, Jazzy Jeff. Except not as cool. That's what they think anyway."

He was sullen, defeated. His arms folded across his chest.

"What's a DJ?"

"You don't know what a DJ is?"

His voice echoed mine; it was gleeful, knowing.

"DJs make music come together. They mix all these different strands of music to make one big flow. It's like art, except they use lots of old bits to make something new. It sounds stupid. You won't get it."

"No it isn't. It's fascinating."

We heard Ora's voice again, more insistent this time. The boy snatched up his radio. We went around to the front of the house, where Ora was loading her car. The boy placed the radio in the boot.

"Bye," he said, his gaze once again directed at the ground.

"Bye, Jazz."

He laughed. It was an unexpected sound, rich and deep. I grinned back. Matthew and I lingered as the car drove off.

"What on earth did you call him?" Matthew said.

"Jazz. After the DJ."

"Don't talk gibberish."

A smile crept onto my face. The idea that I now spoke a language Matthew couldn't understand tickled me. I followed him to the house, my head still throbbing with the sounds.

JAZZ'S THAW WAS gradual. Though he was now an almost constant presence at weekends, he and I travelled in different orbits most of the time. When he wasn't being force-fed history and scenery, he was in his room or in the kitchen with Ora. They hugged each other a lot.

Jazz never read any books, or went outside of his own free will. And he never spoke to us unless we spoke to him. Even when he did speak, he hesitated first, testing the words before he said them. When Matthew spoke to him, he sometimes forgot to reply, just opened and shut his mouth. Maybe it was because he never knew the answers to Matthew's questions. And he called Matthew sir.

To me, Jazz was a strange specimen, a riddle I was determined to solve. I spied on him through a crack in the door of his room. Sounds leaked through the crack, tinny musical notes, the crackle of paper, the scratch of a pen blotting out words. His homework took a long time. I asked him why it took so long and what he was learning at his school, but he wasn't interested in talking about it, said it was boring. When he did talk about school, the stormclouds filled his voice.

On the first proper day of spring, Jazz emerged from his cocoon, lured by pale sunshine. When Matthew and I returned from our swim and walk, we found him sitting at the table at the top of the garden. It was warped; the paint kept peeling off. He wore a T-shirt, exposing bare arms which looked unused to sunlight. They were almost as white as mine. There was a piece of coloured paper in front of him. As we walked over to him, he picked up the paper and tucked it under his jumper, which was beside him on the bench. He began arranging flakes of paint into a neat pile.

"What have you got there, Geoffrey?" asked Matthew.

"Nothing, sir. Just stuff for an art project."

Matthew held out his hand.

"May I?"

Jazz thrust the coloured paper at him. In fact, there was more than one piece of paper; the pieces were stuck together. There were pictures of people on them. Words came out of their mouths in little bubbles. Matthew turned the pages, his gaze intent. Jazz kept his head lowered. The paint pile grew bigger.

"Hmm. Quite well-drawn," he said, handing the papers back to Jazz.

"Thank you, sir," said Jazz.

"Aren't picture books for children?" I asked.

"Ah, but these are comics, Astrid. Comics are different. More of a boy's premise. Eh, Geoffrey?"

Jazz's mouth opened and shut.

"I collected comics as a boy," said Matthew. "They're in the attic in Dublin. I'll dig them out for you and you can peruse them the next time you visit. For your art project."

After that, Jazz stopped calling Matthew sir. He called him Matthew instead.

JAZZ'S FATHER DIDN'T live with Ora and Jazz. Ora told me he lived in Paris and had some sort of complicated job which involved money. When she talked about him, her voice became flat and heavy. Jazz didn't talk about him at all. One day, in the shed, I decided to conduct an investigation.

"How come your father doesn't live with you?" I said.

"Because," he said in his stormcloud voice.

He turned up the volume on the radio. I had to shout to be heard over it.

"That's not a reason."

"Stop asking so many questions. You're always asking questions."

"An enquiring mind is the most useful tool you can have."

"Yeah, well save it for something else."

Jazz turned up the volume, precluding further conversation. I knew from reading the Miss Marple books that patience was the mark of a true detective, so I let the matter drop. His father remained a shadow, a myth. Like my mother.

IT WAS ONLY in the shed that Jazz and I came together. The shed was no longer just a rickety wooden structure in the corner of our garden. It was a magical place. Bit by bit, we created a home among the detritus, not caring about the wind that howled through cracks in the walls and filled the shed with moisture laden air. We stayed there for hours on end; time became meaningless.

After the first weekend, Jazz's radio took up permanent residence on the two upturned metal buckets. It was the metal that made the music sound tinny; Jazz liked that. We sat on two saggy folding chairs in front of the radio, hemmed in by rusting garden equipment and gas canisters. Our knees kept knocking together, so we slouched deep into the chairs to give the illusion of space. We didn't talk about anything except the music. As we listened, we breathed in the smells of creosote and damp earth, which mingled with another smell, of citrus mixed with woodsmoke. I couldn't identify the source of it, but I liked it.

Jazz navigated me through a world which was both alien and exciting, the world of DJ music. That was what I called it, though he called it all sorts of names: techno, rave, house. I was learning Latin with Matthew, but I was learning the language of music with Jazz, exotic words like breakbeat, megamix, four to the floor. Jazz struggled to remember the premise of the novel he was reading for class and it took him hours to learn the conjugations of French and Irish verbs. But he could recite a litany of DJs and dance groups, their music specialties, the

London and New York nightclubs where they played and their top mixes. Some of the names consisted of random letters and numbers. 2 Unlimited, Soul II Soul, Heavy D and the Boyz. Some groups misspelled ordinary words, giving themselves names like Phuture and Sleezy.

"Don't they know how to spell?" I asked Jazz.

"They don't care about stupid stuff like that," he muttered.

"That isn't a sufficient reason."

"Because it sounds cool. Not that you'd know about that."

"Cool," I repeated, relishing the taste of the unfamiliar word in my mouth.

Jazz also knew how the music was created. It wasn't like Bach, who wrote notes on a sheet for orchestras to play. It was a series of sounds mixed together.

"You know, they take a voice out of one song and a beat out of another song," said Jazz. "And they use the recording equipment to put them together, so they match."

"That's a very confusing concept."

"No it isn't. Listen to this. Black Box. They took the words out of an old song and put them to a beat."

He slipped on a tape and a jaunty beat filled the shed. Then a female voice began to repeat the words, 'ride on time.'

There was something compelling about the way she shouted all the words in a rasping voice. Jazz's face became red and he looked at the floor.

"Don't you like it? Why did you play it if you don't like it?"

"I do. It's just the words, you know."

Jazz snorted and brought his hands to his mouth. He made snuffling sounds.

"Have you got a toothache?"

He shook his head. It took me a moment for me to identify the sounds as laughter.

"What's so funny?" I demanded.

"The words. Ride. Two people... you know, doing it."

"Doing what?"

I was becoming impatient.

"Like... sex."

This word prompted further snorts of laughter. My mouth fell open. I kept listening to the words. Ride on time. The words had meanings that only we knew. Like a code in a detective novel. The thought gave me a secret thrill.

MOST OF THE music Jazz listened to was harsher than the Massive Attack piece, but it had the same euphoric quality. The beats filled up all the air in the shed and made our limbs twitch. The music was stored on cassette tapes. Some of them were albums with bright swirling colours. Others were tapes Jazz made himself, with his writing on the covers. The writing was too small for me to read, even with the monocle, so Jazz read it for me.

Sometimes we played music from two tapes at once. When a tune was about to finish, Jazz reached over and started playing the second tape while the first tape was still playing.

"How do you know when to play the second tune?" I asked him.

"It's called mixing. You play two tunes at the same time and make the beats match."

I listened. Apart from the clacking of the play button, it was almost impossible to tell when one tune ended and another one began.

"But this isn't proper mixing. You need decks for that."

"Like on a boat?"

"No. It's equipment. You can play two tunes together. You know, vinyl records. All DJs have them."

"Like Matthew's Bach ones."

"Yeah, but these ones're smaller. 7 inches or 12 inches. 12 inches are best for DJing. You can start a song at any place and drop it in."

"Drop it? Drop the record? Doesn't that damage it?"

Jazz laughed.

"It's not like that. You play one song and then you start the next one in the middle of it, so they're playing together."

"Doesn't it sound strange?"

"Not if you do it right."

"Do you know how to do the mixing?"

"A bit. Mum's friend used to mind me when she was doing her photography course and her son's a DJ. Sam. He let me play on his decks a bit. He says he'll finished with them soon and he'll sell them to me."

Jazz's tours of the DJ world held me in thrall. I listened to him with my head cocked to one side. It was easier to focus on his words that way.

"I like the way the music sounds in here," he said one day.

"It just sounds like music, doesn't it?"

"Well yeah. But it sounds different from how it used to in my bedroom. I don't know why. Deeper, more echoey, you know."

I thought of the echo cave in Ancient Greek mythology.

"It's the sound waves," I said. "They're bouncing off the walls and there's nowhere for them to go."

"Really?"

For once, he was interested in my information.

"I could check with Matthew. But I think that's the reason."

We increased the volume and the beats pounded off the walls.

BIT BY BIT, Jazz revealed his mysteries to me. He stumbled out tales of towels whipping his legs as he stepped out of the dormitory showers, sniggers at missed words and botched answers to questions. Now I knew why he hated school so much.

"Those people sound like Neanderthals,"

"What are those?" Jazz said.

The stormclouds were threatening to return.

"Primitive men. Like apes."

Jazz covered his mouth with his hand, but the laughter escaped and bounced off the walls of the shed, just like the music. I wondered why he always wanted to keep his laughter hidden.

After a while, Jazz showed me how to do the mixing with the tapes. He put my hand on the play button and told me when to press, which beat to listen out for. As he leaned over, our knees knocked together, but this time they forgot to come apart. And the citrus and woodsmoke smell became stronger. Now I knew the source of it: Jazz.

RAIN BOUNCED OFF the roof of the shed, a soft but penetrating summer shower which caused damp patches to appear on the splintered wooden floor. The damp accentuated the smells of creosote and earth. Jazz was playing another of his numbered bands, the B-52s. They sang about a love shack being a little love place where they could get together.

"This place is a shack," I said.

"A DJ shack," Jazz said.

"Is that like a nightclub?"

I knew that nightclubs were the places where the DJs played their records. Jazz said he was too young to go to them. They were full of flashing lights and people danced for hours to the music the DJs played.

"No. They're these sheds in the middle of nowhere with illegal radio stations in them."

"Cool," I said, shooting forward in my chair.

The word now formed a regular part of my lexicon, much to Matthew's disgust.

The following week, Jazz brought a large, flat parcel with him, which he laid on the kitchen table.

"Look at what Geoff did," Ora said. "It was his final project for Technology class."

"Show us your handiwork, Geoffrey," said Matthew.

Jazz's fingers fumbled as he pulled off the brown paper and string, to reveal a wooden board with the words DJ Shack carved in jagged letters. Imprints of headphones and vinyl records were carved around the words. Jazz pressed a button and the sign lit up. He bent his head over the wood.

"That's amazing, Jazz," I said. "Why don't we put it up on the door of the garden shed. For our own DJ Shack."

"I won't have that gaudy thing defacing my property."

Matthew's voice was a thunderclap. Jazz fiddled with the discarded paper.

"It's very well made though, isn't it?" Ora said.

Matthew picked it up and inspected it.

"Well, I do admire the craftsmanship," he said. "I'm sure you'll find another place for it."

I knew where to place the sign, on the folding table near the entrance to the shed. There were bags of seeds on it, but they could be moved. I helped Jazz carry the sign to the shed. We placed the bags of seeds on the floor and balanced the sign on the table, letting it rest against the wall. It was the exact same width as the table, though the wood was a lighter hue. As I leaned closer to examine the imprints more closely, I saw a red squiggle in the corner.

"Is that an 'A'?" I asked Jazz.

"Yeah."

"Matthew says an 'A' is the best grade to get."

"S'pose."

The stormclouds weren't rolling away.

"Why aren't you happy? Are you annoyed with Matthew? He liked it really. If he doesn't like something, he always says so."

"The other boys started throwing it around the place like a Frisbee. Doesn't matter. I was able to fix it."

I studied it again, my head cocked.

"Never mind. When you're a famous DJ, you can tell them they're not allowed to come to your nightclub."

"You know, all the big DJs have assistants," said Jazz. "To hold up the next record for them, help them with the mixes and tuning the equipment and stuff. When I get into a nightclub, you can be mine."

His face reddened.

"Cool," I said.

I switched the button on and off; in the brown darkness of the shed, the letters glowed red blue, red blue. Like flashing lights in a nightclub.

❧ Friendly Fire ❧

WHEN I CLIMBED onto the bus, there was a free seat next to Johno. This was a fortunate development. Mia was on the other side, but that little obstacle could be circumvented.

"A thorn between two roses, eh, Johno," said Kevin as he closed the sliding door.

"Ah yeah," said Johno.

Cliona lumbered up to the front seat.

"Want a hand, Cliona?" said Kevin.

There was no sign of her stooge, but I heard rustling at the back of the bus. He was putting their boots away.

"Oh no, that's not necessary. It's more empowering if I do it myself," said Cliona.

No doubt this was a central tenet of the gimptronics philosophy.

As she lurched onto the bus, she misjudged her step and pitched forward. Kevin's hand shot out and steadied her. She bent over to rub her foot. Kim hovered over her.

"At least there's no damage," said Cliona.

"Been on the beer again, Cliona?" asked Kevin.

Laughter erupted from most of the passengers. Radio silence from Cliona.

"Well, it is quite dark. Such a pity the area isn't better lit. Someone should write to the relevant local authority."

Kevin started the bus with a jerk, cutting short Cliona's polemic. Once again, there was steam on the windows.

"What's your dirty word this time, Astrid?" Kevin shouted.

It only took a second for a word to materialise, inspired by the feel of Johno's thigh pressing into mine.

"Concupiscence," I said. "Strong desire for sex."

"I could go with that," said Johno.

"Sounds like the name of one of them foreign football players," said one of the Greek Chorus.

"No, the fella who's always shooting at the dartboard in Flanagans."

"That's Con Houlihan, you eejit."

A wave of laughter spread throughout the bus. I was forced to concede that my audience was lost. The radio spewed out Complan.

"They play awful shite on the radio here," said Johno.

He shared my belief in the aural aesthetic.

"Volume's on the lowest setting," said Kevin. "You lot must have bionic hearing."

"Yeah, the toilet's flushing in the ski cafe," said one of the Greek Chorus.

"That's if you haven't blocked it," said the other.

A tinkling sound cut through the raucous laughter. It took me a moment to trace it to Mia. She was warbling to the Complan. Kevin turned the volume up and she stopped, inhibited by the fact that she now had an audience. Her face was the same shade of pink as her ski suit.

"Ah, keep going, that's deadly," said Johno.

"I was just messing really," Mia said, aiming her words at the floor.

"That's a pretty voice you have there, love," said Kevin. "Give us another tune."

Mia began to sing again, raising her voice a notch. A reverent silence fell. At the end, they clapped. Johno supplied an eloquent appraisal of her performance.

"I can't stand all that Mariah shite, but you make it less shite," he said.

I looked out the window. The letters on my word were now indistinguishable. Rivulets of moisture streamed from them.

I LAY ON my bed, wearing only my oversize Prism T-shirt, suspended in that funny, loose-end time between skiing and the evening's entertainment. The day's exertions were washed away. I tried to read my Sherlock Holmes book, but my eyes were screwed up after the slopes. Instead, I lost myself in a Sigur Ros soundscape. Mia came back into the room from her shower, gripping her towel in one hand and her cane in the other. I removed one of my headphones.

"Thank God I'm back in," she said, giggling. "I thought my towel was going to fall down."

She began her evening ritual of lugging her suitcase onto the bed, her tiny, straining wrists a reproach I chose to ignore. As she ran her hands over her clothes, she burbled about some incomprehensible television programme that she was missing on account of being away. It appeared to revolve around a woman who wanted to ball her sexy gardener. I reinserted my headphone and tuned her out. My fingers brushed against the whitewashed wall, tracing the Braille bumps in the plaster. The pinpoint lights on the ceiling were switched off; even they felt too harsh after a day under the constant glare. I preferred the soft orange glow of the lamp by my bed.

I picked up my phone and heard the sonic blur that indicated a message. My heart leapt, hope and fear tore at my chest.

    Hope you're having fun and keeping safe.
    Ora.

With her signature of two 'X''s at the end. I deflated, lay back on the pillows, and deleted her text. The emptiness of the screen seeped through me. I filled it with letters, attempting to frame a narrative about my heroics.

    Conqurd slopes 2day. Kikn Cbge Pch Kids
    asses.

Type, delete, type, delete. Hard to match the eloquence of *The Iliad* with 160 characters. *This trip could be good for you.*

"Are you texting your boyfriend?"

Another giggle. How did she know I was texting?

"No."

She said something else, but I turned up the volume and her voice receded.

WE NEVER KISS on the lips; it's an unwritten rule. Instead, we press against each other. I press my lips into the crook of his neck. It is one of my favourite places. The skin is soft and the tang of sweat lingers on it. I trace a line of kisses along his shoulder. My hands move downwards, over taut flesh, start kneading his buttocks. His excitement pulses through the material of his boxer shorts, but the lid remains closed.

PREDATORS SHOW PHENOMENAL patience in their search for prey. In order to regain the ground lost on the bus, I upped the ante with my outfit: deep gold shirt, minuscule black lycra skirt, black suede boots which fit me like a second skin, Gucci shades with mellow brown lenses and gold rims. Still not too hardcore, but a declaration of intent.

This time, some of the guides were sitting at our table. Johno sat between Kevin and his own guide, whose name escaped me. I sat opposite them, with my shadow beside me.

"You tried the schnitzel yet, Astrid?" Kevin asked. "You're a real meat girl, reckon you'd love it. It's pork in breadcrumbs."

"Is it palatable?"

"Johno here's going for it. If it's good enough for him, it's good enough for you."

I decided to ignore his dirty cackle and gave my order to a hovering young waitress. My tendency to pick the same food as Johno was an important weapon in my arsenal.

Moments later, the waitress put a plate in front of me. It was colonised by a puddle of sauce the same shade as oxygenated blood. I gave it an experimental poke.

"I'm not seeing any meat here," I said to Kevin. "Reckon you're pulling my leg."

"Well, I'm not about to rely on your judgement now, am I?"

By the time I absorbed the joke, everyone else was roaring. These people displayed a total lack of discrimination. I parted the Red Sea on my plate and unearthed a chop covered in the requisite breadcrumbs. It landed with a plop on my side plate, showering me with drops of sauce.

"Astrid looks like a murder victim," said Kevin.

"Why?" said Johno.

"She's got sauce all over her belly."

I leaned towards him, again yearning for the impetus created by vodka and beats.

"Care to lick it off?"

"Ah no love, you're grand. I've enough to be getting on with here."

He forked some of the red gloop into his mouth. His lips smacked together as he ate; the sound made me flinch. I diverted myself with my own meat, which turned out to be quite tasty. The chips that came with it absorbed most of the red sauce. When I finished, I went to the bar for my belt of vodka. I always ordered doubles here; the shots were thimble sized. When I came back, Cliona was engaged in a little post-prandial rhetoric, something to do with inappropriate language and labelling, a botched exercise in semantics. Though her voice was loud, her words grated; they failed to deliver the desired impact. They steamrolled over us, obliterating all hope of normal conversation. A pall hung over the table.

"Friends, Romans, countrymen," I muttered.

Cliona's hands dug into her cheeks. Just like Jazz's when he was thinking. Her elbows were spread-eagled across the table. Kim put a hand on her arm, to prevent her from knocking over a glass which was just outside her narrow band of vision.

"It's important to take responsibility for how we are seen by others. For instance, I like to refer to myself as a blindy. I think humour is an excellent tool for offsetting the effects of stereotyping."

"Tool," whispered one of the Greek Chorus, sniggering.

Cliona raised her voice, to stem the incipient laughter.

"We must all be invested in this issue. None of us are immune from the perils of inappropriate labelling."

A sickly, metallic taste was building in my mouth. It was time to shake things up a little. I enjoyed a little dialectic after dinner myself.

"Learn that from your gimptronics textbook?" I asked her.

Cliona bristled. Her cheeks puffed.

"I presume you're referring to my Disability Studies course. In that case, I must ask you to show a little more respect. You might be more sympathetic if your own barriers were greater. Though I'm sure you must face some."

I swirled the liquid in my vodka glass. It made a vortex in the middle.

"No."

None that I wished to discuss with her.

"Still, you're bound to have views on this, in light of your condition."

"Sounds as if I'm pregnant," I said.

Guffaws from the men.

"Nice one," Johno whispered to me.

I smirked, pleased to have a fellow gladiator on side.

"I'm sure you must have noticed the labels people use to describe those with albinism. How do you refer to yourself?"

Everyone lays bets on who can get it on with the albino chick.

"I tend to refer to myself as Astrid. It's common practise in Western cultures to refer to oneself by one's name."

More laughter. Cliona's cheeks were now stained crimson.

"It's regrettable that you should make light of this issue," she said. "Us blindies have to stick together, you know."

"But you're not, are you?"

"Not what?"

We circled each other, waiting to pounce.

"Blind."

"Not as such, but—"

"Then why say you are."

No reply. First blood to me.

"She has you there," piped up one of the Greek Chorus.

Cliona's cheeks deflated with a sucking sound. Johno stood up, cane at the ready.

"I'm going to get some gargle. All this intellectual talk has made me thirsty."

Cliona leaned into Kim and they began whispering and touching each other, two monkeys engrossed in a grooming ritual.

I WAS IN a big crowd all of the time. The roar of noise was everywhere. It was a high noise, full of shrieks and giggles that didn't make any sense. The noise followed me into each room, echoed around the corridors and bounced off the high ceilings and the walls. I woke up in the morning to the sound of feet clattering on bare wooden floorboards. The noise was loudest in the dining room, where I ate at a long table with the other seven girls in my class. We sat at the same table everyday. There was no escape from the noise: clamouring voices, cutlery banging against the table, the legs of the chairs scraping against the ground, water spilling and forming a lake on the table. The girls moaned and wailed about the food, because they didn't like it. But I did. It had lumps in it, like the food Matthew made. The pink ladies fussed over the girls and told them to eat up, eat up.

The noise was a big wave that threatened to knock me over. But my Viking book helped me to block it out. While I waited for the other girls to get ready for bed, I drew my legs towards me and balanced the book on my knees. It smelled of home. The iron bars of the bedpost pressed through the thin pillow, but I didn't care. The noise was gone. I could read some of the words, but most of them were foreign. So I listened to Mathew instead. Sometimes I just opened the first page and looked at the curly writing, trying to figure out what it meant. I looked at the pictures of the goddesses with their streaming golden hair and tried to guess which one was my mother. If she was in Valhalla, then she knew where I was, because the gods of Valhalla knew about everything that happened on earth. But she didn't come and find me. Instead, she waited for me in the pages of the Viking book. The pink ladies always had to take the book away from me. When they took it, the noise came back.

I was the only one who never made any noise. The pink ladies liked that. They asked the other girls why they couldn't be quiet, like me. But I didn't want to make any noise. I never talked to anyone unless they talked to me. After a while, the noise went away, like the noise of the waves crashing on the beach at home.

THIS TIME, AN extra person featured in my pink cage dream: Jazz. He stood just outside the bars of the cage, too far for me to reach. I pleaded with him to release me, but he said, *No. You're one of them now.*

Two nights in a row. Had to be some kind of record. Keeping my face buried in the pillow, I groped for the bedside lamp and filled the room with light, hoping to drive away the last cobwebbed remnants of the dream.

Jazz had witnessed one of my pink cage dreams, during an interlude. As I pushed against the bars, my leg kicked out and came in contact with hard matter: Jazz's leg. I stirred.

"Bars. Couldn't get past," I muttered.

He planted soft kisses on my shoulder, then along the length of my upper arm. His touch stilled my flailing limbs, obliterated the last shreds of the dream. I was able to let myself drift back to sleep.

The cool logic of Sherlock Holmes didn't offer its usual balm. The memory of Jazz's kisses pierced through me, blurring the words on the page. Jazz wasn't there to chase the cobwebs away. My limbs twitched, attempting to seek him out.

I FEARED MY lack of sleep might have erased my new-found skill, but that wasn't the case. The runs passed without incident. I liked to go fast and feel the wind whistle through my hair. But I made sure to stay within shouting distance of Martin. Whenever I strayed, rogue clumps of snow threatened to topple me. He always managed to stay tuned to my gear changes. Wherever I was, he was there too.

The lifts were still a source of anxiety, though less so than the day before. The lift runs were accompanied by a further barrage of questioning. I kept my answers brief, but Martin was undeterred; his questions beat down like incessant rain.

"So this proofreading then," he said. "How'd you get into that game?"

"Providence, I guess."

"Just in the right place at the right time?"

"Yes."

There was a pause, while he waited for me to elaborate. But I saw no need to. My conversations were confined to intellectual jousts with Matthew, or one-line reviews of beats with Jazz. But in the face of his relentless questioning, I gave in, my resistance weakened by the need to distract myself. I expounded on my favourite research methods, the perils of over-reliance on Google, my despair at the ubiquity of misplaced apostrophes.

"You must have had to go to college to learn all that."

"Yes."

"What did you do?"

"Classics."

"All that Greek and Roman mythology stuff? I quite like that."

"There's a bit more to it than that."

"I'm sure there is. It's not gimptronics anyway."

The rope jerked. I held it tighter and the rough cord bit into my hands.

He replied, "Yeah, I heard that little crack of yours last night. Doesn't pay to be a smart arse, you know. You won't be thanked for it."

I shrugged. Proofreading required skill in excising irrelevant information.

THE SUN CAME out just before lunch. Ice crystals formed on the snow and my skis slithered on the slick surface. Only Martin's arm saved me from an unceremonious spillage on the lift run.

"Quite the strong man, aren't you," I said.

"Built like a brick house, that's me."

He flexed his biceps. They were even more well defined than Jazz's.

"More like a brick cottage. You're not quite big enough to qualify as a house."

The lift zig-zagged across the path. My stomach lurched. I couldn't prevent a yelp from escaping.

"What the hell was that?" I said to Martin.

"Eh! No cheek out of you. I'm the one controlling the lift."

When we disembarked from the lift, I shot forward on my skis without warning, determined to avenge him. Fight fire with fire.

"Oi girlie, wait for me," he yelled. "Have to protect you from them Krauts. There's a bloody great swarm of them ahead of us."

AFTER THAT RUN, Martin decided it was time to go into the cafe for a refreshing brew. Though I was loath to admit it, I was quite relieved. My legs were beginning to quiver. When we reached the stopping point just above the steps, Mia emerged with Kevin. Martin started talking to Kevin in a low voice. I concentrated on taking off my skis, shutting out Mia's long monologue about her morning's skiing. Martin always used his poles to take my skis off. I jabbed at the backs of my skis with my own. Nothing happened. I knew there were little holes on the bindings, but they eluded me. After a while, Martin finished his conversation and came over to me.

"You're a determined young lady, aren't you?"

He popped the backs of my skis with ease.

"Just going to fetch your skis, Mia sweetheart," said Kevin.

"I see you're hitting the big time today, Princess Mia," Martin said to her.

All the guides called her that. They were seduced by her limpet exterior. She loved it, greeted it with her helium giggle. I was above such epithets. Kevin came back with both their skis slung over his shoulders.

"Hey Martin, why do you make me schlep my own skis," I asked.

"Don't want to get on the wrong side of a toughie like you."

I smirked. Viking warriors carried their weapons on their backs.

❧ Making Moves ❧

WHEN SUMMER CAME, Matthew's academic rigour relaxed. All I had to do was work through the reading list he set for me every summer. Otherwise, I was free to spend hours on the beach. Jazz didn't have to go to school, so he and Ora came to our house during the week as well. They spent more time at our house than they did at their house in Wicklow. When I wasn't at the beach, I was in the DJ Shack, with or without Jazz, riding on waves of euphoria. It was hot and airless, but its appeal remained strong.

MATTHEW WAS DUE to give one of his lectures in Dublin and display his samples at an exhibition afterwards.

"The vexing thing is that my attendance is required for the whole day," he said to Ora at dinner the night before we were due to go up. "But needs must."

"What will you do, Astrid?"

"She'll stay with me, of course. As she always does. Work through her reading material."

"That won't be much fun for you though, will it, Astrid?" Ora said.

I shrugged. Accompanying Matthew to work was an unquestioned ritual.

"Well, there's no reason why Geoff and I can't stay here another night," Ora said, forking up the last of her salad.

"That won't be necessary," said Matthew.

"It's no trouble. We're not doing anything anyway; I just wanted to check that the house was okay, but we can do that the following day. We'll have a bit of fun here tomorrow instead. Won't we, Geoff?"

Jazz stared at his food. He was a chameleon; they always blended into the background so no-one noticed them.

MATTHEW LEFT VERY early the next day, after our swim. His absence nagged at me, like a missing tooth. I decided to distract myself by spending the day in the DJ Shack with Jazz. But as it happened, Ora's plans for the day were somewhat different.

"I thought we'd have a bit of a day out," she announced as we washed the breakfast dishes. "We'll go shopping and then we'll go to the amusements. And after that, we can go back into town and see a film. I checked with the cinema and there's a film called *Hot Shots!* It's supposed to be funny."

Jazz's head snapped up. He stopped drying the plate he was holding.

"I heard it's good," he said. "There's all aeroplanes and battles and stuff."

"You don't think it might be too violent for Astrid, do you?"

"No, it won't," I said, indignant. "I love battles."

"All right then. We'll do that."

WHEN WE LEFT, it was cloudy, but in town, the sun bounced off the buildings and the pavement. I had to put my shades on. We visited a dizzying array of shops. Ora plied us with clothes: T-shirts, jeans, jumpers. The edges of the jeans were sharp; the material was thick and strong. She exclaimed over the clothes; each item was an undiscovered treasure. The clothes she bought me made me look different, older, more defined. Jazz didn't like his clothes; his voice became sullen and he looked at the ground. But he thanked Ora for each item she bought him.

Every time we left a shop, the glare hit me afresh. It was fortunate that Ora was always looking for something in her cavernous handbag, or asking Jazz to help her rearrange the clothes in the bags. It gave me time to adjust.

My favourite shop wasn't a clothes shop. It was full of CDs and tapes, like the ones Jazz had. It was Jazz's favourite shop too; a smile broke his face in half as we went in. Without my monocle, I struggled to read the names on the records. But then I saw letters that looked familiar and tugged Jazz's sleeve.

"Does that say Massive Attack?"

"Yeah. It's their album. *Blue Lines.*"

"With *Unfinished Sympathy* on it?"

"Yeah."

I kept turning it over and over in my hands.

"You can have one record each," Ora said, appearing out of nowhere.

"But it isn't our birthday."

"Well, there doesn't have to be an occasion," she smiled.

I clutched the tape to me, in case she might take it away. My whole body fizzed at the thought that I now owned a tape, just like Jazz.

THE FAIRGROUND WAS near a beach. The beach was wide, like our beach, but it was crowded with people. I was glad to leave it and go to the fairground, where familiar beats thumped and coloured lights spun. Jazz scuffed his feet along the ground.

We went on a ride with seats that spun around. Above my head, lights flashed and swirled. My face was frozen into position, yet I was flying. A man came over to our seat and pushed it, so that it went even faster. Laughter poured out of me; my stomach clenched and tears streamed out of my eyes. It was only when we stopped that I realised Jazz wasn't laughing.

"Didn't you like it?" I said.

"I don't feel so good."

His voice was thick.

"Will I mop your fevered brow?"

That was what people always did in books.

"Don't be an eejit."

His voice didn't sound as cross as his words.

"Never mind. It's not spinning any more. You'll recover in a moment."

I squeezed his hand. His fingers felt cold and damp. We got out of the seat. My legs were shaking. There were steps just ahead of us. I misjudged the steepness of the first one and started to pitch forward. Jazz took hold of my elbow, steadying me. His touch was light, a butterfly's wing brushing against my sleeve. But it was enough.

WE SAT ON a bench for a while. Jazz drank some water and said he felt better. I still craved speed. We passed a racing track full of cars that buzzed and spun in endless circles.

"Could I go in one of those cars, Ora?"

There was a silence. Perhaps Ora couldn't hear me over the roar of the engines.

"Please?"

"The bumpers are better," said Jazz. "You can crash into people."

I followed them to the ride with the bumpers, my mind still full of the buzzing cars. The bumpers didn't make any noise. They glided along the floor and crashed into each other with a thud. When it was our turn, Jazz allowed me to drive. He showed me how to use the steering wheel and how to avoid the cars that tried to crash into us. But I decided crashing into other cars was more fun. And I was intrigued by the way my driving matched the beats in the background. When we finished, Ora said it was time for something to eat.

"Do you want chips?"

"Okay," said Jazz.

That was what Jazz always said when people asked him questions.

"What about you, Astrid?"

"I don't know."

"Don't you like chips?"

"I never ate chips before. Matthew says they give you high cholesterol."

Ora laughed.

"I don't think you have to worry about that just yet."

We went up to a white van, where a man gave us white plastic boxes filled with plump golden potatoes cut into fingers. They were soft and a little damp to the touch. As I bent over the box, the smell of hot fat and vinegar filled my nostrils. My mouth watered. We ate the chips with little plastic forks, sitting on a bench which faced the sea. When I tried to spear them with my fork, their skins broke apart and white puffs of potato spilled out. It was easier to eat them with my fingers.

They melted in my mouth, explosions of salt and fat. Towards the bottom, the chips became thinner and darker in colour. When I finished, I stabbed the bottom of the box with my fork, trying to scoop out the last crumbs.

"Did you enjoy those?" Ora said, smiling.

"They were ambrosial. Could I have some more?"

"Well, I think you'll definitely have high cholesterol if we let you have more. We'll have some ice-cream instead."

We went to another white van, where Ora bought ice creams for Jazz and I. The ice-cream came in towering cones, with a tall piece of chocolate at the side. Jazz's ice cream was soon demolished, but the mountain of white swirls defeated me.

"Don't you like it?" Ora asked me.

"No. You can have it."

"Oh, I'll put on at least a pound if I eat that."

"You can't put on a pound just from one ice-cream."

"That's true," she said, laughing.

AFTER THE ICE-CREAM, we drove to the cinema.

"Why is the film called *Hot Shots!*" I asked Jazz as we queued for tickets.

"I don't know. Because of all the battles, maybe. It's like *Top Gun*. Did you see that?"

"No. I was never at a cinema before."

"No way! You're so weird sometimes."

"Geoff, that's not nice." said Ora.

"Sorry," Jazz muttered.

After a day in the sun, the cinema was pitch black. Ora and Jazz disappeared. My feet hovered on the edge of a step. I tried to grab the wall, but it was too far away. My feet wobbled. Then I felt the butterfly touch on my elbow again. It was light enough for me to swat away, but instead I let Jazz's hand propel me forward.

We took seats near the front. Ora said it was easier to see the film from there. Jazz had a box of popcorn. He let me try some. It tasted like pieces of paper dipped in salt water. I swallowed it with difficulty and didn't reach for any more. The screen lit up and people moved across it. There was loud music which I didn't recognise. It wasn't euphoric, like the beats in the DJ Shack; it just growled.

"Is that the film?" I said to Jazz.

"No. They're trailers."

"What are those?"

"They show you other films."

"Why?"

"So you know which ones to watch. You'll have be quiet now, the film's about to start."

The screen became busy with activity, people were everywhere. It was hard to keep track of the constant activity. I kept asking Jazz who the people were and what they were doing. Behind us, people asked me to be quiet. Jazz became impatient.

"Astrid, you have to watch the film. That's how you know what's happening."

The planes wheeled overhead, trying to shoot each other out of the sky. One of them did a complete loop.

"Let battle commence!" I said.

"Sssh!" someone said again.

"Why do they keep telling me to be quiet?" I asked Jazz.

"It's a film. You're supposed to be quiet in the cinema. It's like, you know, a library."

The hush of libraries was familiar to me. I settled down in my seat and tried to concentrate. But my eyes grew heavy. My head drifted downwards and landed on Jazz's shoulder. It was wider than I expected. My head fit into the hollow near his neck.

I was woken by the sound of seats clicking back into place.

"We've to go now," Jazz was saying. "The film's over."

I rubbed my eyes and blinked myself awake. My eyes were accustomed to the darkness by now, so I didn't need Jazz to hold my elbow on the way out.

"Thank you," I said to Ora. "That was a most interesting experience."

She and Jazz laughed. I didn't know why.

When September came, Jazz went back to school, but he and Ora still came every weekend, even though Ora's brochure was finished. Other people wanted Ora to take pictures for them. Sometimes they telephoned our house. At first, Matthew was cross, but then he said in a gruff voice that he was pleased with her success. Sometimes he went with her when she was taking pictures. I stayed in the DJ Shack with Jazz. Now that winter was coming, the wind rattled the DJ Shack so much that it threatened to tip over. But we kept the wind at bay with our beats, which were filled with the permanent sunshine of summer.

One day, rain and wind lashed against the house. I made a heroic attempt to access the DJ Shack, putting on my rain slicks and wellington boots. But as I prepared to push through the sheets of rain, Ora intercepted me.

"I'm afraid the shed's not looking like an option for you today."

I followed her inside, dragging my feet. Reading held no appeal; I was in that vacuum between finishing one book and starting another. I sat on the window seat, hugging my knees. Jazz sat at the kitchen table, reading a comic. Now that his reading habits were sanctioned by Matthew, he no longer felt the need to hide them. After a while, he stopped reading and stared into space.

"Well, I never saw two such long faces in my life," Ora said, laughing.

We didn't reply. Ora clapped her hands.

"I know what we can do. We'll make a sponge cake. That'll cheer us up. I'll just see what ingredients there are."

She scrabbled in our presses. Whenever she did that, they always yielded a cornucopia of food. I never knew our presses held such bounty. Jazz got up to help her look.

"Come on, Astrid. It'll be fun," Ora said.

I dawdled over to the worktop, where Ora was mixing all the ingredients in a bowl. She gave me a spoon and guided my hands as I pushed it through the mixture. The spoon made squelching sounds. Bits of mixture clung to my fingers and I licked it off. In spite of myself, I began to thaw. Matthew appeared at the door.

"I hate to intrude into this hive of industry but that man from the Historical Society has tracked you down. Wants to talk to you about a photograph for their next event. They have someone worthy coming. An expert on the holy stones of Wexford, if you can imagine anything so spurious."

"Oh, all right," Ora said, going to the sink to wash her hands. "I'll just be a moment. Keep stirring. We'll start putting it all together when I come back."

Jazz was at the sink, whipping cream. His turned back made him a target. A grin leaked onto my face as I crept towards him, my fingers loaded with cake mixture. I flicked the mixture onto his shirt.

"Hey!" he said.

I danced away, but not fast enough to avoid the gob of cream that splatted onto my face.

"That's mean," I said, in half-hearted protest.

"You asked for it."

I went back to my bowl for more ammunition. Soon, cake mixture and cream flew in all directions. At last, we leaned against the sink, our breath coming out in ragged gasps, our energy spent. Ora was still talking on the telephone.

"We'd better clean up," Jazz said.

He picked up a sponge from the side of the sink and ran it in warm water.

"You've cream all over your face," he said. "I'll wipe it off for you."

He rubbed my face with the sponge. Maybe it was the warmth of the water that caused my cheeks to tingle. Or maybe it was friction from the tea towel he used to dry my face.

"I think it's all gone now," he said. "Oh, wait."

His fingers brushed the hair that covered my left ear. They stayed there longer than they needed to, travelled along the strands. The tingle spread through all the hairs on my head. I knew hair carried static electricity. When he removed his hand, I could still feel his touch. It was bizarre.

"There was another blob of cream, you see. Just by your ear."

His voice was thick. I listened to the crash of the waves. The wind made them louder than usual.

"Your hair feels like silk. I never knew. I didn't mean..."

His face was red. I brought my hand to my face and touched the strands of hair. The static electricity was gone.

"I MUST INFORM you that our plans will be rather different this New Year," said Matthew, as I caught up with him at the top of the cliff path.

I stamped my feet on the unyielding ground; my toes were still numb from our swim. Matthew made no allowances for frigid December weather.

"Ora has invited us to come and visit. We will be staying overnight."

"Could I stay up until midnight?" I asked.

"I don't see why not."

I hadn't seen Jazz in more than two weeks, because of Christmas. As I traced the route to the cottage on a map, my stomach began to fizz.

ON THE WAY to Ora's cottage, Matthew was derailed by a signpost pointing in the wrong direction, so in spite of his expertise with maps, we became lost. The journey was punctuated by bellows of rage and sudden twists and turns. But we found the right road in the end, after Matthew stopped to study the map again.

The cottage nestled at the bottom of a mountain. Plants grew along the white walls. As we got out of the car, Ora appeared at the door. She held a teatowel in her hands.

"Welcome, welcome, did you have an awful journey?"

She kissed Matthew. Then she kissed me, her lips leaving a wet imprint on my cheek.

Inside, most of the space was taken up by soft furniture. All the chairs were covered in scarves. There was a large television in a corner of the room. It was hard to find a path through it all.

"I've made some coffee," said Ora.

"Good. I'm in dire need of it," said Matthew.

"Geoff's in his room, Astrid, if you want to go into him. It's just across the way."

I was already negotiating the obstacle course of chairs and small tables. The corner of one table tugged at the denim of my jeans, one of the pairs purchased during the summer shopping expedition. An ornament threatened to topple onto the ground. The grating sound of china on wood alerted me and I retrieved it in time. I waited for Matthew to reprove me for my clumsiness, but he wasn't there. He was in the kitchen with Ora.

The door of Jazz's room was festooned with stickers and a sign that said 'Keep Out'. I ignored the sign and pushed open the door. Jazz was sitting on his bed, twiddling with a device made up of wires and tubes. He looked up as I stepped into the room.

"Hi," he said.

"What's that? It looks peculiar."

"It's a radio. I made it myself. Mum got me a kit for Christmas."

He returned to his twiddling. I sat on the bed beside him and looked around the room. Every corner was covered in posters of monsters and men holding weapons. Stacks of comics and tapes lined the shelves; there weren't any books. A camp bed was wedged in the space between Jazz's bed and the wardrobe. Jazz pressed a button on the radio and it emitted shrieks and buzzes.

"Are you receiving signals from Mars?" I asked him.

"*Power FM* have a rave on tonight. Sometimes you can get the pirate stations in Dublin. I'll try it again later. If you stick a coat hanger on it, it works better."

I sat beside him and listened for beats through the crackle of static. He showed me how the radio worked, putting my fingers on the buttons so I could distinguish one from the other.

WE ATE ONE of Ora's big dinners. It was an orange stew which tasted nicer than it looked. After dinner, Ora suggested we play a game called Cluedo.

"You'll like it, Astrid; it's just like all those detective books you read."

She was right. It was a mystery in the style of Sherlock Holmes, with clues scattered throughout a house that we had to follow. We played in teams, because Ora and Jazz knew how to play and we didn't. I played with Ora; Jazz played with Matthew. Ora and I emerged victorious, which added to my enjoyment. Matthew grumbled that our victory was a matter of mere chance, but he smiled as he said it, so I knew he was enjoying it too.

Afterwards, Ora switched on the television, because we were using it to tell us when it was New Year. I sat on a big armchair, the one closest to the television. It enveloped me. People on the television were cheering and talking in loud voices. There was an hour and a half to go. I was determined not to miss it. But my eyes had other ideas. They kept closing against my will. Matthew touched my shoulder.

"Come on, Astrid. No point in fighting the inevitable."

"No. Not tired," I mumbled, forcing my eyes open. "Have to stay up for New Year."

Matthew leaned close to me. He smelled of wine and coffee.

"It'll be New Year in the morning, little one."

He never called me that any more. We walked to Jazz's room, his hands on my shoulders. I lay on the camp bed and sank into oblivion.

THE MATTRESS JOLTED. I sat up in bed. It was still dark. I rubbed my eyes.

"Sorry. I hit off your bed."

The sound of Jazz's voice startled the rest of the sleep out of me.

"Is it New Year yet?"

"Yeah. Just about."

Ora and Matthew's voices rumbled in the distance. They weren't in bed yet.

"You think the rave is still on?"

I pulled myself up and made my way over to Jazz, still wrapped in the sleeping bag.

"Course. Those things go on all night," said Jazz.

Jazz attached the coat hanger to the radio and fiddled with the dials. This time, we heard beats through the crackles. There was a hole in the radio for inserting headphones. I put one in my ear and he put one in his. We sat close to each other. Our hands rested side by side; his little finger rubbed against mine. Jazz switched on the lamp beside his bed. It spread yellow-brown light all over the room. The beats made my ears hot. Our shadows danced on the wall in time to the rhythm. His was chunky, a bear cosy in his cave. Mine was a reed swaying in the wind. We listened until white noise swallowed up the beats.

"Happy New Year, Jazz," I said, as Jazz turned off the radio.

"Happy New Year, Astrid."

That was what people said in books. I also knew that they kissed each other. Jazz's face was very close to mine. I leaned over and kissed his lips. They were soft, like pillows. When I drew away, Jazz brought his fingers to his lips.

"Does it hurt?" I asked.

"No. What did you do that for?"

"Isn't that what people do for New Year?"

"Not like that."

His voice was hoarse. The room was filled with his loud breathing. He leaned over to me and his lips brushed against mine. I licked my lips, thirsting for more. We moved closer, until our faces almost touched. Our lips found each other, locked together. The kiss lasted a long time. A warm current spread outwards from my stomach and flowed through my veins. When the air around me became cold, I drew back. Jazz put his fingers on his lips again. His face was an unusual colour, sort of reddish-purple.

"I'm going to sleep now," I said. "Good night."

I slid off Jazz's bed and crawled onto the camp bed. Jazz didn't move. I brought my hand to my own lips. They tingled; Jazz's imprint was still on them.

WHEN WE WOKE up, the house was silent. I jumped out of bed and ran into the kitchen. It was empty. Ora's bedroom was empty too. I ran into the kitchen again and saw a piece of paper on the counter. *Gone for a walk*, said Matthew's almost indecipherable writing. *We won't be long.*

Jazz shuffled into the kitchen and I handed him the note. He read it, yawned and opened one of the presses, which contained the boxes of colourful cereal he favoured.

"He said he was going for a walk with me. We walk every morning," I moaned.

I trailed Jazz as he brought his bowl into the living room and switched on the television. He took out a videotape and slid it into the video recorder underneath the television.

"Do you want to go for a walk?" I asked him.

"I'm watching this. There's cereal in the press."

"I always eat porridge. You don't have any."

Jazz didn't reply. He was engrossed in a battle in which men fought each other with green swords. I sat in an armchair and read *Around the World in 80 Days* without taking in the words. Cold water sloshed in my stomach.

When I heard the rattle of the door, I shot out of the chair. Ora and Matthew appeared at the door of the living room.

"Why did you go without me?"

I put my hands on my hips.

"Hush, Astrid. It's in a good cause," said Matthew.

Jazz was still absorbed in the swordfight.

"Geoff, I'm sorry to disturb your film, but Matthew and I want to talk to you both about something," said Ora. "It's important."

We followed them out to the kitchen. I still held my

book in one hand. They sat facing us at the table, their hands joined. I never saw Matthew hold Ora's hand before. He cleared his throat.

"We have a proposal to put to you," he said.

"Matthew has asked myself and Geoff to come and live in Wexford."

Ora's voice was hushed.

"We've become very fond of each other, you see," said Matthew.

He wiped his forehead with his handkerchief.

"Therefore, we hope to make a life together. But we won't proceed unless you're satisfied."

"We don't want to force you into anything," said Ora.

A silence fell. I tried to figure out why they were attaching heavy weights to the words.

"You might as well come and stay," I said. "Then you won't have the long drive back to Wicklow."

They all laughed, including Jazz. I supposed this was a good thing.

"It will be a bit different now though," said Ora.

Her voice was gentle.

"As I said, we've become very fond of each other," said Matthew. "More than fond, in fact."

He swallowed hard.

"We want for us all to live together, as a family," said Ora.

"Are you going to mate for life, like albatrosses?" I asked.

They laughed again.

"Something like that," said Matthew.

"What about you, Geoff," said Ora. "What do you think?"

"It's okay. I don't mind."

A thought occurred to me. I sat up straight in my chair.

"Does this mean Jazz is coming to live with us too?"

"Yes of course it does, you nincompoop," Matthew said. "Do you imagine he'll be living on the street?"

Now we could go to the DJ Shack all the time. And Jazz could bring his home-made radio.

"Cool," I said.
I looked over at Jazz.
"Yeah," he said. "It's cool."

❧ Tangled Wires ❧

THE TYRES CRUNCHED as Martin manoeuvred the bus over banks of new snow. He was rostered to drive the bus that day. "Back away, Martin, back away," yelled the Greek Chorus.

Martin eased the bus through a tiny gap in the queue of cars attempting to leave the car park.

"You want a go at driving this thing?" he said.

They all honked with laughter. I wrote on the steam. This time the word I wrote was troilism.

"The practise of engaging in intercourse with three or more partners," I informed the group at large.

"How're ya," chimed the Greek Chorus.

"Give you an appetite for dinner," said Johno.

He patted his stomach. Some of his chest hair was visible above the neck of his ski top. I imagined following the trail it made. When I touched Jazz, my fingers travelled across a smooth expanse of skin until my fingers reached the triangular undergrowth which formed the demarcation line.

Once again, Cliona was touting her cause; she revelled in the dank whiff of limitation. This time, the subject of her monologue was inaccessible websites. Some phrases pierced through: 'poor contrast... web 2 compliance... adapt font sizes...' A vile stench distracted me; it contaminated all the available air on the bus.

"Oi, who cracked one off," shouted Martin. "Wasn't you, Mia, was it?"

Mia giggled. The stench curled outwards. Due south, I reckoned. Traceable to one of the Greek Chorus.

"Reckon it was Kim," I whispered to Johno.

"Smells like my sister's baby," he went on, addressing the rest of the bus.

"You a doting uncle, Johno?" Martin asked.

"Nah. Me sister won't let me mind him. She's worried I

won't know how to feed it. I said I'd just follow where the noise was coming from and stick the spoon in there."

Not to be outdone, one of the Greek Chorus chipped in with an anecdote of his own, in which he fell into a puddle and showered an unsuspecting old lady with water and mud.

"She got a bit thick," he said. "I says to her, sorry missus, I just like making a bit of a splash."

"I love them oul ones," said Johno. "They're always tellin' me what a great little fighter I am and that they're prayin' for me. If they only knew I'm beyond help."

Their voices and laughter merged into a dull roar, a wordless battle cry. A YouTube gallery of clips began to play in my mind, featuring images I thought were buried in a safe corner of my mind. The memories laid siege to me and resisted my attempts to pause them. I watched myself as I stumbled on rogue steps and slapped against the ground, flicked the 'V' at cars which materialised from nowhere and became swallowed up by crowds I couldn't outrun. My mouth became filled with the taste of orange drink; this was becoming a regular occurrance.

Every so often, the roar was punctuated by Mia's helium giggle. She didn't contribute any tales of her own; limpets don't carry memories. Still, Johno appeared to find her riveting. As the bus journey wore on, he desisted from exchanging war stories and began talking to her. Their heads were close together; they became enclosed in a bubble.

THERE WAS NO sign of Mia when I got to our room, which was somewhat surprising. Still, I was freed from maid service for the time being. I flopped onto my bed and did my daily phone vigil.

Sx god def n2 me.

The letters were paltry. I deleted them and stared into the screen, became enveloped in its blankness.

SOMETIMES IT'S NOT until the morning after that the interludes happen. I tend to wake up first. The flat is bathed in Sunday morning silence. The sun is already high in the sky, but Jazz's thick curtains keep the room shrouded in brown darkness. With no gel to hold it back, my hair fans my face. In his sleep, Jazz has slung his arm over my body. His legs are tangled up in mine. He stirs; his hand moves. I can feel his touch before it reaches my body; my skin tingles in anticipation. He pushes tendrils of hair behind my ear, reaches for my hand. Our fingers interlace. I bring his hand to my mouth and kiss each one of his fingers, sucking the tips. Then I guide his hands to my small, high breasts and he tweaks the nipples into life.

IMPATIENT WITH MY musings, I went to the wardrobe and stood in front of it, leaning on the open door. I deliberated for quite a while. If I was to stand any chance of dislodging Mia from Johno's attention, I was going to have to emulate her fluff and frippery look. As I rifled through my meagre pile of clothes, a shimmer of blue jumped out. I reached for it. A blue dress with little gold flowers, a sort of Japanese vibe. Lots of girls wore them at Prism. It looked demure at the front, but plunged low at the back. I slid it on and tied the ribbon at the back so that my waist and hips were emphasised. It moulded my body. I risked a somewhat more geotropic flip for my hair. Odd that Mia wasn't back yet. Perhaps the recalcitrant shower was defeating her.

JURGEN THE TEUTONIC Overlord slapped my glass of vodka down with his habitual reluctance. I polished it off as Johno approached the bar with an easy strut. He was the only Cabbage Kid who could approach the bar unaided. He wore a white T-shirt with the Irish flag emblazoned on it and a pair of tracksuit pants with two thick white stripes along the sides, continuous lines to nowhere. The clothes hung from him, obscured his physique. Jazz's wardrobe was a homage to muted colouring and tailored fits.

Johno leaned against the bar counter. His arm was very close to mine, close enough for me to see the veins pulsing under the covering of dark hairs.

"Want me to get you a drink?" I asked him.

"Nah, you're all right. That was some serve you gave Cliona last night."

"Glad you approve. Perhaps we should put her in a cage and feed her bananas through the bars. Think she'd enjoy that."

I laughed, but Johno didn't join in. Lines formed trenches around his mouth. My laughter trailed off into uncertain silence.

"I know she's an eejit, but she didn't deserve that."

Maybe you'll stop being so cruel to blind people.

"Such moral uprightness in one so young."

"Just give her a break, all right. She's enough crap to deal with. We all do."

Before I could defend my honour, Mia approached the bar with a moonwalker's gait, cane at the ready. Johno never used his in the hotel; he appeared to rely on sonar.

"Straight ahead, Mia, that's it," Kevin yelled, acting as an aural signpost.

Mia bumped against Johno. Smart move, initiating physical contact under the guise of clumsiness. She was dressed in a cowgirl get up, with a pink and white gingham print shirt, pink earrings and jeans.

"Seems you can get dressed without my help," I said to her.

"Oh I just..."

Her words were suspended in mid-air; she appeared to have no intention of finishing the sentence.

"Ah, she came into my room," said Johno. "We were doing something."

"Why are you being so cryptic? Should I be suspicious?"

Johno laughed, his gurgle back in full force.

"Ah no. All will be revealed."

He leaned over to her and spoke to her in an undertone, his posture an eerie caricature of Kim leaning over Cliona.

"I was gonna come up and get you. Thought you'd be ages getting dressed, being a girl."

She giggled.

"No, I was grand. I got down the stairs myself."

A latter-day Scott of the Antarctic.

"Will ya have a scoop?" Johno asked. "It'll warm your throat for later."

Mia asked for her customary glass of watered-down beer.

"I'll have a vodka please, Johno," I said. "What's later?"

Best to feign interest.

"Oh, myself and Mia're planning a bit of entertainment, aren't we, Mia?"

Mia giggled. As Jurgen plonked our glasses onto the counter, Martin arrived.

"Well, aren't you the lucky one, Johno," he said, "surrounded by girlies. Astrid the Swedish model and Princess Mia."

I smirked.

"A Johno sandwich," said Mia.

They laughed, far more than the quip merited. More than they laughed at my steamy words.

"Not for much longer," said Johno. "C'mon, Mia. We'll be back in a minute."

They disappeared, their feet clattering on the spiral staircase. The others were moving towards the dining area, where chairs were arranged in a semi circle. Two chairs stood apart, at the top of the semi circle. I hung back, weighing up seating options. A seat materialised near the two empty chairs. The Greek Chorus were on my other side, but I took it as the lesser of two evils. It turned out to be a smart move. When Johno and Mia returned, they took the two empty chairs and Johno chose the chair to my immediate right; his leg was within touching distance. A guitar hung from his neck.

"Howya," said the Greek Chorus as I settled myself in my chair.

"What did we do to deserve this?"

"I'm thanking my lucky stars."

One of them stretched his hand out, this time landing on target. I feinted to the right and bumped against Johno's knee. He jerked away, no doubt anxious to protect his guitar. Still, he came to my rescue, distracting my suitor by striking a chord on the guitar. Everyone broke into song. They sang as if their lives depended on it, some in keys not found on the tonic scale. When Johno finished, they clapped and cheered. He accepted the praise and handclasps from his worshippers. The light gave his face a soft glow.

When the applause died down, Johno began to play again. The songs blended into each other, turned into an incomprehensible mush. Their voices were thick curls of smoke, clogging the air in the room. Belts of vodka made the din more bearable. Johno downed beers with long swallows; some of the liquid dripped onto his shirt. He played on, uncaring. At intervals, I allowed my leg to brush against his. He appeared not to notice, but I still relished the feel of it through his jeans. Johno's legs were thinner than Jazz's, less dense, but still hard and firm.

When I sat down after yet another refill, Martin was sitting on the couch just behind my chair. He roared out the words to the song, blasting my ears. I flinched. He leaned over to me.

"This not your thing?"

"You could say that."

"What gets you moving on the dance floor then?"

"Electronic music."

"That bleep bleep bleep music? That's what blows your skirt up?"

I struggled to stifle my amusement.

"So you won't be treating us to any tunes then."

"Not unless you got a DJ box."

The words came unbidden. I had no intention of allowing myself to be exposed to ridicule. *How come you haven't DJ'd since Eclectica?*

"Oh, you're a DJ? Where do you strut your stuff?"

"An Internet show. Kind of obscure."

"You'll have to tell me the website, might give it a whirl. You don't do nightclubs, do you?"

I shook my head.

"Good. Awful places. Used to have to raid them when I was in the force. Music was loud enough to make your ears bleed."

He laughed.

"DJ Astrid. Has a nice ring to it."

"It's DJ Ice White, as a matter of fact."

It baffled me, the ease with which he extracted information.

"That's a cool name."

I stood up. My thirst was building again.

THERE WERE TWO places we went to when we weren't in the classroom. When it rained, we went to a big room called the playroom. The shelves in the playroom were filled with books and coloured objects, like the ones in the classroom. There were two houses where the girls played with their dolls. One was made of plastic and held together with poles. It looked like a tent and it was big enough to crawl into. The other one was made of wood and looked like a real house, with furniture in it. I didn't play in the houses. There were too many people in them.

On dry days, we went into a yard with red brick walls around it. The pink ladies called it the playground. They stood in a corner and watched us play. There was no grass in the yard, only small stones. Some of the stones were stuck to the ground, other ones were loose. The loose ones didn't have any animals underneath, like the ones on the beach. Maybe it was because they were too small. When the sun shone, the stones sparkled. Coloured lines were painted on the stones. Some of them were straight and some of them made shapes and crossed over each other. I walked around the edge of the yard and listened to the squeals of the other girls as I attempted to balance on the lines. The girls played games which involved standing around in circles and singing songs, making houses with their dolls, or rolling balls to each other. They asked me if I wanted to play, but I decided I didn't like games. I wanted to climb trees, roam the beach looking for samples, swim in water that moved and made splashing sounds. Sometimes, as I walked on the coloured lines, the other girls zig-zagged in front of me and I knocked them over. They gave loud, piercing cries and always waited for the pink ladies to pick them up. The pink ladies said, "Now, now, Astrid." But it wasn't my fault they kept getting in the way.

JURGEN'S VODKA STORES were depleted. He was none too happy either. I ordered a sparkling mineral water and slumped back into my seat. Johno stopped playing as I sat down, but the reprieve didn't last.

"Lads, we've a bit of a treat for you," he said, in that mellow, husky voice. "Haven't we, Mia?"

Mia lowered her head and said nothing.

"We've been working on a tune," he went on. "Hope ye like it."

He started to play; the chords were more delicate and gentle than before. Then Mia started to sing. At first, her voice was so low and hesitant that everyone had to lean forward to hear it. After a while, her voice picked up pace and volume. The song was a dirge about a rose that came in springtime; it activated my gag reflex.

When the song ended, everyone cheered and whooped. Johno leaned over and kissed Mia's cheek. Mia covered her face with her hands and giggled.

"Fair play to you, Johno," shouted one of the Greek Chorus.

"I saw her first, though, remember."

They snorted with laughter; Mia and Johno joined in. As the applause died away, my gag reflex subsided and my mind became clear. It was just part of the act. Had to be. Though I was forced to concede this battle to Mia, the war was not yet won.

I LAY UNDER the tree in the corner of Mrs O'Brien's living room, breathing in the smell of pine. The branches were covered in lights, red balls and pieces of string that sparkled. The tree was always there at Christmas time. We didn't have a tree like that at home. Matthew said it was because we were humanists.

My belly was warm and full, but my legs were restless. I got up and went over to the boys, who were marching their toy soldiers up and down on the carpet.

"Let's play," I said, tugging at their hands.

"We're playing soldiers," they said.

"That's boring. I want to play something else."

We went into the boys' bedroom and started jumping on my mattress, making it move up and down. Then the boys decided to launch themselves from the top bunk-bed onto the mattress. There was no space on the floor between them. The boys made pow-pow-pow noises as they landed.

"We're bombers," they cried.

After a while, I tired of watching them. I climbed up the ladder to the top bunk and hovered at the edge, curling my body up like they did.

"You can't," the boys said. "It's too far."

"You can't stop me."

I edged forward and let myself drop. My body flew through the air, very fast. The mattress rose up to meet me. I bounced onto it; my face rubbed against the blanket. Then the boys jumped onto it too, whooping as they went. The mattress rippled under their weight. I giggled. They started tickling me and I squealed with laughter. But then they stopped. When I sat up, Mrs O'Brien was standing at the door. I waited for her to give out about the messy beds. She didn't like it when we played our jumping game. But she didn't.

"Astrid, you're wanted on the phone," she said.

Only grown-ups used the telephone. Matthew didn't like the telephone; he was always cross with it. Mrs O'Brien didn't have a telephone, so we went to the cottage next door to use theirs. We didn't have to walk far, because the next-door cottage was stuck to Mrs O'Brien's. Their telephone sat on a table near the front door. It was black, like Matthew's. The family that lived in the cottage stood in a circle around the telephone. The O'Brien boys joined them. Mrs O'Brien placed my hand on the receiver and put her own hand over mine. She helped me lift the receiver and pressed it against my face, adjusting it so that my lips rested against the bottom part. Then she took her hand away. The receiver felt heavy and cold, but my breath warmed the bottom part. I rested my face on it.

"Say hello," Mrs O'Brien whispered.

"Hello," I repeated.

"Astrid?"

A fist formed in my throat, squeezed it tight.

"Can you hear me?"

The voice sounded like Matthew's, except that it cracked in a lot of places. The receiver began to slip away from me. I tried to hold onto it, but it clattered to the ground.

"It's all right, pet. I've got it," Mrs O'Brien said.

She put the receiver in my hand again. This time, I heard a bleeping noise.

"Matthew?" I whispered.

But this time there was no voice. Just the bleeping.

"Not to worry," said Mrs O'Brien. "He'll ring again."

She took the receiver out of my hand and put it back on top of the telephone. The circle was still behind me; breath blew on my neck. Mrs O'Brien talked to the woman who owned the next door cottage in a low voice.

"Go on outside and play," she said. "There's too many of us in here."

The boys moved towards the door with the next-door boys, who were their friends. I stayed where I was.

"I'll come and get you if he rings again," said Mrs O'Brien. "Off you go, pet."

She gave me a gentle push on the back. I put on my coat and followed the boys outside. They ran up and down the street with a ball, which moved too fast for me to follow. I walked away from them and stood at the end of the street. They didn't notice. In my head, Matthew was calling my name. In front of me, there was a bigger road; it was blue with white stripes in the middle. It was the road Matthew and I drove on when we went to Dublin. Matthew's hospital was in Dublin. If I kept walking along the road, I could find him and explain what happened. My legs pushed me forward, onto the road. I was going on a quest. Viking warriors went on quests to find treasure. But I was going on a quest to find Matthew.

I walked near the edge of the road, my head down. The road stretched on and on. There were no people on the road and no houses either, only bushes. As I walked, the sky grew darker, until it became black. I put my hands into the pockets of my coat to stop them getting cold, but the air crept under the coat, sending shivers through my body. My legs became heavy; they dragged along the ground. The ground pressed into my shoes, making my feet hot and sore. The heaviness spread through my body and I couldn't make my legs go any further.

As I came to a stop, the road became flooded with light. It stung my eyes, like the machines at the clinic. I squeezed them tight shut and covered them with my hand. There was a loud purring sound and warm air brushed against my legs. I thought it must be a cat, but it wasn't. It was a car. My legs wobbled and I tumbled onto the wet grass. Leaves scratched the back of my neck. Cold water seeped through my dress.

A dark shape appeared in front of me. It was a ghost. I wanted to run, but I couldn't move. There's no such thing as ghosts, I told myself. Matthew said only simpletons believed in such things. Hands picked me up, began brushing leaves and twigs from my clothes. I stretched out my arms, trying to push the ghost away, but my fingers brushed against wool and the ghost became a person, a man. Energy coursed through my body. I opened my eyes and stood up straight. The man squatted in front of me. Spots danced around his face.

"I'm looking for my father, Matthew Johnson. Do you know where he is?"

"You're Astrid, aren't you?"

How did he know my name?

"I'm Dr Murphy. Do you remember me?"

I nodded. He was the person Matthew took me to see when I wasn't well.

"I need to find Matthew. Do you know where he is?"

"Well, yes I do, but—"

"Has he gone to Valhalla to live with my mother?"

"Not that far."

Why was he laughing?

"Then could you take me to see him?"

Dr Murphy stopped laughing.

"I'm afraid I can't. It's a very, very long way, even in a car. And much too far to walk."

"But I need to tell him something."

Tears stung the back of my eyes, but I didn't let them fall. I had to carry on.

"It's late now. He'd be asleep by the time we got there."

His voice was gentle. I couldn't stop shivering, my eyes were full of grit. Drops of water kept running out of my nose. I looked at the ground; my head was too heavy to lift.

"You must be tired after walking all this way. Why don't I bring you back to Mrs O'Brien's?"

He reached for my hand and led me to his car, where he wiped my nose with a tissue and covered me with a red blanket which scratched my face.

Light beamed into my eyes; it was softer this time. I was in Mrs O'Brien's living room. It was filled with people who were all talking at the same time; their voices were too loud. This time, I couldn't stop the tears from falling. I was too tired to make a proper crying sound, so I made gulping noises instead.

Dr Murphy brought me into Mrs O'Brien's bedroom. He undressed me and put me into bed. I wanted to tell him this wasn't where I slept, but I couldn't speak. Mrs O'Brien came in with my pyjamas and a hot water bottle. The shivering slowed down. Mrs O'Brien put a cup in my hands, filled with milk. I didn't like the milk, but I drank it because it warmed me up. While I drank, Mrs O'Brien rubbed my feet. Her hands were soft and they made my feet tingle. I kept gulping. Matthew wasn't here. I couldn't find him. Couldn't tell him I was sorry for dropping the telephone.

I let Mrs O'Brien wrap me in her arms. She murmured soft words in my ear and rocked me until the gulping noises stopped and my eyes closed.

❧ Vitriol & Vodka ❧

As soon as my preparations for skiing were finished, I cloistered myself with the militaristic beats of Kraftwerk. Mia's tug on my sleeve was quite insistent that morning, but I still managed to ignore it. That night, we were embarking on an odyssey, venturing beyond the confines of the hotel to a restaurant in the village. This was it. Do or die.

The sharp focus of my mind was reflected in my skiing. Martin often had occasion to say "That's the way." He came from the Matthew school of flattery, but from the tone of his voice, I knew it was high praise.

The lifts were their usual hideous selves, this time because a wind buffeted them about.

"Nasty beasts," Martin said, "but they have to be done."

This time, Martin's interrogation centred on my childhood in Wexford, my unorthodox education, my experiences at college. I no longer bothered to mount a defence against the barrage of questions.

"Regular Poirot, aren't you?" I said to him.

"Well, I was in the force for 25 years."

He threw back his head and roared with laughter. Jazz laughed like that, but only when we were alone, in the DJ Shack or the studio. The rest of the time he produced his quiet, fit-for-society laugh, though at least he no longer stuffed his hands in his mouth. It was becoming harder to dislodge him from my mind.

Martin was now giving me a potted autobiography.

"Anyway, I got my silver jubilee, my pension, all that jazz," he said. "And I sold off all me worldly goods to come out here and get paid to go skiing."

More laughter. It was fortunate that we were close to the top.

"Pity this has to be our last run," Martin said to me as I adjusted my shades. "Some of 'em want to go shopping, so we're going into Schmullingen. It's the nearest big town."

"Oh, okay."

An irritating diversion, but at least it gave me more time to consider my plan of attack. And there was always the lure of bargain shades.

SCHMULLINGEN WAS MOSENBACH with more buildings. The bus took us to the outskirts of the town, where a shopping mall perched near a roundabout. As we stood in front of the shopping centre, a pair of trademark golden arches came into view. McDonalds rated low on my list, but I was never one to turn down an opportunity for chips. Besides, they had good coffee.

"Happy days," said the Greek Chorus as we went inside.

"Do they have those sausage yokes in here? If they do, I'm ordering 'em."

"Why, do they remind you of something?"

I moved towards the counter, anxious to disengage myself, but the Cabbage Patch Kids were everywhere.

"I don't really eat McDonalds," Mia was saying behind me.

"Sure they've chips," said Johno.

I turned to face him, glad of a chance to soften the ground.

"My sentiments exactly," I said.

Mia brushed her hair out of her eyes.

"It's just, you never know if they've been cooked in animal fat. I hate being awkward."

Liar.

"I'll get you some water so," said Johno. "That shouldn't have any animal fat in it."

We all laughed. Johno was quite a wit, in his earthy way.

"They've got a frankfurter meal here," Martin said.

"What a trip." I grinned. "I'll have to order that."

"Deadly," said Johno.

"I wish the menus were more disability-friendly," Cliona said. "It's not right to position them so far from the counter."

"It's McDonald's, Cliona," I retorted. "Chips and burgers. Even you shouldn't require an accessible menu for that."

Her tut was audible through the 900 bpm gabba house that pumped out of the speakers. My meal appeared on the counter. The fraulein hovered. I always took care to ensure my money was in my hand when I reached a cash register, but now I was caught unawares, distracted by white noise. Gold coins bulged under the leathery skin of my wallet. When I opened it, they merged into each other. I was forced to burrow through the mound of shrapnel.

"I help you," said the fraulein.

"No way," I muttered.

I thrust a fistful of coins at her and moved away, ignoring her calls. There was a table near the window. Johno was sitting at it, with Mia in tow. She was proving quite an obstacle to my battle plan, but at least there was space at the table. I couldn't afford to lose ground at this stage. The rest of the Cabbage Patch Kids arranged themselves at the tables beside ours. Martin came over to our table and sat opposite me.

"Like the sound of them beats, Astrid?" he asked.

"Central European delicacy, Complan mixed with speed."

Johno gurgled. Mia looked perplexed. Another small advance.

"No, it's like the shite they play at that club. What's the name of it? Near Temple Bar. Cube or Triangle," Johno said.

"Prism?" I asked him.

"That's it. I was there once. That was enough."

"Pity," I kept my voice light. "Regular haunt of mine."

"Might have guessed," Johno muttered.

I figured I must have misheard him. After all, the music was quite loud.

I tucked into my meal. The Greek Chorus were asking

each other what they were eating, even though they already knew. One of them was masticating with his mouth open. Gobbets of burger flew out of it. The other shoved his fingers in his mouth and sucked them. Even Johno allowed ketchup to drip down his chin without a care. Feeding time at the zoo.

ONE DAY, WE didn't go to the classroom. The pink ladies told us we were going to the zoo instead. The other girls squealed. I didn't say anything, but my insides burst with happiness. Maybe Matthew was there, waiting for me.

But he wasn't there. A zookeeper met us instead. It wasn't any of the ones I knew from visits with Matthew. My insides flattened. The zookeeper took us to the places where the animals lived and described them all. I didn't listen to him; Matthew's voice blocked him out.

Near the end of our visit, we went to the Pet's Corner. Matthew and I never went there; we preferred more exotic creatures. These creatures were covered in fur and almost all of them were asleep. They lived in cages, or in small pens where they could run around. The zookeeper opened one of the cages and lifted a white ball into his hands. He told us it was a mouse.

"Anyone like to hold this little fella?" he asked.

The other girls squealed and clutched each other.

"I will," I said.

"Aren't you a brave girl?" one of the pink ladies said.

The other girls' sounds of disgust came from far away as the zookeeper lowered the mouse into my cupped hands. Its hair felt soft; it was the same colour as mine. When the zookeeper took it away, I kept my hands together, even though they were empty.

After that, our visit was over. We climbed onto the bus and I pressed my face against the window. The glass was cool. I was in a cage too, except that mine was pink because there was pink everywhere. There were other colours in the school, but pink was the only one I saw. I knew I was going to be in the pink cage forever.

AFTER LUNCH, WE ventured into the main body of the mall. First, we went to a supermarket. I broke away from the others to purchase a bottle of water and a bottle of vodka, which were instrumental to my plan. Then we did a tour of various tat shops that blurred into each other. I eschewed the shades, which were of the cheap-and-nasty variety. The Cabbage Patch Kids spent a long time fondling the items; every purchase was of great import. The only items that piqued my interest were the baseball caps which hung on a rack. I spun it around and a few hats flew off. When I picked them up, I saw my name on one of them. None of that sort of merchandise ever featured my name. I tucked it under my arm. Then I took a lazy browse through the other hats and stumbled on a Matthau. Pretty close to Matthew, though the idea of Matthew in a baseball hat was so ludicrous I couldn't help grinning. I gave the rack another savage spin and looked in the 'G's. No Geoffrey. Didn't know why I even looked.

"You buying that?" Martin asked.

He tweaked the Astrid hat.

"Suppose. Though it is kind of naff."

"I get the feeling you think this holiday's naff."

He said it in a tone low enough for me to ignore if I wished. I decided to take that option. A surreptitious swig of vodka in the mall toilets helped the process along.

MY WORD THIS time was priapism. A state I had high hopes of inducing in Johno later on. When I announced it, he made a primitive yawping sound and said, "Don't mind if I do!"

It augured well for the evening ahead.

I STOOD OUTSIDE the bedroom door, wrapped in a towel that was a fraction too short, my hair slicked back. The door refused to open. I shoved it and squeezed through the gap.

"Ow. Jaysus," said a deep, growling voice. "Steady on."

A tall, lean figure blocked my view of the room. Johno.

"Have I stumbled into the wrong room?"

Such unparalleled access was not to be sneezed at. As I moved into the room, I allowed my breast to brush his arm. He moved away as if scalded, no doubt surprised by the sudden advance. Mia was on the other side of him, staring into her suitcase as if it contained the answer to all her dilemmas.

"Oh, hi Astrid. We were just..."

"Here," said Johno. "This fluffy yoke. That what you're looking for?"

He held up a pink fleece and thrust it into her hands.

"That's it. Oh, you're so good."

She buried her face in the jacket's folds.

"Right, come on. We're leaving."

"I'm changing in Johno's room," Mia clarified.

"Why?" I asked.

"You know why," said Johno ominously.

The caramel-coddle texture was gone from Johno's voice, leaving just a jagged edge. I had no idea what could have aroused his ire. At least Mia was out of the way. It gave me time to work on my look.

I WENT BACK to the bathroom and emptied half the bottle of water down the sink. Then I tipped the vodka into the bottle. It was a trick from my early days of clubbing with Jazz, always got me toasted. Some of it spilled down the side; I never managed to achieve a direct aim.

Back in the bedroom, I searched for suitable music to accompany me while I dressed. Nothing in my collection was particularly dancey, apart from some early Prodigy. On the way to sourcing their album, I came upon an hour-long mix recorded by Jazz. The mix that propelled him into Prism. The mix I helped him create. I rested the iPod on the end of the bed and clamped the earphones round my head, stretching the lead as far as it went. This gave me leeway to extract the silver dress from the wardrobe.

I laid it on the bed and surveyed it. It was a masterwork. My fingers trailed along the fine silver mesh that covered the metallic material underneath. Then I took off my iPod and shrugged myself into the dress, smoothing it down over my hips. The material was similar in look and feel to chain mail. At first glance, the dress did not appear to show much flesh. Only my shoulders and shoulder-blades were bare. But there were two slits on both sides which travelled the length of the dress, allowing a lean column of flesh to be seen. Thin bands of material zig-zagged along the slit, acting as a bridge between the front of the dress and the back. The skirt hugged my hips and skimmed the top of my thighs. Other girls had Fuck-Me boots. I had a Fuck-Me dress. It resulted in a score every time I wore it. *You think you look shit hot in those clothes.* The words buzzed at the edge of my mind. I quashed them; they were mere flies.

On this occasion, I teamed the dress with fishnet tights and a pair of silver stiletto heels. The heels were somewhat crumpled from being squished at the bottom of the rucksack, but they straightened out when I put them on. They raised me to Johno's height. I reached for my overcoat. The inside pocket was a perfect fit for my water bottle. I inserted it, then left my coat open so my ensemble was visible in all its glory.

After that, I put the finishing touches to my hair. I kept it soft, minimal gel, just enough to make a wavy fringe that flared outwards and parted at the centre. Jazz liked my hair that way. Figured the mix must have triggered the thought. My head needed to be clear. I took a deep breath, reached for my bottle and took a swig. The fiery taste of the vodka drove everything else from my mind.

This was an occasion that called for my Roberto Cavalli shades. They were the real deal, one of my rare extravagant purchases. Their rims were the same shade of silver as my dress. As I inspected my reflection, a tingle shot through me. My hand drifted downwards, under my skirt. I was already wet, in anticipation of what was to come. My finger burrowed into the soft undergrowth. I removed it and licked the tip, tasting salt. Sometimes I let Jazz lick my finger and taste flesh that was not quite forbidden. I squared my shoulders, a young gladiator headed into battle.

THEY WERE ALREADY there when I arrived. Johno was leaning against the wall, wearing some sort of hideous rag covered in bobbles, which still managed to complement his physique. His guitar was balanced on his shoulder. Mia was on his other side. A reddish-pink polo-neck jumper poked out from under her fleece. Her hair fell in soft waves around her face. It shone in the dim light. I stood at the edge of the throng, waiting for my dress to elicit gasps of admiration.

"You do know it's minus 10 outside, don't you, Astrid," said Martin.

"What's she wearing?" one of the Greek Chorus stage-whispered.

"Kind of a silver yoke."

"That's not a colour for clothes, is it?"

"I'd say she looks like my brother's Opel Corsa. It's silver."

They laughed. Johno whipped his head around and laughed too. I looked at them, took in their worn slacks and woollen jumpers.

"You're hardly the arbiters of sartorial elegance," I said.

They stopped laughing.

"What's she on about?" they muttered.

"All right, gang, let's get cracking," said Martin.

There was a melee as everyone paired off. No chance of getting to Johno; he and Mia were hooked up with Kevin and Martin. Somehow in the shakedown I ended up without an elbow. Not that this was a cause for concern. Easier to strut that way.

Outside, a snowdrift lay in wait, in a cunning position just behind the exit. I was about to plunge headlong into it when a hand yanked me up. It was Kim. I didn't look at him, just shook him off and checked that my bottle was still in situ.

"You might as well walk with us," said Kim, in his nitrogen voice.

"I don't think so. That was an aberration."

"It's no trouble."

I decided to take the line of least resistance, since I wanted my dress to be presentable when I reached the restaurant. We crocodiled along the street. Cliona walked with agonising slowness, treating Kim's arm as a lifebelt. Her cane ploughed tracks through the snow. The town was a lunar landscape, the streetlights casting grey shadows. I went into my usual flight mode and kept striding ahead, my feet lurching over hidden cracks in the pavement. I took perverse pleasure in yanking Kim's elbow and hearing Cliona's disapproving yelps.

"Astrid, you'll have to slow down," she said. "My night vision is very poor."

There she was again, waving her career gimp's get out of jail free card.

"So you keep saying."

I took intermittent swigs from my bottle. Given the company I was being forced to keep, I was glad of the sustenance. In the distance, I made out a yellow glow, a beacon.

"That's the restaurant," Cliona said. "Didn't Kevin say it was called Brumhilde's?"

"Thought you couldn't see in the dark."

When we reached the door. I dropped Kim's elbow as if it were a brick of uranium and pushed open the door.

"Astrid, wait." Cliona said.

"And to think you wanted me to slow down," I said over my shoulder.

AGAIN I WAITED, leaning against the wall, until the Greek Chorus, Cliona and Kim were seated. Then I sat alone on the bench nearest the wall. Johno approached with Mia; he still hadn't managed to extricate himself from her clutches. He looked to be headed for where I sat, but he was rendered unreachable by a gulf of noisy bodies, as a group of guides slid in beside me. I needed the bathroom, so I decided to make good my escape. There was still some vodka left in the bottle; I took another restorative swig.

When I returned, a plate of dark meat was being placed in front of me. It was served with these weird little white potatoes instead of chips.

"Where's the chips?" I said.

The vodka was wreaking havoc with my voice, turning it shrill. It sloshed in my stomach.

"You don't get chips with that one, love," one of the guides said. I couldn't work out which one. Not Martin or Kevin. Their faces blurred into one. A waiter came around with the drinks order. I ordered vodka. Not my usual style with a meal, but I needed to maintain momentum. In the background, there was a soundtrack of people masticating with their mouths open.

"I didn't realise I was eating with swine," I said.

My words disappeared into the ether.

ALL DAY THEY talked about my birthday. All day, I waited for Matthew to come. He was always there when my birthday came.

At teatime, the girls were wailing about the food, like they always did. Little balls of half-eaten food sat on their tongues as they talked. The pink lady who ate with us said we were having a special treat because it was my birthday. My chest tightened. I knew what it was. For a moment, the noise at the table stopped.

"Look, Astrid," a voice said. "That's for you."

Something was being placed in front of me, a pink mound with candles burning on top of it. I counted them; there were six. I became lost in the flickering dance of the candles. The light from the candles made their faces disappear. Voices sang, urged me to blow the candles out and to make a wish. I puffed out my cheeks and the air came out, making the sigh a balloon makes when it goes flat. I closed my eyes and wished for Matthew. When I opened them, he wasn't there. He wasn't coming. I heard cheers from far away.

"We'll have to give the birthday girl the first slice," said the voice.

I plunged my fingers into the cake. It was soft; full of finger-shaped holes. Icing spattered all over the table.

"Don't want any stupid cake," I said.

I heard the refrain, *Now, now Astrid.* A dull throb of satisfaction pulsed through me. They brought me to the bathroom to wash off the icing. When I came back, the other girls were crying that they wanted cake. But it was gone.

AS THE PLATES were cleared away, I became aware of a presence on my left. I turned around. Johno stood there, offering the promise of salvation from Hades.

"I want a word," he said.

I was impressed he knew where I was sitting. Further evidence of his remarkable powers of sonar.

"No room here," I said. "Unless you want to get personal."

"Outside."

A bolt of heat shot through me. It was time. I stood up and put on my coat. He put his hand on my elbow. Only the tips of his fingers rested on my sleeve; he was determined to prove his independence. Or his trust in me. I manoeuvred us towards a bare, whitewashed wall at the back of the restaurant. We leaned against it, beside a water pipe. Its faint gurgling was the only sound. I pressed my mouth close to his ear.

"Good thing you wanted a word. I was planning to seek you out myself."

I was back in Prism, with shapes dancing on the walls. Jazz was in the DJ box, watching from on high. My hand traced the line of his hip and reached for his fly. His hand stretched towards me. My stomach lurched and fizzed.

The ferocity of his push sent me sprawling. I tried to right myself, but couldn't find my footing on the soft snow. My legs parted. I wondered if my underwear was on display. Good thing he couldn't see it. I heaved myself up, leaning against the wall. Water trickled down my legs.

"What are you like?" he said. "There's no way I'd touch you. Not after how you treated Mia."

What was he talking about? Where did she fit into the equation?

"Don't pretend you don't know what I'm on about.

Ridin' her up the arse. Acting like you can't hear her when she's asking you for something."

Maybe you won't be so cruel to blind people.

"She says you keep your stupid headphones on the whole time. That's just ignorance. She's blind, Astrid, she's not an eejit."

"So you fancy yourself as a gallant knight, going into battle for her? How very noble of you. Can't she fight her own battles?"

"She just needs a bit of help sometimes. And she's not getting it off you. You don't have the decency. You won't even talk to her."

I raised myself up to my full height.

"I have no interest in talking to her."

"You've got issues, you know that? You're a bully."

Words splintered into little pieces in my brain... ruined... cruel... don't know what it's like. I closed my eyes, trying to squeeze them out. Johno's cane tapped against the ground. He was leaving. Going back to Princess Mia. Freezing water trickled into my shoes. Drip, drip, drip. Like the erosion of rocks, invisible, pernicious. I finished the vodka bottle; its warmth sustained me, readied me for the final skirmish.

JOHNO SAT AT the top of the table with his guitar, Mia beside him. I strutted towards him. Far away, I heard a juddering sound, a clatter. Jazz's mix looped in my head; I couldn't remember which part. A pinpoint of light guided me to Johno. Voices called my name, but I pressed on, determined to complete my mission. Johno carried on strumming chords. Mia had a microphone in her hand. Her mouth was open. It was always a little open, as part of her gormless act. I snatched it out of her hand. Time to move in for the kill. Johno's mouth waited. I thrust my tongue between his teeth, forcing his lips open.

The only way I could get your attention is if I do this.

Johno snapped his head away. My tongue flailed. I stared at him, dazed. They were the wrong lips. Too thin. I wanted fuller, cushioned lips.

182

"Jaysus," he said, from somewhere far below me. "You're a witch. A white witch."

His arm was around Mia's shoulder.

"Can't handle a proper woman," I said. "Rather have that little invertebrate."

I spoke into the microphone. My voice echoed in my ears. Electricity surged through me. I was going to show them. Vanquish them all. Starting with Mia.

"Not as stupid as you look, are you, Mia? Got everyone dancing attendance on you. Let them think you can't do anything for yourself. You thrive on that, don't you? Being a pathetic child."

My words were hot fat flying into the air, into the silent crowd. All that could be heard was the murmur of the Greek Chorus.

"What's she doin'?"

"Tryin' to give him one. He's knockin' her back, though."

"Ah yeah. Man of taste."

"Jaysus, I'd love two women after me."

"Chance would be a fine thing."

Were they speaking about me? I turned towards them.

"That your party piece? State the obvious and repeat it ad nauseum?"

"I think you've said enough, Astrid."

Cliona. Taking up her cudgels, joining in the crusade.

"I don't recall asking for your input."

An obstacle materialised, a warm brush of flesh, but I ignored it. I was a warrior from my Viking book, thirsting for vengeance, wreaking havoc with a flaming sword.

"We expect a certain standard of decorum on these trips. We made an effort to accommodate you, because your name was put forward by a very important fundraiser. It's obvious that we made a mistake."

"Least I don't pretend I can't see in the dark in order to get on the trip. Fraud!"

"Astrid, I have *retinitis pigmentosa*. It affects night vision."

"That's convenient, isn't it? A neat label for you to hide behind. Strip that away and there's nothing there. You need that label. Tell everyone how brave you are. Have a servant boy do your bidding."

Another hand brushed arm. Thought I saw Kim's face swimming in front of me. Yes, it was. He was the only man I knew who wore purple shirts.

"Get off me. Nitrogen."

I propelled myself forward, towards the door. Leaning on the handle, I turned around to face them. Their faces clumped together, indistinguishable from each other.

"But believe it or not, you are right about one thing. It was a mistake for me to come here. I don't know why I came. Allowed myself to be surrounded by idiots. You're all weak. Pathetic. Can't do anything for yourselves. Let them all wipe your ass for you. Stupid Cabbage Patch Kids. Had enough of you."

I pushed the heavy door open, burst through it, into the lunar landscape. Moved from lamp post to lamp post, setting a crazy, determined course. I was free of limpets, fallen gods. Didn't need well-meant, interfering elbows, the drip-drip-drip condensation of patronising remarks. A voice floated towards me from time to time, but I ignored it. The ground threatened to give way. I took off my shoes and the ground became firmer, but the bottoms of my tights were soaked in an instant. A Latin verb hovered at the edge of my mind. I seized on it. A perfect stream of conjugations flowed: *dêleô, dêlêre, dêlêvî, dêlêtum*. To destroy, conquer. I showed them. The words pushed me on, beyond cold, beyond all feeling.

The hotel loomed in front of me, offering shelter. I crashed into the bar, landed on top of a stool. There was a random young guy behind the counter. Least it wasn't Jurgen, who conveyed disapproval in a syllable.

"Vodka," I said.

A glass slid in front of me. I aimed it at my mouth but missed. Liquid slopped onto the counter. My head became heavy. It rested on the surface, which was as unyielding as Johno's mouth. Liquid trickled into my hair.

"Want 'nother," I muttered.

"I think you've had enough."

The voice again. It was following me.

"Fuck you, Jazz."

My tongue felt thick. Hands pulled me upright, propelled me forward. Then I was being lowered into a soft bed. 'They lay bets on albino chicks,' a voice said. It sounded like my voice. Then I heard a strangled, high-pitched laugh. A blanket surrounded me and everything went black.

JAZZ WAS OUTSIDE the pink cage again; the dream was now a nightly performance. His reproaches were louder than ever. I jerked awake, my mind endeavouring to banish the images. When I touched my cheeks, they were covered in wet track marks. I didn't know where they came from.

❧ Dark Rooms ❧

I thought Ora and Jazz were going to move in straight away, but instead, the procession of boxes began. Every weekend when they arrived at the house, their arms were full of boxes. The boxes spilled their contents throughout our house. Our bare rooms became filled with clutter, objects which were exotic to my eyes. Colourful ornaments took up residence on tables beside Matthew's African artefacts. Books of photographs claimed space on our crowded bookshelves. They burst with lush colours; the pages were thick and reflected the light. Scarves began to cover threadbare patches on our couches and chairs.

The most curious of these new objects was the television. It made its presence felt even before its arrival, when, a man came and climbed onto our roof to attach an aerial. I watched with my mouth open as he balanced himself on a long ladder. Another man went into Jazz's room with a box of tools; Matthew and I conjugated Latin verbs to the sound of his hammering.

"Why are all these men coming to the house?" I asked Matthew.

"It's for Geoffrey's television," he said.

"I thought you said television was the opiate of the masses."

"Well, Ora imagines that Geoffrey can't do without it, so I felt obliged to accommodate him. I only hope you won't fall prey to its powers."

The procession even made its way to the empty, echoing rooms, rooms I now knew were once my mother's. Matthew inspected the rooms. I followed him and stood in the corridor, listening to him as he walked up and down. His heavy tread made the floorboards squeak. Even by the standards of our house, they were cold; the wind whistled through cracks in the floorboards. The sun slanted through the windows, exposing the thick layer of dust that covered the bare floorboards.

Some men delivered furniture in a van and Matthew helped them install it in the rooms. In the bigger room, there was a table with a vase in the centre, a green couch with a matching armchair and a box full of children's toys. In the smaller room, there was only space for a desk and chair. The rooms no longer echoed.

Matthew spent a lot of time in the rooms, arranging the furniture. He nailed a piece of dark cloth over the window in the smaller room. As he hammered in the final nail, the room was plunged into darkness.

"Why did you do that?" I asked him.

"It will be Ora's darkroom. She needs darkness to develop her photographs."

He stepped down from the ladder he was using to reach the top of the window and turned to face me.

"It's good to see life in these rooms again," he said.

Ora spent a lot of time in the rooms too, moving items from one place to the other and wondering aloud whether they looked all right. I watched her as she dusted the furniture in the bigger room with a yellow cloth. She sprayed the table with furniture polish. The room looked smaller now that the furniture was in it. The smell of the furniture polish tickled my nose and made me sneeze. Ora looked up when she heard the sound.

"Oh, there you are. I'm nearly finished this. Then we'll have some lunch."

She straightened up and came over to stand beside me.

"I hope you don't mind me taking over like this," she said.

"Taking over what?"

"The rooms, you know."

I shrugged. They were just rooms.

THEY MOVED IN the weekend after Jazz finished school for the summer. Ora's car was filled to bursting with boxes; this was the last part of the procession. A removal van followed the car. It was filled with furniture. Ora directed Matthew and the removal men as they carried the furniture in. She found corners for it which I never knew existed. Our hall became a sea of boxes. I retreated to the windowseat and listened to the sounds of scraping and banging as the furniture was placed in its new home. Ora filled the presses with gleaming objects which looked more suited to a spaceship than a kitchen. Our house was splitting open.

"Why do you have so much paraphernalia?" I asked her.

She laughed, but didn't answer my question. I got off the windowseat and went to find Jazz. He was in his room, knee-deep in boxes of his own. The homemade radio was on the windowseat. Matthew came in, holding a silver television. It was the television from the cottage in Wicklow. He grunted as he placed it on the rickety half-moon table at the end of Jazz's bed. The table buckled under its weight.

"I trust that will be sufficient for now, Geoffrey," Matthew said, wiping his forehead.

"Yeah. That's okay. Thanks."

When Matthew left, Jazz said he had something to show me. I followed him down to the hall. He stopped next to two boxes which bulged even more than the others. When I leaned closer, I spotted a metallic gleam. Jazz picked one up.

"This is so cool," he said. "It's the greatest thing ever."

His smile split his face in half. Ora came to the door of the kitchen. Her face was red.

"Is it all right if we bring these to the DJ Shack, Mum?" he asked her.

"Oh. Of course it is. There's not much more you can do here anyway. You've been so helpful."

She leaned over to kiss him.

"Here, you can carry the other box," he said to me. "It's not as heavy as it looks."

I picked up the box and followed him out the back door, struggling under its weight but feeling important.

JAZZ TOOK HIS ghetto blaster off the table and began unveiling the metal equipment. First he took out a device which looked a little like his radio, a flat board filled with knobs. He placed it at the centre of the folding table. Then he lifted out two small record players and placed them on either side of the board. His movements were careful, reverent. In the second box, there were two speakers. Jazz placed them on the gas canisters, because there was no room for them on the folding table. He balanced them against the wall. When he finished, he stared at the equipment, his wide smile still in place.

"What do you think?" he said.

"I don't know. What are they supposed to be?"

"They're decks. With a mixer and speakers."

"Like the ones you told me about."

"Yeah. They're just basic ones, but they'll do for a start."

"Where did you get them?"

"Mum got them as a surprise. For the move. She got them off an ad in the *Buy and Sell*."

The decks injected life into his voice.

"Do you know how to make them work?"

"I think so. Remember I told you Sam let me use his a bit. Come on, we've other things to get."

We went back to the hall, where Jazz picked up his sports bag. When we returned to the DJ Shack, he opened it. It was full of records.

"I've been saving these," he said. "Been buying them with my pocket money every week. Now I've something to play them on."

"Are they 7-inch or 12-inch?" I asked, proud to display my knowledge.

"7-inch."

He took out one of the records, slid it out of its white paper covering and handed it to me. It felt cool and smooth. I ran my fingers back and forth along the grooves. They started to tingle.

"Only hold it at the edge," Jazz said, sounding worried. "It'll scratch otherwise."

My fingers detected a nick in the bottom right-hand corner.

"I think it might already be."

"Where? Where?"

Jazz was frantic. I decided it was best not to say any more, so I covered the spot with my finger.

"Oh, phew, that's okay. That's the bit where the needle goes in."

I looked at the label on the record, but without my monocle, I could make out only a faint scrawl.

"What tune is this?"

"It's Sam's; he made it himself. Imagine. Here, give that to me and I'll slip it on."

He placed the record on one of the record players and fiddled with buttons and wires. It took him a long time. Squealing noises came out through the speakers. Jazz didn't say anything. He kept his face bent over the equipment, sometimes muttering under his breath. At last, beats began to pound through the shed.

"It's brilliant," shouted Jazz above the din. "Real pumping beats. Proper acid."

Jazz often described the music he played as acid. It was short for acid house. His head went up and down; it always did that when he liked a piece of music. The beats became interspersed with the sounds of breaking glass, saucepan lids banging together. Then there was a cymbal clash, the hammer blow of Thor. I covered my ears, certain that the roof of the shed was going to blow off. Jazz turned it off.

"Let me pick the next tune," I said. "I can pick proper music."

Jazz slid out another record; the name 'Jack' was printed on it in bold red letters.

"Think you'll like this one; it's a bit mellower. It's called *Strings of Life*."

He was right; it was mellow, almost stately, a linear pattern of beats interspersed with swirling piano notes. We listened, rapt. Jazz pressed his knuckles against his cheeks.

"I want a go," I said, when the tune finished.

"No way. I have to know how to work it before I can show you. We better go back. Mum's brought soup for lunch."

As we reached the back door of the house, I said, "You're a proper DJ now."

"No I'm not." He blushed. "But at least it's a start."

I pushed open the door.

"You'll have to choose a DJ name. Like one of your bands with numbers."

"Maybe something with Jazz in it."

As we ate our lunch, we kept smiling at each other. When Ora asked us why, we were unable to tell her.

THAT NIGHT, I found it hard to sleep. Voices murmured in the next room. It took a while to realise there were no people in Jazz's room; it was just his television. The sound of his breath travelled through the walls. I was used to him being here as a guest, but now it was his room for always. My veins tingled. When sleep came, it was restless; my blankets kept falling to the ground.

ORA LEFT A trail of smells everywhere: the chemical smell of the fluid she used to develop her photographs, the pungent, itchy smell of flowers, rich cooking odours. She was a constant, hovering presence, apologising, tidying up, enquiring about our welfare. The kitchen hummed to the sound of her stirring, chopping, frying. She poured mixtures into the gleaming pots and pans, pressed buttons which made her space-age contraptions buzz and whirr. Matthew said I wasn't to worry; she was just feathering her nest. But to me, she was a cuckoo, trying to implant herself in ours. I was used to her going away after field trips. Now she was there every time I turned around.

Her furniture battled for position in our house. The overflow of furniture turned familiar walkways into alien territory. I was forever banging my legs off low tables which popped up out of nowhere, or sending tiny ornaments clattering to the ground. It was exasperating. She filled the rooms with colours, a riot of yellows, oranges, reds and purples. Matthew said it was like living in a sunburst. Ora muttered apologies from behind her cloud of hair. In the end, Ora's furniture won; even our chessboard was forced to surrender during one of her tidying sprees.

Visitors kept invading the house. They came to have their photographs taken by Ora, in the bigger of her two rooms. Some of them came into the kitchen to drink the strange-smelling tea with her. The telephone rang a lot too, but since most of the calls were for Ora, she always answered it. It was fortunate that Matthew and I were out of the house a lot of the time. That summer, I was given the honour of helping Matthew collect his samples during his field work. We spent hours observing the teeming life in unexpected corners of Wexford's beaches.

"You already have a scientist's thoroughness," Matthew said to me. "You should be up to it."

Jazz stayed behind, to help Ora arrange her furniture and cook meals. When he wasn't with her, he was in the DJ Shack hunched over his decks, or in his room watching the television.

The changes in our house scratched at my insides, made me restless. I flitted from room to room, trying to find an anchor. Ora was always reaching towards me, trying to swaddle me in a blanket of affection, but I danced away before she could reach me. It wasn't deliberate; I was just used to affection that came in sudden fierce bursts rather than in a constant stream. I retreated to the windowseat, one of the few unravaged parts of the house, where I worked through Matthew's reading list. That summer, I was in thrall to the world of Greek and Roman legend, where battles and love affairs were conducted on an operatic scale. From time to time, the sound of Ora's cooking cut through the narrative.

I never realised how often I fell asleep while I read at the windowseat until Ora came to live with us. She was always finding me with my cheek resting on the cool glass, my chin drooping. I shrugged off her entreaties to lie down and rest. It was only my eyes that were tired. Though Ora was an alien presence, she was also a benign one. She was nothing more than a minor irritant, a fly in the background.

ORA KNEW A lot about unexpected things, such as hair. I never thought much about my hair, just tied it back from my face with an elastic band when I was looking for samples. One day, she stood behind me as I brushed my hair at the bathroom mirror. I turned around.

"Oh, look at all the hairs on your brush!" she exclaimed, her voice full of consternation.

I shrugged and began pulling the hairs out; it was a daily ritual.

"You'd be much better using a comb, your hair's so fine," she said. "Come down to the kitchen and I'll show you."

She took a comb out of one of the drawers and began to run it through my hair, teasing out the strands until they fell around my face. I squirmed at the tugging motion, but was soon seduced by the smooth, deft motion of her fingers. It didn't hurt as much as the brush and when she finished, there were very few hairs on the comb.

The next day, Ora had to go into Wexford to collect film. When she came back, she said she had something for me. It was an elastic band covered in soft material. She positioned me in front of the small mirror in the kitchen and started drawing strands of my hair towards her, enough to make a small ponytail. The ponytail hugged the base of my skull; the rest of my hair formed a waterfall beneath it. A grin crept onto my face as I savoured my new, grown-up appearance. Just then, Jazz and Matthew emerged from their separate corners of the house. Ora turned me around to face them.

"Look at Astrid," she said. "Doesn't she look glamorous?"

"Yeah," said Jazz, unsure of what he was supposed to be admiring.

"What have you done to her?" Matthew asked.

"I've fixed her hair. Don't you see?"

"You can't expect us men to notice something as trivial as that. Isn't that right, Geoffrey?"

Jazz went to the sink and started washing his hands.

"S'pose," he said, his words muffled by running water.

I kept sneaking looks at myself in the mirror, marvelling at the alteration in my appearance.

The small ponytail became a fixture in my hair. Jazz kept creeping up behind me to pull on it when we were in the DJ Shack. I tried to move away but never succeeded; his fingers always found their target.

"Leave it alone," I said to him one day. "I like it this way."

"So do I," he muttered to the floor.

"That isn't true. You're always pulling it. It's tedious."

"I do. It's pretty."

He lifted his head.

"Here, I'll do it up for you."

I submitted to his touch. His hands fumbled, but they were gentle.

DURING THAT STRANGE, scratchy time, Jazz and I found each other in darkrooms of our own. When I wasn't scouring the beaches with Matthew, I was in the DJ Shack, watching Jazz perfect his act. His hands were surer now; he could fit the songs together and play them without any gaps in between. He also knew a few tricks; with the flick of a button, he made the voices on the tracks sound slow and sluggish, or so fast that they were more rodent-like than human. The altered voices tickled us, made us laugh until our stomachs ached.

I was entranced by the sounds he created, longed to emulate him. Jazz was reluctant at first, but I persisted. He pointed out the different components of the decks and sound desk, but my eyes failed to follow the trajectory of his finger. As far as I was concerned, he was pointing into oblivion.

"Have you got that?" he asked when he was finished.

"Yes of course I have."

I injected scorn into my voice.

"Right so. Push up the fader for the left-hand decks."

I stared at the buttons, picked one. Nothing happened. I stared at the clumps of soil covering the wooden slats on the floor, a hot lump rising in my chest. As I reached out for another attempt, Jazz's hand covered mine. He guided it towards the correct fader. Then he placed it on the other buttons and told me their names. His grip was firm. As he leaned over me, I breathed in his smell.

"We can try a mix if you want," he said.

"Oh. Right. Cool."

My stomach fizzed. Jazz loaded up two of our favourites, *Chime* by Orbital and *Charley* by The Prodigy. We did a trial run; Jazz showed me the buttons to use to slow down the Prodigy track and mesh it with Orbital.

"I'll tell you when to do it," he said.

I felt for the groove with my finger and eased the needle in, handling the record with the same delicacy as I handled Matthew's samples. The beats filled the shed. My head was cocked to the side; my whole body was poised, waiting for the moment. Then I heard it, a subtle change in the beats that acted as a cue. I leapt forward, pressed the button and did a slow fade, following Jazz's instructions to the letter. The two tunes began to meld. I moved down the other fader, letting *Charley* die out and *Chime* take over. Fierce joy surged through me, causing a grin to spread across my face.

"You knew?" Jazz said. "I didn't have to tell you."

"The beats matched. Like you said."

I was in a daze; beats swirled in my head. Jazz held his hand in the air, palm facing outward.

"High five," he said.

I didn't move, unsure of what he expected me to do.

"Slap your hand on mine."

My hand stretched out in a slow arc. As it reached his waiting hand, my palm became magnetic, fused with his. Warm currents travelled from his skin to mine. His fingers were thick; the skin spilled over the edges of mine. But my fingers were long, so our hands were almost the same size. We stood for a moment, the heat of his hand radiating into mine. When he took his hand away, I wiped my own on my jeans, because it was moist.

Jazz and Ora were living with us for about a month when Jazz's father made an appearance. Not in person, but in the form of a letter. Matthew found it on the doorstep when we came back from our walk, an exotic cream envelope among the brown bills. There was a splodge of red at the top.

"Hmm, Paris postmark. A missive from the snake oil salesman, no doubt."

"Who's the snake-oil salesman?" I asked.

"In this case, Geoffrey's father."

"They don't have snakes in Paris, do they?"

"I'll explain later, Astrid."

"But—"

"I said later."

Matthew never evaded my questions.

When we came into the kitchen, Ora and Jazz were eating breakfast. Ora said good morning, but Jazz didn't say anything. He never talked in the mornings. Matthew thrust the letter at Ora. She slit the envelope open with her knife.

"It's from your father, Jazz," I said, proud to be the bearer of interesting news. "Is he going to come for a visit?"

"I should hope not," said Matthew. "I couldn't be held responsible for the consequences if he were to turn up here."

Jazz gave a furtive laugh, his hand over his mouth, his shoulders shaking. Ora chewed her lip and Jazz stopped laughing.

"What's he want now?" he said in his stormcloud voice.

He slathered two slices of bread with thick layers of butter and jam, folded up one of them and stuffed it into his mouth.

"Goodness, it says he's going to send extra money for you to have grinds," Ora said, her voice bright and eager.

Matthew snatched up the letter.

"In view of Geoffrey's poor academic performance during this past school year, my client has directed that extra funds be made available for grinds, so that he will be better equipped for his state exams next year."

He slapped the letter on the table.

"What qualifies him to decide that?"

"I think it's very good of him," said Ora. "At least he's thinking about you, Geoff."

Jazz swallowed his last bite of toast with a loud gulp.

"No he isn't. He just wants a progress report. Like I'm one of his stocks."

His remark was directed at his plate.

"Write to him and tell him we won't be requiring it," said Matthew.

He began eating his porridge. His spoon clattered, attacking the bowl.

"On second thoughts, that man from the Historical Society is a retired schoolmaster. He could be approached about giving Geoffrey grinds. What do you think, boy? That suit you?"

"Yeah, okay."

Jazz always said okay. It was hard to know whether he meant it or not.

THE LETTER LEFT a crackle in the air, the electric crackle that precedes a thunderstorm. Ora bustled from room to room, wiping, dusting, sweeping, a slave to perpetual motion. Her industry drove Matthew and I out of the house in search of samples. When we came back, I went in search of Jazz. It was easy to trace him to the DJ Shack; the beats were so loud that the building appeared to shake. I was about to join him when Matthew intercepted me.

"I'd like you to help me archive the journals on my desk. The pile is in danger of creating a landslide."

"But I'm—"

"There's one article about the reproductive methods of bivalve molluscs that I've been meaning to discuss with you. I noted your interest in the topic when we were examining those specimens the other day."

MATTHEW KEPT ME busy with various tasks all day. At some point, Jazz and Ora left the house. Later, they returned with bags of shopping. At dinner, Jazz once again gave his food his full concentration. We didn't talk much; the crackle grew thicker.

Sometime after going to bed, I got up to use the bathroom. On the way back, I heard voices from Jazz's room, the sound of gunfire. The door was ajar. I crept in. Jazz didn't turn around. He kept his eyes on the film he was watching. The images on the screen were reflected in his glasses. Since he wasn't telling me to go away, I risked moving towards the bed. As my hand brushed against the blanket, I heard a crackling noise. My fingers made contact with a piece of paper. I held it close to my face. It was a sweet wrapper. I moved my hand along the bedspread and followed a trail of them.

"Why are you eating all these sweets? You already had your dinner, you couldn't be hungry."

"I can eat sweets if I want to," he said, in a lacklustre attempt at defiance.

He opened a packet of crisps and stuffed them into his mouth, so fast he almost inhaled them. I listened to his stolid munching, the rattle of the crisp bag. The screen on his television became very bright, bright enough to spot a sheet of paper on the bed beside him. It was cream, with a splodge of red on top.

"Is that the letter?"

"Yeah."

"Why did you keep it? I thought you didn't like it."

"I don't. It's garbage."

He scrunched the letter into a ball and threw it on the floor. I picked it up and smoothed it out. The splodge of red turned out to be curly letters, spelling out an alien name. The paper was thick and smooth.

"Does it say anything about him being a snake oil salesman? That's what Matthew said he was. Do you know what a snake oil salesman is? Matthew forgot to tell me."

Jazz didn't answer, just kept staring at the television.

"Well? Is he?"

"No. He's a stockbroker. Got a fancy job in Paris, making people rich. Means he can pay a solicitor to do his dirty work for him."

"Why doesn't he write to you himself? He's your father, isn't he?"

"No he isn't. He's dead as far as I'm concerned."

Jazz began to gather the crumbs and sweet papers into a bundle, making angry, sweeping movements. He leaned over to put them in the bin by his bed. Then he turned off the television and stared at the blank screen. I perched on the edge of the bed. Jazz moved over and I lay beside him, facing away from him. Through our pyjamas, our skin touched, creating a layer of static electricity.

"But he's not dead. He writes to you."

"You don't get it."

Jazz released a gust of air.

"I haven't seen him since I was seven. Mum said he was going to live in Paris because he had a new job. And that was it. He had a new girlfriend too, but I didn't know that. Found out after. That's why he didn't come home. He thinks we're boring. We're just like rubbish he wanted to get rid of."

I'd never heard Jazz say so many sentences at once. And I never knew his voice could be so loud. He was almost shouting.

"Maybe you'll visit him in Paris. Matthew says there are many interesting historical sites there."

Jazz gave another sigh. It filled the darkness.

"You don't know what you're talking about. You're just a kid. And anyway, Matthew never left you."

"Yes he did."

I addressed my remarks to the pillow. Jazz made a loud sucking noise as he inhaled.

"He didn't mean to. It was because of my mother. She died, you see. When I was born."

"Yeah, I know. Mum said. I didn't mean..."

Jazz put his hand on my shoulder.

"D'you miss her?"

I thought of the picture in my dresser drawer, the Viking book whose meaning I now knew.

He continued, "Mum used to try and act cheerful. But I

could hear her crying through the wall. So it's easier, you see."

I waited for Jazz to continue. When he didn't, I decided to prompt him.

"What's easier?"

"Pretending he's dead."

A silence fell. It was a warm silence; the crackle was gone. We knew what to say to each other without having to say it. Jazz folded the letter in half and reached over to put it on his bedside locker.

"So what happened?" he asked.

"What do you mean?"

"When Matthew left. Where did you go?"

"I had to go to a school."

"You went to school!" said Jazz, incredulous.

"Immaculate Heart School for Visually Impaired Girls."

I said the words very fast, to get rid of the taste in my mouth, the orange drink taste.

"How long was he gone for?"

"A long time. Forever."

"At least he came back."

His arm crept around my waist; his hand sought mine. It was damp and sticky from the sweets. I rubbed the soft flesh on the base of his thumb. We crawled under the blankets and his body curved into mine.

MATTHEW WAS LESS available than before. Our everyday rituals, listening to Bach, playing chess, discussing items of interest in Matthew's newspaper, fell by the wayside. Instead, he walked with Ora on the narrow country roads that surrounded our house, or went to her darkroom to look at her photographs and help her decide which ones were the best.

Jazz and I no longer travelled in separate orbits. During the day, we were in the DJ Shack. In the evenings, we went to his bedroom, which now looked like his old room in Wicklow, with posters on the walls and comics on the shelves. His smell was stronger now that he was a permanent resident. And he never opened the curtains, so it was always twilight in there. We sat on the windowseat, where his radio perched. Jazz said it was the best vantage point for picking up radio stations. After much persistent tweaking, we were able to locate pirate dance radio stations from Wales. The signal was much clearer than in Wicklow. Sometimes we were able to pick up BBC Radio 1, which played a lot of dance music. We sat on either side of the radio with our eyes closed, wrapping ourselves in beats. The music sounded better when my eyes were closed, the beats were sharper, more concentrated. Sometimes we leaned over to adjust the sound at the same time and our fingers brushed against each other. The friction sent a jolt through me, the sort of jolt I felt when I touched something hot by accident.

Other times, Jazz turned the lights out and put on his television. We topped and tailed each other; my head rested next to his feet. I pressed my face close to the television, trying to see between the lines that filled the screen. But the flickering images were hypnotic: they sent me into a fitful doze. Our bodies hovered close to each other, so close that my skin prickled. But they didn't touch. There was a hum in the air. At first, I thought it came from the television, but when Jazz turned the television off, it was still there.

EVEN AFTER JAZZ returned to school, we continued to seek each other out; the darkrooms became our world. Beats lined the walls of our world, which was populated by new numbered bands: SL2, Altern 8, Opus III.

I worked hard to master my mixing technique. The groove where the needle went was invisible to me, but if I held the record a certain way, I was always able to locate the groove and insert the needle. Still, the process took more time than it was supposed to. I persevered, determined to emulate Jazz's fluid movements and rich, deep sound.

Even though I still spent a good portion of my days with Matthew, he drifted away from the centre of my world; he and Ora were dim figures on the fringes. When Jazz went back to school, I spent my evenings on the windowseat in his room, listening to his radio, breathing in faint traces of his scent.

JAZZ WAS NOW a master of the decks, but his fingers itched for more sophisticated equipment. By happy circumstance, his old DJ mentor Sam was willing to relinquish his vinyl decks. Ora told Jazz he could take a loan from her and pay her back. As Jazz's state exams closed in, he spent as much time agonising over how to raise the funds as he did studying. In the end, it was Matthew who came up with the solution. He announced that a photographic subject of Ora's, who owned an apple farm, was taking on summer labour. Jazz could pay Ora back with his wages.

When the exams were over, Jazz and Ora went to Dublin and came back with the decks. He installed them on the folding table, relegating the other decks to a corner of the shed.

"No more kiddie decks," he said. "These are serious decks. Technics. They're the best. All the nightclub DJs use them."

The new decks had a bigger mixer with more buttons, which made the sound easier to control. It took less time for Jazz to learn to operate them; they were more responsive to his touch. Soon, beats hammered off the roof of the shed with even greater intensity than before.

THE FOLLOWING MONDAY, Jazz started at the apple farm. Matthew drove him there every day and collected him afterwards. We woke him up when we came back from our walk and he sat pale and hunched over his cereal. He hated mornings. But he didn't mind the job; his desire to pay back Ora's loan made his fingers nimble. Calluses appeared on his hands, but he didn't mind. He said all proper DJs had calluses. When he came home, he exuded sweaty contentment. He talked more than usual; names appeared in his conversation, of boys that he worked with. Soon, faces and bodies appeared in the house to match the names. Ora served Jazz's friends huge slices of cake and sandwiches; the exertion made her face pink. I stayed at the windowseat, gazing at them over the top of my book. They filled all the available space at the table with their banter and loud laughter. Sometimes they talked to me; they teased me the way the O'Brien boys once did, tickling me and ruffling my hair.

But most afternoons, we cloistered ourselves in the DJ Shack, experimenting with the new decks, which offered far more possibilities than the old. We found all the places where one tune could undercut another. Jazz made scratching sounds on the records by running his fingers over it while they played.

WE STILL SPENT our evenings in Jazz's bedroom, but they took a different form. When we reached out to change the station, our fingers connected. We held hands for a long time, then wiped them on our jeans. And when Jazz watched television, we didn't top and tail each other anymore. Instead, we lay side by side, our bodies pressed together. We faced away from each other and we never spoke, in case we broke the spell. Messages pulsed through our skin. And we didn't kiss, the way we did for New Year in Wicklow. Instead, we became explorers, tracing the maps of each other's bodies with furtive strokes. Static electricity travelled all over my body, not just the places Jazz touched. Some of the places we found were soft and damp; others were harder, more substantial. Jazz made a strange sound when I touched him, somewhere between a grunt and a moan. When Jazz touched me, my skin shivered, but I didn't make any sound.

AS THE SUMMER passed, my body began to behave in strange ways. The jeans Ora bought for me no longer fitted over my hips and my legs became too long for my body. Though I was all wire and sinew, buds began to sprout on my chest, which became visible through my clothes. When I touched them, I was filled with a hot stabbing sensation, a pleasurable sort of pain. Ora took me shopping for clothes which accommodated my new shape. Matthew took books off the shelves containing diagrams of the reproductive system. I read the labels which appeared beside the diagrams with my monocle: vulva, labia, uterus, satisfying Latin words. Matthew accompanied the diagrams with factual explanations about hormonal changes, the process of fertilisation, the menstrual cycle.

"You're becoming a woman now," he said in a gruff voice. "You need to know these things."

Matthew's dry, clinical explanations bore little resemblance to what I was experiencing; they only served to further stoke my curiosity. I kept studying the diagrams, even when Matthew wasn't there. My fingers left an imprint on the thin, gauzy pages. As I examined them, I felt Jazz's hands on my skin, even though he wasn't there. His phantom touch bewildered me.

Jazz noticed my new shape too. His touch became more certain, more insistent. When he touched my buds, they became hard, the way they did when I touched them. And the sensation of pleasurable pain was greater. He ran his hands over the jutting curve of my hips and stroked the silky skin on the inside of my thighs. A hard, hot object pressed against me; I didn't know what it was, but it caused heat to travel through me, spreading outwards from the depths of me.

JAZZ'S SHAPE WAS also changing. His face began to lose its roundness and the sun turned it a warm brown colour. Hair began to sprout on his body, thick, springy hair that had a different texture to the hair on his head. Dumb-bells appeared in his room, lent to him by one of the boys he worked with. Matthew showed him how to use them and he practised with them every day. He didn't like me to be in the room when he practised. The results of his efforts were pleasing. Though he was still soft in the middle, there was a new hardness in his arms; muscles rippled under his skin. My own arms were pale twigs compared to his. His legs were harder too, from moving around all day on the apple farm. His new muscles made his skin taut, as it stretched to accommodate them. And his voice was deep now, like Matthew's, but with less gravel. I mapped the changes with my fingers, during our night-time interludes.

WARM AIR CIRCULATED through the DJ Shack, moisture-laden air which covered my face with droplets of water and turned the dust on the floor into mud. The smell of creosote was stronger than ever. I was listening to *Love Sex Intelligence*, by The Shamen, a new record which Jazz deemed worthy of a one-off withdrawal from his apple farm funds. Jazz came in as I was resetting the record. The scent of apples mingled with his usual smell.

"This is a good one," I said to him. "It's about sexual intercourse, isn't it?"

"You're such a weirdo, you know that?"

He gave me a playful punch on the shoulder.

"How do you know about that stuff anyway?"

"I've been studying it," I said with a flourish, my chin jutting outwards.

"You're such a know-it-all," he snapped.

"It's all in Matthew's books. I can show you if you don't believe me."

Jazz scuffed the ground with his foot.

"Do you want to see them or not?"

"Yeah, okay."

I sped to the house, retrieved the books and ran back to the shed. When I returned, Jazz was still standing in the same spot. The record was finished, but the needle remained in the groove. We returned to the chairs and I found the pages. Neither of us said a word as we looked at the diagrams.

"Wow!" said Jazz. "They're way better than the ones in my science book."

"Matthew always says the best way to gather information is from a live specimen."

Jazz's head snapped up.

"What do you mean?"

His voice was thick. I stood up, leaned against the wall, lifted my skirt. My knickers fell to the ground. Only the sound of Jazz's ragged breathing broke the silence.

"You shouldn't," he said.

In the silence, his voice was magnified. I stayed still, entranced by the unexpected tingling that spread through me. Jazz didn't look away. Instead, he stood up and began moving towards me with slow steps, until he was in front of me.

"Can I... can I?"

I reached out and guided his hand under my skirt. He stroked the pearl-smooth surface, then burrowed into the folds of skin underneath. The skin began to throb and the tingling intensified. The hard hot object pressed against my hip. Tumescence; I knew what it was now from Matthew's book. Jazz kept rubbing me, his fingers moving back and forth, soft at first, then harder. Hot liquid spurted out of me. My lips parted and I sighed. Jazz made a strange grunting noise and took his hand away.

"I have to go," he muttered.

He ran out of the shed and slammed the door. I stayed where I was. Warm waves crested over me. When they began to recede, I lifted my hand up to my face and examined the liquid. In the semi-darkness, my fingertips glistened.

JAZZ BURST THROUGH the door of the kitchen. The noise he made caused me to drop my book. His excitement was palpable.

"You'll never guess," he said.

"Not if you don't tell me."

"There's a party next week after we finish. Well, in the evening. There's going to be a barbecue and a disco after. And they want me to do the disco."

Ora rushed over to him and flung her arms around him, even though her hands were covered in flour.

"Oh, Geoff, that's wonderful news," she said.

"Is it going to be a rave?" I asked.

Jazz disentangled himself from Ora.

"No, it's just a kid's thing. Just for a couple of hours."

But his smile belied his words. His teeth looked very white against his tanned skin. I stood up.

"Could I go?"

The smile left Jazz's face.

"It's just not right," said Jazz. "There'll be, you know."

He looked at his shoes.

"What will there be?"

"You're a bit young, Astrid," Ora said.

"No, I'm not. I'm almost a teenager. In some countries I could be married."

"I'll tell you all about it after. And you can help me put my set together. I'll need a hand."

I pulled myself up to my full height.

"This is indeed a great honour," I said, in my deepest voice.

Jazz punched me on the arm.

"Eejit," he said.

But he was smiling. I smiled too, a secret, knowing smile. Nobody was going to prevent me from witnessing Jazz's first proper DJ set.

As soon as Jazz came home each day, we raced to the DJ Shack, where we spent hours creating his set. Jazz tested mounds of records, most his own, but some belonging to his new-found friends. He used me as a sounding board, asking me which tunes I thought flowed best. I endeavoured to give him my considered verdict. Without prompting, I handed him records and pulled up faders. The set took shape, became a continuous rush and gurgle of beats, like a river flowing into the sea.

When Jazz and Ora arrived at the car to load the equipment, I was already there, leaning against the boot. I wore a straw hat, a check shirt and one of my new pairs of jeans. My hair was arranged in its grown-up style and I wore a pair of dark shades which wrapped around my face. They were a present from Ora.

"What are you dressed like that for?" Jazz said.

"Don't I look rustic?"

"Oh yes, you do. You look lovely," said Ora, sounding anxious but eager.

"You're not going," Jazz said, his arms folded across his chest.

Though his voice was still soft, there was a new tone to it, full of confidence and authority.

"Yes I am. All good DJs need an assistant. That's what you said."

I folded my arms across my chest too. Jazz sighed.

"All right. Fine. But you're to stay with me the whole time."

WE ATE THE barbecue in a field, at a long wooden table. Ora presided over one of the barbecues and helped serve plates of food. Jazz's friends began their usual tickling and punching routine.

"Don't," I squealed.

"Leave it off," Jazz growled.

But I didn't want them to stop. It felt good. Grown up.

We ate juicy steaks, sausages which cracked in the middle and big floury potatoes. The food was delicious, but for once, Jazz didn't eat much. He kept disappearing to check on his music and equipment. One of Jazz's friends was supplying a proper DJ system, with huge speakers and lights. As I approached Jazz to see if he needed help, my path was lit by big revolving discs that flashed and spread pools of colour all over the field. The DJ system was perched on another long table. It was dusk now, almost time to begin, but there was no sign of Jazz. I called his name and a shadow emerged.

"Are you ready?"

"Yeah. I was just rigging the lights. There's loads of requests already. Good thing most of the songs are on the set anyway."

"Cool."

"Time to go," he said, with a loud intake of breath.

His fingers hovered over the decks, zeroed in on a fader at the centre of the mixer. He pulled it up and pressed a button. The sound wobbled a little, then settled. A mellow trickle of beats leaked out over the field. People began to appear, the setting sun turning them into long-limbed shadows. It was hard to tell them apart from the trees which lined the field, keeping watch. They stood in black clumps, not moving.

"Aren't they supposed to be dancing?"

"No-one dances at the start," Jazz said.

His voice was calm, but there were vibrations in it. I picked up a record from the pile and handed it to him.

"Maybe this will help," I said.

A white flash of teeth told me that Jazz was grinning. He inserted the record. A voice urged us to pump up the volume. There were loud cheers. As the beats built, the people began to move, their limbs waving, buffeted by imaginary winds. Midges burrowed into my skin, but I brushed them aside. As it grew darker, the lights became more visible. They turned into beams which bounced across the field, casting a glow over the crowd. Here and there, I saw splashes of colour, similar to the colours of the lights. The crowd turned into cartoon figures, paper-thin, insubstantial.

The beats became more frenetic and the bodies formed strange shapes, trapezoids, hexagons, oblongs. All of Jazz's numbered and lettered bands made an appearance, some of them unexpected.

"Why are you playing that?" I hissed at Jazz, as the air filled with the sound of mice being heated in a microwave oven.

"Got a request."

"But it isn't on your set."

"Doesn't matter. You've got to give them what they want."

There was a chair beside Jazz, but I didn't sit on it. I took requests from the dancing figures as they emerged from the darkness. Under Jazz's direction, I searched for the records he needed. Whenever he reached for a record, it was there, waiting for him. Apart from the requests, I forgot about the dancing figures. I just let myself be carried forward by the current of beats, which swelled as the set reached its climax. Jazz finished with The Prodigy, *Everybody in the Place.* As he pushed up the fader, I pressed a button and the bassline thrummed through the speakers. The limbs of the crowd flailed, made scissor motions.

"Cool," said Jazz. "I never thought of doing that."

As the song neared its end, Jazz pulled the fader down in a long, slow movement, letting the beats die away. The crowd filled the silence with cheers, which we heard from a distance. Jazz pulled me towards him and threw his arms around me. Everything disappeared. There was just the heat that rose from his body and the feel of his arms around me. Then he let go and I became aware of figures surrounding the decks, returned to their earthly form now that the lights were dimmed. They clapped Jazz on the back and hugged him. I stood to the side and let the lingering warmth of his touch seep into my skin.

✺ Martin the Merciless ✺

I SWAM TO the surface. Light hammered my eyes. I squeezed them tight shut, flinching away from it. My hands fluttered at my sides and made contact with rough material. My dress. Why was I still wearing my dress? With my face buried in the pillow, I reached out for my shades. My hand hit something hard, which sloshed and wobbled. A glass of water. Where did that come from? My fingers clamped around it. I unpeeled myself from the sheet and brought the glass to my lips. The room tilted; my stomach tossed and heaved. My head was transformed into a bag of cement; it sagged under its own weight. The sips of water failed to wash away the orange drink taste that flooded my mouth. Mia's side of the bed was empty. Unslept-in. The silence echoed. Where was she? Oh yes, Johno. She was clinging to a different rock, but her departure left no scar. I tried to retreat to my ice fortress, but Jazz waited for me there, pinning me down with his cold, quiet words, crushing my lips. I couldn't keep him at bay now. The covering veil was torn away. Bile rose in my mouth and I covered it with my hand, swallowed it back.

I sat up, looking for escape, my movements as slow and careful as an old woman's. As I swung my feet around, something pierced my flesh, cut through the fog in my brain. It was the heel of my shoe. I moved my foot away and something skittered across the floor. An orange basin. What was that doing there? *Think you've had enough.* I bent over it and watched as a river of bile gushed into it. When I was finished, I sank to the floor and rested my head on my hands. My insides were emptied, raw.

An eternity passed before I felt able to stagger to the wardrobe. The face that greeted me in the mirror was dishcloth grey. Behind my shades, my eyes wandered, unable to find their still point. I moved away from the mirror, from the spectre of myself in clown clothing. *Hologram. White witch.*

I sank back onto the bed and flipped my phone open, filling the screen with Jazz's face. I traced the full outline of his lower lip and typed the words:

```
Got it on wit rock god. Shwd him wots

wot.
```

The words looked hollow on the screen and filled me with that grey, Sunday-morning sensation of waking up on grubby polyester sheets. I deleted them. I stood up and ripped the dress off of me. The material tore. I bunched it in my hand and shoved it into the bin in the corner. Gulps of water fortified me as I struggled into my ski suit; I willed the liquid to remain in my stomach.

As I pushed open the door, I heard a babble of voices. My head tightened. The Cabbage Patch Kids stood in their phalanx formation, talking and laughing as they waited for the bus. Their laughter was alien. As I reached the bottom, the babble began to fade, creating a vacuum. Oh yes, last night. Snatches of conversation began to play in a loop... *can't handle a proper woman... hate to interrupt your Greek tragedy... neat label for you to hide behind... invertebrate... tired of fighting... tired of fighting.* The last sentence snagged, like a CD fallen victim to scratches.

They were loitering, blocking my escape path. I rammed through them. Shoved them aside like skittles. The babbling rose again, increased to the level of a dull roar. In the midst of it, I detected a shrill nasal whine. *Not even an apology. Well, she needn't think she's coming back next year.* The words swirled in the air, but they passed over me. I was drowned; the water was closing over my head.

Mia and Johno stood closest to the door, nose to nose, whispering. *Well shot of her, stupid bitch.* Jazz's sweet-and-sour breath blew into my face. My stomach heaved. I reached for my trusted store of Latin verbs, but only one came to mind: *amo amas amat.* To love. Generic.

Outside, cold air blasted into my face, but failed to lift the fog from my brain. A wave of dizziness passed over me; the world was tilting on its axis. I leaned against the wall and closed my eyes. After almost a week, I still wasn't accustomed to the light; it bludgeoned me with its hammer blow.

"Oi, sleeping beauty."

My eyes jerked open. Martin was standing in front of me. His decibel level was off the scale this morning.

"Ready to be bested?"

"I don't think skiing will be possible for me today."

I injected my voice with as much dignity as I could muster. Martin leaned in close to me.

"Don't think you're getting off that easy," he said.

His voice was low this time, but its message was clear.

THE GREY LADY'S room was different from all the other rooms. It was a soft room. The carpet was the colour of Mrs O'Brien's vegetable soup when she put carrots in it. There was a fireplace, but it didn't make the same sound as the fireplace at home; there was a hiss, but no crackle. A table stood by the window. Its legs curved at the top and it was covered in pieces of paper, like Matthew's, except that these papers were in neat piles. A cup stood on a little mat at the edge, but it didn't have any coffee in it, only pens. There were no curtains, but there were blinds on the windows, so the room looked a bit dark even in the daytime. The light came from two lamps on either side of the fireplace.

I was only in the grey lady's office twice. She was the grey lady because her hair was grey and she always wore grey dresses. The first time was with Mrs O'Brien and the brown lady. I wore my pink dress and pink hair slides to match. The hair slides were a going-away present from Mrs O'Brien. They didn't hurt, but they stuck to my hair. I kept reaching up to touch them. My dress smelt of washing. The material was stiff and made my skin itch. The grey lady sat at her table, under the window. Mrs O'Brien and the brown lady sat opposite her, on two pink armchairs. I leaned against Mrs O'Brien's armchair.

Mrs O'Brien ran her fingers through my hair. The grey lady asked me if I wanted something to drink, but I said no. Cups clinked on saucers. Conversation floated over my head. I got up and wandered over to the fireplace. There was a small table next to it, covered in green balls. I wondered what the balls were for. There was a round space in the middle of the board. When I pressed it with my finger, I found a little hole where a ball was supposed to be, so I moved one of the balls into it. It was heavy and made a clacking sound. But now there was another space. I kept moving the balls to try and fill the spaces. The clacking sound they made was satisfying. Holes kept appearing, no matter how often I moved the balls. Before I reached the end, one of the balls slipped out of my hand. I crawled on my hands and knees, but couldn't find it, so I went back to Mrs O'Brien's chair. Words floated down towards me and became stuck together. The warm air made my eyes droop.

The second time was after I smashed the cake. This time, I didn't play with the wooden board; I sat on one of the chairs. My feet poked over the edge and dangled in the air. I was hungry; my stomach made growling noises. The grey lady sat at her desk, far away. Her words were far away too. *Don't you like it here? Aren't you well looked-after?* I didn't tell her about the weight that sat on my chest, the orange drink taste which was in my mouth all the time. She used more words. There were too many of them: *your father... grateful... rest of the year.* I wanted to ask her about Matthew, but I didn't. This was a place that didn't like the word 'why'. Her voice didn't go up and down; it was low and heavy. I pulled my legs towards me and sank down into a cool, silent place. After a while, the words disappeared.

THIS TIME, THE bus took us in a different direction. A constant whispering current flowed around me, but the roaring in my ears blocked it out. Jazz's words of reproach accompanied my journey, mingling with the sound of the engine.

When the bus jerked to a halt, I dashed out and gulped lungfuls of cold air. We were surrounded by gleaming white buildings. A humming noise emanated from the buildings; it pounded through my head. I moved away from the others and leaned against the walls of one of the buildings to put on my boots. Martin came over to me as I was fastening the Velcro.

"Fancy a gondola ride?" he asked. "Best offer you'll get all year."

"Don't you need water for those?"

"Not these ones. Come on, I'll show you. You'll like this, I promise."

We passed through turnstiles similar to the ones on the other lifts. As we approached, the humming nose grew louder and long wires appeared above our head. Attached to them were capsules with seats inside, rather like carriages at a fairground ride. They were the source of the humming noise.

"Them's the gondolas," Martin said. "Cable cars."

One of the cable cars came to a halt in front of us. Martin took my skis and slotted them into mystery pouches at the side.

"Hop in," he said.

I squeezed myself through the mouth of the cable car. Two seats faced each other. I collapsed onto one of them and stretched my legs out.

"Told you. Easy peasy. Much more civilised than them other lifts."

The door clicked shut, there was a hiss and we were off, sailing above the snow-covered tops of fir trees.

"So what've you got against jazz then?" Martin said. "I'm quite partial to a bit of Sinatra myself."

His voice bounced around the confined space in the gondola. My head tightened again.

"I don't know what you're talking about."

"You were blabbing on about jazz last night. Cursing it to high hell, you were. Suppose it hasn't got enough bleep-bleep in it for ya."

Think you've had enough. The voice was Martin's.

"It's not music."

I muttered the words, to ensure they were audible only to myself. But Martin was able to pick them up.

"Well, what is it then? It better be good."

"A person."

The words were heavy weights in my mouth; saying them took a supreme effort of will.

"A fella?"

He was a skilled interrogator, capable of unmasking me. Just like Jazz.

"Yes. My—"

I was no longer sure where brother ended and lover began.

"That why you made a play for Johno?"

Johno. A shadow now. Jazz's lips superimposed themselves on Johno's, crushed them into oblivion with their white-hot touch.

"Johno's not right for you anyway. You need a fella who's up for handling a moody mare like you. We're not worth it, most of us, honest."

This one is. The words hovered, but I didn't say them. There was another hiss and the doors opened.

"Come on, we've got a slope to conquer."

I followed him out of the cable car, holding the door tight to prop up my shaking legs.

As WE CAME out of the hall where the gondola stopped, we stepped into a white world. The clouds touched the top of the slope and obliterated even the trees.

"You can't expect me to ski that," I said.

"Yes I am as a matter of fact," said Martin. "Don't wuss out on me now, girlie."

"What is this? Punishment?"

"Course not. You're up for it."

I inched forward and my skis began to slide. The steepness of the slope pulled at my legs, drove the oxygen from my body. The turns came fast, one on top of the other. My skis scrunched on the soft snow. Short, shallow gasps of breath echoed in my ears. I surrendered to the speed, let myself fly.

The wind whistled past my ears. My skis moulded themselves to the slope. I was blanketed by trees, soft snow, the distant tinkling of bells. Though I couldn't see the mountains, I knew they were there, a benevolent force. Martin's voice guided me through the fog. I was grateful for the speed; it wiped my mind clean.

The runs blurred into each other. Time and again, Martin asked me if I wanted to take a break, but stopping meant thinking, so I shook my head. Halfway down one of the runs, my legs began to protest and I wobbled to a halt. Martin pulled up beside me. My head was clear now, my stomach raw but calmed. I swallowed, trying to banish the last lingering traces of metal from my mouth.

"Here, we'll sit by this rock, have a bit of a breather."

There was a small overhang behind us. I lowered myself down and rested my body against the rock's smooth surface. The snow blended with the sky; silence formed a cloak around us.

"Thirsty?" Martin asked.

I nodded.

"I know what'll cure that. Some snow. Mind you, it's a bit yellow, we need a fresh fall."

"Matches my hair."

He laughed.

"Try some then. You'll be colour coordinated."

I scooped up a handful and crammed it into my mouth. Its fresh, clean taste banished the previous night from my mouth. It tasted of life.

"By the way, you heard the others talk about Franzi's?"

"Huh?"

"The local nightclub?"

My ears pricked up. I scanned my internal database for mentions of nightclubs in the village.

"Well, it's a hall really, but the locals have a disco there every week. We always go on the last night. Only thing is, the local Johnny's cried off. How d'you fancy spinning a few records?"

My stomach lurched. The orange drink taste returned.

"That's what you call it, isn't it? Spinning?"

"Told you I don't do discos."

"Well, if I were you, I'd do this one."

Once again, his words found their target, pierced my Achilles heel.

"You've got ground to make up after your performance last night. You were pretty free with your insults."

I shrugged.

"You do remember what you said, don't you?"

My mind was too clogged with other conversations, other memories.

"Don't you even give a stuff?"

"I have no interest in ingratiating myself with them."

Martin stroked his beard.

"You said you didn't know why you'd come. But you do. Your other trip went skew-whiff, cos of your eyes?"

I drew my legs up to my chest, trying to deflect the blows.

"Because your sight isn't as good as you think it is. You're more like rest of 'em than you know."

You pretty much are one of them. The rock was starting to press into my back. I stood up and stretched, moved towards my skis to put them on. Martin began a new line of attack.

"So how come you don't do discos? Give DJ Ice White a chance to strut her stuff."

"Tried it once. Didn't work out. Stylistic clashes."

"Well we're a bit easier to please. Suppose we'll have to get in a vat of vodka for you."

I shook my head. My stomach revolted at the thought.

"We got a deal then?"

He held out his hand. I capitulated. Reached over and shook it.

"Right then, let's get a move on," he said. "My bum's getting cold."

FOR THE REST of the day, a curious peace descended on me. We made only a brief stop for lunch; when we did it was late and none of the others were there. Now I was certain of where

I was going, my skis sliced through the snow. The watchful fir trees and the small wooden huts blurred as I passed them. The swishing sound my skis made filled me with quiet pleasure. On the wide, flat part near the bottom, Martin let me turn on my own, but I didn't feel the rush of liberation I expected. The absence of his voice created a vacuum.

The rest of our gondola rides passed in blissful silence; Martin suspended the interrogation. The only interruption came from his phone, which jangled in his pocket.

"All right, mate... yeah, it's going good... nearly over now... got one of them looking at me right now, in a manner of speaking."

It took a moment for my fuddled brain to grasp the import of what he was saying. A wave of laughter caught me off guard. I didn't make a sound, but my body shook.

"Good," said Martin. "I was wondering if you knew how to laugh."

ON A DAY when the sun was high in a blue sky, they took us for a walk. It was almost warm. I had to wear my sunglasses, because there were no clouds to block the sun. They called it a nature walk.

The other girls walked in clumps, holding on to each other to stop themselves from falling down. I walked on my own. The other girls stretched their hands out towards me, but I walked too fast and their hands went away.

The nature walk was in the forest behind the school. The trees were tall and the sunbeams slanted through the branches. They said we were going to play there. I lost myself among the trees. My shadow followed me; it copied everything I did. Dead leaves squelched under my feet. I wanted to send them to Matthew with the correct labels on them, to show him that I remembered. But when I picked them up, they were too wet. The squeals of the other girls came from far away.

At the end of the forest, there was a stream with stones in it. I put my hand into the water and picked up a fistful. They were smooth and round. All of them were the same colour brown. I plopped them back into the water and ripples spun out.

Then I took off my shoes and socks and edged my feet over the low stone wall that surrounded the stream. The stones slipped away from me and I landed in the water with a splash. The water was so cold that it cut into my skin, but I didn't care. I made little fountains with my feet.

When I got out, blood hit my feet in a fierce rush. I jumped around in the mud and they tingled. They came for me and said *Now now, Astrid*, because my skirt and blouse were covered with brown stains, but I didn't care. My skin tasted of sun.

I DIDN'T GO back on the bus with the others after skiing. Instead, Martin took me to Franzi's hall to look at the equipment. His sturdy red jeep turned out to be the ideal vehicle for negotiating the unending stream of sharp bends that led to Franzi's. The road cut a swathe through the mountain. We travelled so high that even the trees fell away. Driving to Franzi's reminded me of the go-kart track Jazz took me to once a year. He never partook himself, just waited while I quenched my thirst for speed on the rutted paths.

"You're going to have quite an audience tomorrow night, girlie," Martin said, turning towards me.

"Shouldn't you be watching the road?"

"S'alright. Know it like the back of my hand."

"At least one of us is."

"What?"

"Watching the road. In a manner of speaking."

A small smile played on my lips.

"I declare. Was that a joke? Wonders'll never cease."

He roared with laughter.

"You ever try any of this driving malarkey?"

The smile left my face. I looked at my lap. There was a small stain on my ski suit, near my knee, a trace of red sauce from my lunchtime schnitzel.

"Might have done."

"Who came off worse, you or the other bloke?"

"Neither."

"Glad to hear it."

Staring at the endless fir trees made my eyes heavy. I closed them and let my head rest against the window.

HIS NAME ESCAPES me now. All I remember is his car. I first heard its siren-call on a damp, empty summer day. I was sixteen, a no-man's land of an age. Nothing satisfied me: not the reading lists Matthew set, not the household jobs Ora fabricated for me, not even field trips. Matthew was away a lot, at conferences and meetings. Tagging along with him no longer held the same appeal. And Jazz was in London, gaining valuable work experience at a recording studio as part of his sound-engineering course. I was filled with restlessness, which was fuelled by the dull, aching awareness that I was being left behind. Long walks and beats stilled it, but their effects soon wore off.

I was pounding along the beach on one of my endless walks when I first heard the car. As I approached the carpark overlooking the beach, the noise grew louder. Cars spun in circles, sending gravel flying. Beats pounded from the cars, faster and more aggressive than anything Jazz played. One of the cars stopped right beside me. The driver rolled down the tinted window and rested an arm on the door. It bulged with thick veins. A tattoo poked out from under his T-shirt.

"Howya," he said.

I nurtured a violent wish to be wearing garments that were more alluring than frayed shorts and a faded navy jumper.

"Hi," I said. "How do you do that? It's cool."

"Hop in and I'll show you."

I got in and he took off. The engine buzzed in my ears. We spun in circles; flying without leaving the ground.

EVERY NIGHT, I sped down the cliff path to the carpark, where he waited for me. Ora and Matthew were deep sleepers, so I was never caught. I plundered the stash of clothes at the bottom of the wardrobe which I was saving for when I was old enough to be admitted to nightclubs. Sophisticated clothes, similar to those worn by the girls who attended Jazz's discos.

We drove along country roads, sometimes taking corners on two wheels. He put his hand on my thigh as he drove, his fingers working their way under the material of my skirt. We drove to different carparks, or raced along beaches. When he wasn't driving, we drank vodka out of paper bags. He gave me rough, hot kisses which left me aching for more. His moustache tickled and he smelled of petrol and sweat. As time went on, being a passenger failed to deliver the same thrill. I began to dream of gripping the wheel, feeling the car leap forward at the slightest touch of my foot.

Some weeks into my new regime, Jazz's work experience came to an end. He turned up for a visit in a beat-up white car, bought with money from DJ sessions in London. On his second day home, I lay in wait for him outside the house.

"Teach me to drive it," I pleaded, as he unlocked the car.

"Are you nuts?"

"Never mind. I know other people who can teach me."

"Yeah, I heard."

His mouth was set in a grim line.

"Heard you've been running around with boy racers all summer."

"Who told you that? One of your apple farm cronies?"

"Yeah. I met Tom when I was getting petrol. He thought I should know. Stay away from them, Astrid. They're bad news."

"Like you care," I said, turning back towards the house. "You've been away all summer."

A plan crystallised in my mind. I was due to meet him in the carpark, as usual. And Jazz was meeting Tom for a drink, so the coast was clear.

THAT NIGHT, I selected a black crop top and a faux-leather skirt, also black. I opted for strappy sandals; low-heeled shoes were a better option. The occasion merited an outing for my first-ever pair of designer shades: Guccis, bought with birthday money. They were black too.

Tonight, we were going to a big carpark twenty miles away which served as a regular meeting point for boy racers. When we got there, he passed me the brown paper bag. I shook my head.

"You're not sick, are ya?" he said.

"Far from it."

I moved my hand up his thigh. His jeans were streaked with oil. I paused at his bulge, testing the power of his gear stick.

"I want you to teach me to drive."

He shook my hand away.

"I'm not lettin' you wreck my car."

I leaned over and flicked my tongue across his lips.

"I'll make it worth your while."

"All right babe. Anything you say. Just one spin though."

The others did donuts while he showed me where to position my feet and how to change gears.

"Let's go," he said after an eternity.

I pushed the clutch downwards, four to the floor. The buzz of the engine drowned everything else out. The car was moving forward. It was happening at last. Power surged through me. It was happening. I was driving.

The pole came out of nowhere. The car juddered into it with a sickening crunch. My head pitched forward, bumped off the steering wheel. When I straightened up, my shades fell on the floor. Laser beams assaulted my eyes. I bent forward and began to grope for my shades. They were on the floor under the brake, cracked in half.

"Shit," he screamed.

As I straightened up, he grabbed my arms. His fingers dug into my flesh.

"Get out of my car, you stupid bitch."

Dazed, I pushed open the door and wobbled out of the car. The bonnet was bent out of shape, the metal twisting in odd directions. He got out too.

"I'm sorry," I said in a small voice.

"What are you, blind?"

Some of the others came up to us. The air was thick with expletives.

"We better split," one of them said. "Bet the guards'll come."

"I'll come with you," he replied. "Get the lads to collect it in the morning."

The others began to climb back into their cars. It took me a moment to realise that the cars were full.

"What about me?"

Fear made my voice squeak. It sounded pathetic.

"Should have thought of that before you trashed my car."

They drove off, their brakes squealing. I leaned against the wrecked car, trying to steady my wobbling legs. My brain scrambled for figures to calculate the amount of time needed to reach my house. If I walked fast, I stood a reasonable chance of arriving before Matthew sought me out for our morning swim. As I summoned up strength for the journey, another light dazzled me. Tyres crunched as a car came to a stop. Two figures climbed out, moved towards me.

"We received reports of a disturbance," one said.

There was a flash of luminous yellow. The guards, as predicted.

"Did you crash this car?" the second figure asked.

I nodded.

"You'd better come with us."

They were arresting me. Least I didn't have to worry about walking home. I stumbled forward and cannoned into one of them. He steadied me.

"Easy now," he said. "Have you been drinking?"

I shook my head.

"We'll see about that."

He held out a clear plastic bag and told me to breathe into it as hard as I could. When I finished, he said,

"Well, at least that's clear anyway."

Then he gripped me firmly by the elbow and led me to the squad car.

THE LIGHTS IN the station burned my eyes. I tried to create a shield with my hand, but it was ineffective. They brought me into a room which contained only chairs and a table, an interrogation room. They sat opposite me and asked me questions about what we were doing in the carpark. I kept my answers brief. Their pens scratched the paper.

Then they handed me a form to fill out. I hunched over the piece of paper. It was divided into sections asking me to fill in my name, age, address and phone number. I filled in the blanks with painstaking strokes. The letters refused to land on the dotted lines; they spider-crawled across the page. My head came to rest on the pen. Their eyes were on me the whole time as I formed the letters. The pen hovered over the question about my date of birth. I decided to risk writing my real date of birth; after all, I was in my 17th year.

"Not exactly Sherlock Holmes, are you," I said, as I pushed the form towards them. "This all you can manage by way of investigation?"

One of them, the guard who brought me to the car, slapped the piece of paper down in front of me. He was young, with bristling dark hair.

"You forgot to sign your name," he said.

I tried to find the place where I was supposed to sign. The letters swam in front of me.

"At the bottom," the other guard said.

He was older, with hair a similar colour to Matthew's.

"Now, do you think you could tell us why you were behind the wheel of that vehicle?" said the young guard.

"Driving it."

I folded my arms across my chest.

"But you don't have a licence, do you?"

"So?"

"It says here you're 16."

Their mathematical ability was greater than I imagined.

"You know we could charge you for being an unlicensed driver, underage."

"Whatever. Go right ahead."

I tried to swallow the hot, sour ball of panic that rose in my throat. The younger guard stretched his hands behind his head.

"You haven't driven before, have you?"

"Course I have. Lots of times."

The older guard decided to intervene.

"You didn't see that pole, did you?"

His voice was gentle. I heard the pity in it and flinched.

"It was dark. What do you expect?"

"Well that's funny," the younger guard said. "It's the only one in the car park."

There was a sneer in his voice.

"It's a great big red yoke. You'd want to be blind to miss it."

"I can assure you I'm not blind."

I kept my voice tight and clipped, forcing the words past the ball in my throat.

"Can you see that poster in the left-hand corner?" said the older guard.

I looked in the corner he indicated. It took a while for the zoom in my eyes to locate a blue and green poster covered in black writing. Below the writing, I saw the outline of a car.

"Can you read what it says?" the older guard asked.

"Yeah. It's road safety stuff."

Figured I could bluff it out.

"Tell us what's on it," said the younger guard.

The glaring lights in the room bounced off the poster, turning the letters into hieroglyphs. My shoulders slumped. The air hissed out of my body.

"Thought as much," the older guard said. "Right. I think it's time to call your parents. And you'd want to be careful picking your friends in future, all right?"

They directed me to the waiting room and offered me tea, which I refused. I sat on a plastic chair, grateful that at least I could now shut my eyes. They continued their hummingbird flutter behind my eyelids. I was unable to stop shivering. The chair welded itself to my bare legs. My shades were still in my hand; the pointed ends dug into my flesh. I braced myself for Matthew, flinging open the door of the station, bellowing with rage, or for Ora, full of gentle reproach and promises of herbal tea. But it was Jazz who came through the door. The older guard went up to him and talked to him in a low voice. Then Jazz came over to me and held out his hand. I took it and hauled myself up. My legs made a soft sucking noise as I peeled myself off the chair.

"My shades broke," I whispered.

Tears sprang out of my eyes and slid down my cheeks. I covered my face with my hand. This was just too random. I waited for Jazz to say I told you so. But he just covered my shoulders with his leather jacket.

"Come on, let's get you home," he said.

We left the station, his arm around my shoulder. Nestled against his substantial warmth, my shivering began to ease.

"ANYWAY, THE LOCALS come up for the disco Saturday nights," Martin was saying. "They love all that bleep-bleep music."

My stomach lurched, as Martin negotiated a steep bend.

"You won't have to do it for long. Just 10.00pm until 12.00pm. The Austrians like to go to bed early."

I stared out at the purple sky. A text flashed into my mind. *My own 2hr set.* I reached into my pocket, but it was empty. No point sending it anyway.

FRANZI'S HALL WAS a squat building, a typical ski chalet, whitewashed like all the others. Inside, the walls were lined with dark wood. A bare lightbulb above my head cast a weak glow; the dim light was welcome, a break from the coruscating glare of the ski slopes. The room was almost devoid of furniture, apart from a bar counter and a few warped tables propped up against the walls. A set of antediluvian decks perched on top of a rickety light system designed in the style of a ghetto blaster. The decks were vinyls. Not my natural medium. Finding the grooves was still a scramble. A table stood beside the decks, with two cardboard boxes underneath it that bulged with vinyl records. It was all very school-disco circa 1993. I was back at the apple farm barbecue with Jazz, as he held back the darkness with his beats.

"Right then, I'll leave you to it. Come back for you in two hours. That do you?"

Martin's voice dragged me from my reverie. I stared at him, dazed.

"You all right?" he asked.

"Oh, yes. Fine."

There was an obstruction in my throat; I swallowed it down and ignored the stinging behind my eyes. There was a job to be done.

THE TWO CARDBOARD boxes awaited my inspection, treasure chests eager to spill their bounty. The weight of their cargo caused them to list to the side. I took the records out in blocks of 10 and isolated possibilities for the set. Jazz could play up to 15 records in an hour; his tunes came in short sharp bursts and were designed to set limbs flailing. My tunes meandered through soundscapes; a length of 8-10 minutes per tune was not uncommon. Jazz built his set on the bedrock of his 30-minute mix, played when the crowd's euphoria was at its height. I didn't have that luxury. Still, it was fortunate that there was so much to choose from.

Without my monocle, I was forced to eyeball each of the records. There was a preponderance of the Complan-speed mix favoured by the ski-cafe owners: classic Euroschlock. Figured it was best to leave some of it in. *You've got to give them what they want.* Again, Jazz's breath blew on my neck as I bent to lift out the piles of records. The air in the hall was thick with the mingled smells of creosoted wood and damp; the smell of the DJ Shack.

PERHAPS IT'S JAZZ'S fingers which excite me the most. They still carry a trace of fatboy pudge; the fingertips are soft and wide. These are the fingers that can create electric dreams at a stroke. They burrow under my Prism T-shirt and run down the length of my body, searching for my soft places, using the map of blue veins under my skin as a guide. They mould my ass, my narrow hips, my taut belly, the soft skin of my inner thigh. Sometimes they linger in the smooth place around my groin. They leave a trail of prickles, pinpoints of light which cause my skin to glow. With one touch, they peel away all my layers, yet somehow I never feel exposed.

As I DUG further, I stumbled upon electronic gems. Every Kraftwerk album known to man. *Jackpot* by Tocotronic, last played the night before I left. A rollcall of Scandinavian greats, Lali Puna, Amina, Jori Hulkonen. And early Sigur Rós bootlegs. I managed to resist the urge to bury my face in the piles of records and moan with pleasure.

At the very bottom, I blew dust off some vintage records, weird central European electropop from the 80s, early 90s rave and hardcore. Pure Ementhal: 2 Unlimited, Snap, SL2, K-Klass. Jazz still rated *Rhythm is a Mystery* as one of his all-time favourite tunes; he always played it at Prism's 'Old-skool Nites'. No Massive Attack, but with so many riches to plunder, I didn't feel the lack.

Next, it was time to tackle the machinery. My fingers took me on a journey around speakers, wires, faders. I played with the buttons, listened for tiny gear changes in sound. At first, the wires were a jumble, but I was soon able to negotiate the maze. As I moved my fingers up and down, Jazz's hands covered mine, his touch light and reassuring. Perhaps tiredness was making me fanciful, or the remains of last night's vodka was still coursing through my system. Nonetheless, my movements became deft. The hall throbbed with sound; the wooden walls created a deep, lush acoustic. I worked the lights and watched pink, yellow, red and blue shapes dance on a crazy, wobbling orbit on the rough floor. The tidal wave of beats pulled me along until all the thoughts in my mind were crowded out.

When the door to the hall opened, I was fading *Enjoy the Silence* by Depêche Mode into *Running up that Hill* by Kate Bush. *Come on, Jazz; let me have this one*, I muttered.

"Talking to yourself, girlie?"

I whipped my head around. Martin stood beside me, grinning. I lowered my head then removed the record from the decks and returned it through its case. My movements were deliberate and meticulous. I didn't look up.

"Sorry, didn't mean to startle you," he said. "You're sounding good anyway."

The hall reverted to its drab, huddled self. Martin's voice was amplified by the silence. I checked his words for hidden sarcasm. There didn't appear to be any. Nonetheless, orange drink swamped my mouth.

"What are you doing here?"

I folded my arms.

"Hate to disrupt an artist at work, but grub's up."

"You're early. You said two hours."

"I gave you an extra half-hour as it is. Looked in on you and you were bangin' away to your heart's content. Didn't think it was right to stop you when you were in the groove."

I threw a last wistful glance at the records, then heaved myself out of the chair.

BACK AT THE hotel, I bypassed the bar, where the distant roars of the Cabbage Patch Kids could be heard. The stairs were steeper than ever. I showered, washed myself clean. When I returned to the bedroom, I put on my Prism T-shirt, crawled under the covers and stared at Jazz's face until I could no longer see it. I listened to all of his mixes, even the Tiesto one which I despised. For once, my sleep was dreamless.

ᦒ White Night ᦒ

My FINAL DAY of skiing passed in a blur. I bombed down the steep slope until my legs tingled. We stopped only to neck down glasses of sparkling water. At two o'clock, Martin called it a day.

"Best to end on a high," he said. "Besides, you've got your hot gig tonight."

We stopped to eat in the cafe near the gondolas; then Martin drove me back to the hotel to change my clothes. I stared into the vast expanse of wardrobe, picked up garments and discarded them. They were tawdry now, stripped of their allure. I dug through the pile until I came upon my travelling clothes: the jeans and T-shirt, the faded jumper. They were a comfort blanket. I rested the jumper against my cheek and thought of Jazz in his black and white T-shirts, his camouflage gear. I composed a text,

Got shit hot gear 4 1st nite. Hp u apprv.

I hovered for a long time over the send button before I deleted it.

I threw on my clothes, ran a desultory brush through my hair and a quick browse through my stock of shades. There didn't seem any point to them where I was going, so I stuck to my glasses. I put on my overcoat, equipping myself for the ice-box air in Franzi's hall; he didn't appear to believe in insulation.

THE RECORDS WERE still in situ when I arrived at the hall, old friends waiting to greet me. A desk light with a button switch was now positioned beside the DJ decks. When I touched it, a cloud of dust rose up from it.

"Where did that come from?" I said to Martin.

"Franzi dug it up. Thought it might come in useful."

Words of protest bubbled on my tongue, but they refused to form sentences. It was something of a relief to avail of light that came at an angle, rather than shining straight into my face. Martin said something else which I didn't catch. Then he was gone.

I decided to refine my set, test it for meld and flow. Unlike Jazz, I liked my sets to be tight, calculated to the last second. I timed the rise and fall of the beats and listened for the subtle key changes which acted as markers to bring in the next tune. *Yeah, that's it*, Jazz said each time I achieved a perfect fit. I shook my head from side to side, trying to shake off his voice, to convince myself it was fancy, but it was lodged in my brain. Some of the tunes I chose refused to flow into each other. I kept reaching into my pocket for my phone, to seek Jazz's advice, but it was always empty.

IT WAS JAZZ who set up the gig at Eclectica. His recent appointment as resident at Prism meant that he was now at the centre of all the happenings in the dance music world. He heard that a warm-up DJ was being sought for a new electro night established to act as an alternative to the frenetic weekend party scene. The resident was a friend of a friend; Jazz let it be known that I was in the frame. My proofreading client base was expanding at a steady pace; I worked with a small publishing company and with a portfolio of academic clients acquired during my degree. But the prospect of my own DJ set was too tempting to relinquish. I compiled a 30-minute demo, submitted it and was summoned to deliver a two-hour test set. In front of real punters. For a solid week prior to the gig, I holed myself up in Jazz's studio, tweaking, experimenting with various combinations, until the pads of my fingers were bruised and the beats became a blur. The set I chose veered towards the more mainstream end of my collection: Air, DJ Shadow, Zero 7, Daft Punk. But I wanted to demonstrate the diversity of my collection, so I tempted fate and added a few more obscure titles. The venue was aiming for a retro vibe, so the decks were old-skool Technics. No mp3 signal, no laptop screen to act as safety net.

On the day of the set, I slotted the records with care into my briefcase, a handsome black leather number presented to me by Matthew and Ora on my successful entry into college. The records were in perfect symmetry; even the needle grooves were aligned with each other, to ensure ease of access.

Jazz walked with me down the dim, derelict street to the club. He was due to go to a birthday party later with one of his nut-brown maidens, but he still planned to witness my launch. I wore black skinny jeans and a matching T-shirt with the word Jagged emblazoned on it in graffiti-style hot-pink letters.

I can still pinpoint the exact moment when it all went wrong: when I fell over the amp. It was placed near the door, a landmine waiting to explode. Jazz tried to grab my arm, but it was too late. I pitched forward and landed on the ground, my limbs splayed. When I picked myself up, a man was standing there, staring at me. Jazz introduced him as the resident. I took several deep breaths, stood up, shook his hand. He told me in curt tones to go to the DJ box. I strode over to it with as much purpose as I could muster. A maze of faders and buttons stared up at me. With the resident's eyes on me, I was unable to implement my trusted sound-and-feel method of navigating unfamiliar sound desks. A light shone into my face, robbing me of all signposts. I reached into my briefcase for my shades.

"Make it snappy," the resident said to me. "They're lettin' em in now."

At least my records were in order, arms at the ready. I took a deep breath, loaded the first record. Took a gamble on a fader. A nearby speaker let out a screech. From a distance, there came the sound of voices. The hairs on the back of my neck stood up. A cold teardrop of sweat trickled down my back. Civilisations rose and fell before I managed to produce recognisable sounds. Air hissed out of my mouth. No chance to take a breath. Had to line up the next record. The light bored into my eyes; impeded my search. A silence opened up as I loaded the record, but I was able to plug the gap. The crowd were invisible to me. Couldn't even see Jazz, though I knew he was nearby.

My second record was long, an extended DJ Shadow mix. I sat back, took a gulp of air. A finger prodded the space between my shoulder blades.

"Wake up," said the resident. "There's people looking for requests."

I straightened up. My T-shirt was clinging to my back.

"I have a set," I told him, in the coolest tones I could muster.

"Yeah, well we operate a loose format here. Punter's choice. Deal with it."

A thin guy stood in front of the decks.

"D'you have any Daft Punk?" he asked

As I struggled to locate the whirl of electricity that graced the cover of Daft Punk's *Discovery* album, the DJ Shadow record ground to a halt. The silence yawned. I found the Daft Punk and began a frantic search for the groove. The situation was not helped by the fact that my fingers were shaking. As I inserted the needle, my elbow sent one of the records flying. I picked it up. It was intact, but my pile was in complete disarray. What was I planning to play next? Oh yes, the Sigur Ros bootleg, a gem unearthed during one of my cybertrawls. That was bound to silence him. Show him I was no dilettante. But the glaring light rendered the letters on the record sleeve invisible. By the time I located it, the room was silent once more. On the rare occasions that Jazz made a mistake, he carried on, acted as if nothing were amiss. I took my cue from him, forced myself to continue loading the record. But then the silence was filled, by the sound of slow handclapping, hisses, whistles. Missiles which punctured my skin, rendered me immobile. Another man stood beside the resident. His finger jabbed the air, pointed at me.

And then Jazz was in front of me, pulling me to my feet, putting his hands on my shoulders and moving me to the side. The noise was drowned out by beats. My beats. Jazz was at the decks, his fingers working the sound desk. He bent over and gathered the dropped records, straightened the pile. Then he touched my arm.

"What? I don't..."

My lips were frozen.

"He's asked me to do the set. I'm sorry."

I collapsed onto a chair. The beats whirled and closed over my head. Though the music wasn't Jazz's usual style, the set was flawless, faithful to my original intentions. Some people even danced. As the beats died away, the resident came over and started talking to Jazz. I shoved the records into my briefcase, no longer caring about order or alignment. The clasps on the briefcase protested as I wedged it shut.

"What are you playing at, wasting my time with some wannabe chick?" the resident was saying. "I'm not running a charity."

Jazz's reply was inaudible.

"Anyway, she looks a bit weird. Don't want her frightening off the punters."

I got up and made for the exit, every muscle in my body straining in an effort to avoid the amp. Neither Jazz nor the resident noticed my exit.

Outside, a light drizzle fell, soaking into my clothes. I gripped the handle of the briefcase until my fingers turned white and the leather made an imprint on my palm. The street was illuminated by pools of orange light. I heard footsteps behind me, but I quickened my pace and they grew fainter.

I was within touching distance of a taxi rank when my hip crunched against one of the poles at the side of the footpath. Pain seared through me, stopped me short. The footsteps were louder now, but I couldn't outrun them. I leaned against the pole, breathing in ragged gasps, waiting for what was going to happen. The pain became lodged in my chest. A butterfly touch landed on my arm.

"Come on, we'll go back to mine," Jazz said.

"For what? A post-mortem? Besides, aren't you expected elsewhere? You're already late. That won't go down well."

"I told her something came up."

His hand was still on my shoulder; the warmth of his touch leaked through my skin. My legs turned against their will. I walked in front of him, my shoulders hunched, my grip on the briefcase still vice-like.

When we reached his apartment, I sat on my chair, my head resting on my hands, listening to the soothing sounds of coffee being made. Jazz didn't drink coffee, but he knew how to make mine just the way I liked it. I looked up as he set the cup down on the coffee table. He sat on the armrest of my chair. Mist filled my eyes, obscuring my view of the room.

"Equipment's pretty shoddy," he said. "And that light didn't help."

"There's no need to make excuses. I blew it. Nothing more to be said."

"You're too purist for that place anyway. Guy's a jerk."

"That's not the point."

"I know."

"You know I had everything tight."

"Yeah, I know."

He rubbed my back in circular motions, until the mist cleared.

As I NAILED down the last loose ends of my set, the door opened. Martin was back, this time accompanied by a burly man who I figured must be Franzi. I stood up and came out from behind the decks. He pumped my hand with even more vigour than Martin. His handlebar moustache dominated his face, bisecting his glowing pink cheeks. He said something guttural to Martin.

"All that DJ work must be making you hungry," Martin said. "Franzi's asked us to dinner. He wants to thank you for stepping in."

I had no thought of food; the weight was back in my chest, restricting my digestive tract. But I figured it was best to play along. I wasn't in the best position to negotiate.

As it turned out, the dinner was restful. Since no one else could speak English, I wasn't obliged to make any contribution to the conversation. Words ebbed and flowed around me. The food consisted of big sausages which were the same consistency as Franzi's skin and potato salad laced with vinegar. It slid past the weight in my chest. I washed it down with an enormous mug of coffee, strong enough to last until closing.

THE CABBAGE PATCH Kids were spilling out of the bus when Martin and I arrived at the hall. I ducked inside, grateful that they were unable to see me. As I took up my post, other people began to arrive, big men in check shirts and girls with gleaming blonde hair arranged in plaits. The men were covered in hair, bearing the hallmarks of their marauding barbarian ancestors. My stomach somersaulted. A makeshift bar was now situated in a corner of the hall, the one nearest the decks.

"Franzi's nephew, real family operation," whispered Martin. "Will I get him to slip you a voddy for courage?"

I shook my head. My stomach was too raw for vodka.

"By the way, Franzi heard you earlier. Said you're better than the local Johnny."

I continued adjusting the amp.

AS THE BELLS in the village chimed the hour of ten, I launched into my first record: *No Limits* by 2 Unlimited. A rather cheap ploy, to lure them onto the floor with cheese, but to my surprise, it worked. Shadows began to appear on the floor, reflected in the pools of light. The lights danced too; they bounced around the hall, turning it into a cave of wonders. My second record flowed from my first with such ease that it was impossible to tell where one ended and the next began. A warm glow began to seep through me. Now I understood the pleasure Jazz took in being positioned high above the crowd at Prism. Behind the decks, I was liberated from the scrutiny of others, free to be an unobserved guest at the party.

The vintage-rave medley gave way to 80s synth pop. The figures were becoming clearer now, a sea of check and flowers. The men were flinging the girls around the floor in an unending dervish whirl. The lights gave their bodies an orange-brown sheen. Their hands flailed; they danced with blithe unconcern for their appearance or for the actual rhythm of the music. No hip-grinding here. The heat of their bodies rose in a cloud and wafted towards me. My clothes were sticking to me.

I couldn't identify the Cabbage Patch Kids among the throng, but there was no time to dwell on that. My attention became absorbed by lights, the need to tweak buttons. The fierce thrum of the beats drove the other sounds away. I was grateful for it. It was only when Martin tapped me on the shoulder that I realised people were gathered around the decks.

"Please to play DJ Otzi," said a man with a handlebar moustache which rivalled Franzi's.

"Ja, und Scooter," said a girl.

Her voice rang a faint bell. It took a moment for me to identify her as a waitress from the hotel; she was unrecognisable without her traditional garb. Neither artist featured in my playlist. Darts of panic shot through me. I dove into the cardboard boxes and grabbed piles of records. In the dim light, the letters were almost invisible. The music ground to a halt. A bedlam of voices rushed to fill the vacuum. I held the records in my lap, frozen to the spot. Sweat dripped from my armpits, my back. This was Eclectica all over again. I waited for the boos, the hisses. But instead, people were clapping their hands. Not in slow, sardonic motion, but in applause.

"All right, girlie?"

Martin. I opened my mouth, prepared to tell him that I was fine, that I didn't need his help, but couldn't summon up the energy. *Why do you always turn everything into a fight?*

"I'm searching for a record."

"What one?"

"Scooter."

Martin gave the records a cursory inspection, selected the right one and handed it to me. *Rise above it*, whispered Jazz. *Act like nothing's happened.*

I managed to stop the record from slipping out of my damp hands and inserted it into the decks. Relief flooded through me; my body went limp. There were whoops from the waitress and handlebar man.

"Nice recovery," Martin said. "Need an assistant?"

I shrugged my assent; this was no time for Viking heroics.

"Want a voddy now?" said Martin.

I shook my head.

"Just water. Thanks," I croaked.

He reached over and kissed the top of my head.

"You're doing a bang-up job, girlie,' he said, from far away.

Time passed in a blur, as a stream of people approached the 'DJ box.' Martin took their requests and helped me unearth CDs from the cardboard boxes. Most of the requests were for Belgian hardcore and forgettable Eurodisco. My playlist was in tatters; beats piled on top of beats. But no one cared.

Jazz appeared behind me. He placed his hands over mine, guiding their movements. His voice murmured in my ear, telling me when to fade in the next tune. I kept reminding myself that it was a hallucination, the product of a fuddled brain. Yet I made no attempt to shake it off.

Martin tapped me on the shoulder, signalling that it was time to bring the set to a close. I returned to my playlist for the last two, my Depêche Mode/Kate Bush indulgence. As *Enjoy the Silence* faded away, the crowd began to cheer. Their voices travelled down a tunnel.

"They're cheering for you, girlie."

I slumped in the chair, the adrenalin of the last two hours leaching out of my body. Martin understood that I wasn't capable of speech. He said something to the crowd and they began to disperse. As they moved away, I became aware of the Cabbage Patch Kids, sitting at one of the warped tables near the wall. Johno and Mia. Kim and Cliona. The Greek Chorus. Two, two and two. I remained behind my decks, letting them act as a buttress. Their voices were easy to distinguish through the high, happy babble.

"Those people have no respect. After all these years, they should be more aware of our needs. We'll have to talk about a brighter place next year."

Cliona.

"Do you think they'll be doing last orders at the hotel? I'm gasping."

"Yeah, the beer tastes like piss here."

The Greek Chorus.

"Thank fuck we don't have to listen to any more of that shite. That's what you get for putting a poser from Prism on the decks. We'll play some real music back in the hotel."

Johno. No longer a Roman god, just another random baller. I knew that somewhere in the darkness, he and Mia were touching. A stray beat pulsed through my head. I listened out for Jazz, for his quiet words of praise. But he was gone.

MARTIN HELPED ME to pack everything away before we went back to the hotel. He spewed out a stream of chatter about the gig, how well it went, the response of the crowd. I lacked the energy to respond. As we drove back to the hotel, my mind played the set in an infinite loop. Martin stopped the car, but neither of us made a move to get out.

"I hope you know how well you did," he said. "Franzi wants you to come back next week."

There was no surge of triumph. Just a cavernous space with nothing to fill it.

"Thanks. For, you know, everything."

I looked at my shoes.

"Don't mention it."

A silence fell, leaving space for a hug, a handshake. But I wasn't one for mawkish gestures.

THE HOTEL WAS silent. I guessed that the others were ensconced in their bedrooms. The spiral staircase was more difficult to climb that night. My limbs were weighed down; it was hard to lift my feet.

In the bedroom, the air was cold. The wardrobe door was open; my rucksack waited to be filled. I knew I should lie down, try to sleep, ease the throbbing ache in my muscles, or shower to remove the layers of sweat from my skin. Instead, I retrieved my phone and iPod and lowered myself onto the windowseat, pressing my body against the cold glass. My legs were bent, wedged against the wall. The iPod and phone rested on the windowsill, under my legs. An icicle hung from the window; it was at least a foot long. The ice fortress was all around me, but it offered no protection.

I reached for my phone, positioned it so that I was almost nose-to-nose with it. Jazz's features were indistinct. I traced them with my index finger. Then I filled the screen with the letters of his name. *Jazzjazzjazzjazzjazz.* I tried to resurrect him, but there was nothing left. The fissure inside me kept widening.

There was only one thing to do. I sucked my breath inwards. No point in putting it off. I typed,

> U wr rite. Abt trp. Abt evrtn. Go bk to J.
> B happy. Wont gt in ur way.

This time I didn't delete it. This time I pressed send. *He will never touch me again.* The thought pulsed through me. I wrote conjugations on the frosted glass. *Amittô, amittere, amîsî, amissum.* To let go. I was a defeated Viking warrior, willing to cast myself into exile.

I threw down the phone and picked up the iPod, attempting to fill the cracks inside me with beats. I plumped for Massive Attack, with its rollcall of memories featuring Jazz as central protagonist. *Unfinished Sympathy*, the music which altered the direction of my life. *Safe From Harm. Protection.* That was what Jazz did. With his steadying arm, his voice in my ear, the warmth of his body. And his touch, which reached into the depths of me and set my neural passages aflame. He helped me navigate a world full of obstacles I couldn't outrun. When I was with him, I laid down my arms.

When the Massive Attack finished, I started on *The Well-Tempered Clavier.* Matthew always said that Bach was a suitable replacement for a God. But that night, the stately notes failed to offer their usual solace. I switched off the iPod and heaved myself off the windowseat. My legs hurt from being bent into position. I shoved the clothes into my bag and looked at my watch. It was still inky-black outside. I closed the door and steeled myself to face the nuclear winter.

SOMETHING ALWAYS JERKS us back to reality. A shaft of sunlight stealing through the curtains. Pins and needles. A pressing need to urinate. A ringing phone. Without saying a word, we get up, dress, make breakfast, convene in the studio. Revert to type.

❧ Finis ❧

IT WAS SUNNY. We were standing in a circle. Break time was over, but the teacher was letting us stay outside for longer. A warm breeze blew across my face. They said we were going home for our holidays soon. I knew what holidays meant now. We were let out for a little while, but we always had to go back in again, behind the gates.

The teacher rolled a large ball to each of us, with coloured stripes on it. The other girls squealed with laughter as they hit the ball. There was an itch on the back of my left leg, near my ankle. It was too far away for my hand to reach. I tried to scratch the itch with my foot. Doing little tests like this made the games more fun. As I edged my shoe towards my ankle, the teacher called my name. The ball was coming towards me, so fast that the stripes disappeared. Before I could right myself, the ball slammed into my stomach and I fell on top of it. It rolled away and I slid onto the ground. The teacher picked me up and brushed little stones from my clothes. I scuffed my shoes against the ground as I waited for her to finish, but I didn't wriggle away. They left me alone faster if I stood still.

When she stopped, long shadows appeared in front of me. I turned around. Two figures stood next to the circle. The sun made it hard to see who they were. They were covered in dust. One looked like the grey lady; the other wore grey trousers and a blue shirt. He was tall, with silver hair. Like Matthew. My mouth fell open; I forgot to breathe.

"Aren't you going to say something? Or have they turned you into a complete imbecile?"

The words punched me in the stomach, harder than the ball. Matthew was here. And he was cross with me. It was too much. My chest became tight. I tried to speak, but could only make gulping sounds. His blue shirt became hazy as my eyes filled with tears. He picked me up and pressed me close to his chest. I clamped my arms around his neck and buried my face into his shoulder.

"Come on, Astrid. We're going home."

He began to take big, jouncing strides. Tears poured out of me in a loud gush.

"Dr Johnson, you can't do this," the grey lady said. "She still has another month of lessons."

Matthew's head whipped around.

"I think you've done enough."

He kept walking, away from the yard. I looked up. We were in the carpark at the front of the building. At the car, he set me down with a jerk.

"Get in," he said. "I'll be back in a moment."

He opened the back door and strapped me into the car seat. The straps were very tight and bit into my stomach. I wanted to tell him, but he was gone.

When he came back, he was carrying my suitcase. It thumped as he put it into the boot. He got into the front seat and the car shot forward. It squealed. Every time we turned a corner, my stomach jumped up and down. The only sound in the car was my sobs. I couldn't stop them; I couldn't be a Viking any more. Maybe that was why he wasn't talking to me.

When we stopped, we were at the Dublin house, parked at the end of the path that separated our house from the bigger one. Matthew undid my straps; they left sore spots on my skin. As I climbed out of the car, hot liquid streamed down my legs and into my socks. A sour smell reached my nostrils. Matthew always said that only babies and animals soiled themselves. He didn't say anything; he was busy taking my suitcase out of the car. But the dark stain on my blue dress gave me away. I ran through the gate and plopped onto the grass, my whole body shaking with sobs. The hedge that surrounded the house gave me shelter. Matthew came over and stood in front of me, his breath coming out in little gasps.

"Please don't be cross," I said, gulping.

"I'm sorry, Astrid. I'm so sorry."

His voice was full of cracks, like the voice on the telephone. He dropped onto the grass and knelt in front of me. When I stood up, I was almost the same height as him. This time when he pulled me towards him, his hands were gentle. He held me tight, not caring about my soiled dress or the sour smell. I buried my head in his chest. After a long time, we broke apart. There was a dark stain on his shirt, like the one on my dress. He wiped my face with his handkerchief. It smelt of dust and pine. I breathed in the smell of him.

"All right then," he said. "Let's go inside and sort you out."

His voice no longer cracked or sounded cross. It was his old voice.

I FOUGHT OFF sleep as I waited for Matthew to come in and say goodnight. He was taking a long time. We were still in Dublin, because Matthew had business to do, but we were going back to Wexford the next day. The light in the room was soft and yellow. Dark furniture kept watch over me. The pipes gurgled. They gurgled a lot; Matthew said it was because they were old.

The Viking book was on my lap. When Matthew came in, I held it out to him.

"Do you know," he said in a slow voice. "That was your mother's favourite book when she was young. Why such a gentle soul was held in thrall to such a bloodthirsty people, I will never know."

I sat up with a jolt, the sleep banished from my eyes. Matthew sat on the bed beside me and put his arm around me. I leaned closer to him. There was an object in his other hand, a square brown parcel. He thrust it at me. I didn't pay any attention to it; his words were squeezing all the other thoughts out of my head.

"Are you going to open that or not?" he asked, his voice speeding up again.

I balanced the parcel on my knees. The brown paper was rough and there were bumps around the edges. My finger found a small hole in a corner at the top and burrowed through it. The paper came away to reveal a picture of a woman in a wooden frame. I held the picture up and tried to touch her face, but it was covered with cool glass. The woman smiled at me. She had two dark circles for eyes. Her hair was the colour of the conkers I picked in autumn. She wore a square black hat on her head and a black gown. There was a piece of rolled-up paper in her lap. Her mouth went up at the edges.

"That's your mother," said Matthew. "Mary Johnson."

She didn't look like any of the women in Valhalla. Blood rushed through my ears. Matthew's heart thumped, so hard I felt it through my clothes.

"You look like her," Matthew said.

"No I don't. I'm the wrong colour."

"That's just a genetic quirk."

I decided not to ask him what a genetic quirk was. He took my hand in his and moved it around the edge of my face. Then he moved it around the outline of the woman's face. The shape he made was the same. The shape of an egg.

"You see? The same face."

Matthew sounded pleased, so I was pleased too, but I was more interested in the book. I moved the picture to the side.

"Aren't you going to read me a story?"

"Not tonight. Tonight I want to tell you a different story. One I should have told you a long time ago."

His voice slowed down again, like a toy with its battery running down.

"Is it about my mother?"

"Yes."

He picked up the picture and looked at it.

"Such a beautiful woman. A gentle spirit. This was taken on her graduation from university. I didn't meet her until long after that. My father died, you see; it was quite sudden. So I obtained leave from the research project in Africa and came home to settle his estate. I intended to stay only a short while."

He rubbed his eyes and adjusted his glasses.

"A few weeks after my return, a friend of my father's asked me to dinner. I don't care much for social fripperies, but

I went nonetheless. And she was there. Sitting on a swing seat at the bottom of the garden. She moved her hands when she talked. Her fingers were long and slender. Like yours."

I tried to keep up with his words, to fit them together in my mind.

"I decided not to return to Africa. She accepted my offer of marriage. The house in Wexford, it was hers. After a while, you came along. We weren't expecting you, but there you were."

He opened the Viking book at the front, where the curly writing was.

"She chose your name. Let me show you."

He brought the book close to me and I followed the movement of his finger.

"That's her name when she was a girl."

His finger moved to the right.

"And that's your name."

I examined each of the curly letters.

"It doesn't look like my name."

"She wrote it in runic letters. You've seen them in the illustrations. Viking letters. Your name means beautiful, fair goddess in Old Norse. She told me that that was how she saw you in her dreams. I told her she was being fanciful. But then you were born and her prediction was true."

"She knew who I was?"

"Yes. She held you. Said your name. And then she was gone. I couldn't stop her. Couldn't do anything. I wanted her to have you at home. I thought I could keep her safe."

He didn't say anything else, for a long time. His breath rattled; it was trapped at the back of his throat. The corners of his mouth turned down.

"Maybe she'll come back from Valhalla for a visit."

"No, Astrid. People don't come back from Valhalla."

He took another breath. It whistled past my ear.

"Did you go on a quest to find her?"

I thought of my own quest, on the long, dark road.

"You could say that."

"I thought you had a fever."

"It started that way. I had malaria, a fever that comes from Africa. It went away, but I still wasn't well."

"Did you have a cold?"

"No. Nothing like that. Some illnesses don't have names. I was just very tired. And sad."

"About my mother."

"Yes."

As he talked, I traced the outline of the woman's face, but I couldn't make her real. Matthew's words blocked her out. He was here again. That was all that mattered.

"You won't go away again, will you?"

Matthew placed his hands on my shoulders and turned me around to face him. His grip was tight, but I didn't wriggle.

"Astrid, I promise you. I will never leave you again. No more wretched schools. It'll just be the two of us from now on."

He let go of my shoulders and looked down.

"My absence was longer than intended."

"But you're back now."

I touched his face. There were drops of water on his bristles.

"Why is your face wet?"

"Just moisture. It's a hot night."

I leaned over and perched the picture on my locker, on top of the Viking book. My eyes were heavy now. I let them close.

I BARGED THROUGH the crowd towards the carousel, to an accompaniment of tuts and clicking tongues. It took me a moment to realise that my bag was sailing past me. I loped forward and grabbed it. My legs wobbled and I almost crashed into the guy next to me, but I managed to right myself and the crowd parted, like the Red Sea.

The Cabbage Patch Kids stood in a huddle, their huge suitcases in front of them. Cliona and Kim's heads were close together, as usual. The voices of the Greek Chorus foghorned in my direction, proclaiming their need for 'an honest-to-Jaysus cup of tea.' Johno's arms were wrapped around Mia. I didn't stop. I pushed on, past the ache in my chest. It was best this way, a quick, clean exit, no phoney goodbyes.

There was a knot of people at the partition. None of them looked familiar. I didn't know what I expected. I made for the coach park, my gaze directed at the ground, my legs weighed down.

The wind bit into my face as I left the building. Cold damp air settled into my bones. Sunlight beamed at an obtuse angle through the low clouds, filling the sky with a strange greenish-yellow light. A suitable colour for exile. Sigur Ros swirled through my head; the windscreen wiper thud of *Takk* filled the empty spaces inside me.

I buried my chin in the collar of my overcoat and fished in the pockets for my hat. I tried to scan the poles next to each of the bus shelters for the Aircoach sign. A tan leather jacket flashed past me, then vanished. It looked like one of Jazz's favourites. I shook myself. Jackets like that were commonplace. A hiss alerted me to the arrival of a bus. I looked up and saw a familiar blur of blue. People appeared from nowhere, surging towards it. I pushed through them, eager to be cocooned in its warmth. As I reached the queue, I saw the leather jacket again. It was coming towards me. A butterfly touch landed on my sleeve. *Takk* swelled to its climax, a thundering chorus filled with hope and yearning. My feet carried me away from the queue, the butterfly touch propelled me towards the bus shelter. My legs threatened to collapse from under me. I grabbed the pole which held the timetable. My hand made a fist around it, white on grey.

"Hey," he said.

His hand was still on my sleeve. He scuffed the ground.

"What are you doing here?" I managed to croak.

"Well, you know, since I didn't bring you."

He shifted from foot to foot.

"I'm amazed you dragged yourself out of bed after the club."

I kept my voice steady, trying to mask the hope that flickered in my chest.

"I didn't do it last night. Called in sick."

In three years, he had never missed a set.

"Guess I was DJing for both of us then."

He took a step back.

"You were DJing?"

I nodded; a blush rose on my cheeks.

"For the Cabbage Patch Kids?"

"No way. A real gig, local Austrians and everything."

I reached out to give him a playful shove. He trapped my hand and placed it on his chest. His heart thumped through the solid wall of bone and muscle.

"How was the trip?"

"You could say it was interesting."

He laughed, his wonderful, resonant laugh. When his laughter faded, it left a silence that fizzed with electricity.

"That text you sent."

"Listen, I was strung out. There was this guy and I blew it and—"

"There's just one problem with it."

"What's that?"

"You know those Greek women. What do you call them? The ones that inspire people."

"Muses."

"Yeah. You're my muse."

Words welled up, but I was unable to squeeze them past the obstruction in my throat.

"I can't do it without you. Guess I kind of want you to get in the way. And that thing about people laying bets on the albino chick? It wasn't true."

"Well, that's a relief. They'd never afford me," I laughed.

He didn't smile back. Instead, he let go of my hand and

touched my face, his fingers tracing the curve of my cheek, Brailling it into his memory. My skin tingled as his fingers moved across it. They moved towards my hair and pushed the rogue strands behind my ear. There was no need to hide now, no need to face away from one another. In the distance, the coach revved up to take off.

"You look tired," he said.

"Didn't sleep last night," I muttered.

"Too high from DJing?"

"Not as such. I was thinking."

I took a sudden interest in my shoes.

"What were you thinking about?"

His voice was gentle. I moved closer to him.

"I was thinking that you get in my way too. That..."

The blockage was still in my throat. I swallowed it down.

"There've been lots of guys. But there's only ever been one you."

My voice wobbled. The last vestiges of the ice fortress were crumbling.

"Let's go home," he said, grabbing my hand.

A smile crept across my lips.

"There's something we should do first."

I leaned forward and eased my tongue into the salt marsh depths of his mouth, until my mouth became enmeshed with his. His arms enveloped me. Everything else disappeared. I let myself unfurl.

❧ Acknowledgments ❧

To my family, who put up with my crazy ways.

To my publishers, Book Republic, who give a wonderful platform to new authors.

To the tutors who have guided me on my writerly journey: Jim Boylan, Catherine Dunne, Anthony Glavin, John McKenna. I owe a special debt of gratitude to Suzanne Power. Without her faith in me, this novel would not have been possible.

To Declan Meade of The Stinging Fly for his considered opinion.

To the writers who supported me during those nights drafty classrooms, especially Mary O'Gorman and Michael Flynn.

To Dan Ruane and Kenno, who guided me through the world of beats.

To the ski guides who've made it possible for me to scale the heights. Thanks for the banter and thanks for making me believe I can do it.

To Suzanne Dalton and Ulla Quayle, who shared their experiences of schools for the blind, which were far more pleasant places than the 'pink cage' Astrid experienced.

To Patricia Galvin, who gave me information about malaria facilities in Ireland in the 1980s.

And to Norman, who told me that there are some for whom the garment would fit perfectly. How right you were.

❧ About the Author ❧

Derbhile Dromey is a freelance writer, originally from Clonmel, Co Tipperary, but now living in Waterford. She holds a BA in English and History and an MA in Journalism. Her work has appeared in the *Irish Independent, Irish Examiner* and numerous trade magazines. Five essays about her life as a visually impaired person were broadcast on Lyric FM's Quiet Quarter slot and one of them found its way into a book called *The Quiet Quarter, Ten Years of Great Irish Writing* (New Island). She was shortlisted in the 2011 West Cork Literary Festival Short Story Competition and her work will be featured in an anthology, *From the Well*. When she isn't writing, she worships at the altar of music, walks on the beach and does silly voices.